KUMARI

**GODDESS
OF DESTINY**

For Delilah

*Thanks to my agent, Peter Cox, and to everyone at
Piccadilly Press, especially Brenda Gardner, Mary Byrne,
Becky Cole, Melissa Patey, Vivien Tesseras and Anne Clark.
A big thank you, as ever, to my family and friends for putting up
with authorial angst, and a special mention for classes 8L and
8P at QEGS (07) for helping me choose the title. Most of all, I
would like to acknowledge all the brilliant booksellers,
librarians and readers I have had the privilege to meet. Your
feedback has been wonderful and it makes it all worthwhile.*

First published in Great Britain in 2008
by Piccadilly Press Ltd,
5 Castle Road, London NW1 8PR

Text copyright © Amanda Lees 2008

A catalogue record for this book is available from
the British Library.

ISBN 978 1 85340 992 9

1 3 5 7 9 10 8 6 4 2

Printed in the UK by CPI Bookmarque, Croydon, CR0 4TD
Cover by Anna Gould and Simon Davis
Typeset by Carolyn Griffiths, Cambridge

Set in Stempel Garamond and Trajan

KUMARI

GODDESS
OF DESTINY

AMANDA LEES

Piccadilly Press • London

THE STORY SO FAR

Kumari is a goddess-in-training who lives in a secret valley kingdom, destined to stay young for ever. Her dear Mamma was murdered mysteriously, but when Kumari tries to summon her to find out the truth, she finds herself in downtown New York!

So Kumari starts a new life in the World Beyond. She lives with foster-mother Ma, makes her first real friends and meets a boy called Chico, while all the time acquiring her goddess powers. But she has only a year and a day to get back home – or she will die. Her life is also threatened by Simon Razzle, a cosmetic surgeon in search of eternal youth, and by the Ayah, her former nurse and now her deadly enemy. Kumari escapes death, thanks to her Mamma, who appears just in time to save her and despatch the murderous Ayah. With her time running out, Kumari leaves the World Beyond, vowing to avenge Mamma and liberate her from limbo.

Back in the Hidden Kingdom, disaster strikes: the king falls desperately ill and the fires of Happiness go out. Kumari must follow mysterious clues from her dead Mamma to find the secret ingredients which will relight the fires. She is helped by Ma and Theo, who have come to warn her of terrible danger. Captured by Razzle, the Kumari is shocked to discover that the Ayah is alive – and still wants the girl goddess dead. Summoning her powers, Kumari escapes and succeeds in restoring the fires and saving Papa and the Kingdom.

Theo and Ma leave the Kingdom, but give Kumari a special pendant which will allow her to return to the World Beyond some day . . .

CHAPTER 1

The top of the Empire State Building was on fire, flames shooting up from the one hundred and second floor. Clinging on to the steel mast that soared like a spire into the sky, Kumari could feel the heat scorching her feet, surging towards her from the observation deck.

Thick black smoke seared her eyes and tears began to stream down her cheeks. Coughing and spluttering, she looked to the sky for salvation. Except there was no escape; no way of descending or ascending. Unless, of course, she used her Powers and attempted to fly. Power No 6, the Power to Levitate or to Fly Through the Sky. It had worked for her back home, but then she had not been so high up. The tallest building in New York City, the Empire State, hundreds of metres above the ground – if she tried to fly from here, there was no guarantee she would make it.

And then she heard a voice call her name.

'Kumari!'

'Mamma, is that you?'

Through the smoke a figure emerged, loving hands stretched towards her. Kumari stared at her Mamma's wrists – they were bound up in chains.

And then another voice shrieking from somewhere above: 'She's mine! You keep your hands off her.'

Tilting her head upwards once more, Kumari could not believe her eyes. The Ayah, face twisted in hatred, was clambering towards her down the mast.

'Mamma, help me!' she tried to shout, but somehow the words would not come out. The smoke was choking her, filling her throat. 'Mamma,' she tried again, peering desperately through the belching clouds. A hand grabbed her by the shoulder.

'I've got you now!' the Ayah crowed, her fingers digging deep into Kumari's flesh.

'Let me go,' screamed Kumari. She could feel the flames licking at her clothes. 'I'm burning!' she cried. 'Please help me.'

Someone was still shaking her by the shoulder.

'Kumari, wake up. Kumari, my darling, open your eyes.'

She was back, no longer clinging to the Empire State. It had all been a dream. Except that the smell of burning still filled the air and her eyes were once more starting to stream.

'Kumari, the palace is on fire. We must get out of here at once!'

She was fully awake now, staring at her Papa, her mind desperately trying to catch up with what was happening. Behind her Papa she could see the RHM holding out one of her cloaks.

'Here, Kumari, put this on. There is no time to get dressed.'

Beside her on the pillow, Badmash stirred. Without another thought, she scooped him up. As she scrambled from her bed, the RHM flung her cloak around her and then they were hustling along the corridors. From all around Kumari could hear frantic shouts.

'The fields are burning!' someone cried.

Through a window, Kumari caught a glimpse of smoke spiralling up from the valley below. If the crops were destroyed, the people would starve.

'Come, Kumari,' Papa urged, his face etched with worry. He, too, had seen the fires. He too knew what they meant.

The guardsmen were evacuating the building. Outside in the main courtyard, people simply stood and stared as flames gushed from the palace roof. Vivid orange against the pre-dawn sky, they guttered amidst the golden spires.

All of a sudden, the crowd let out a collective gasp as a fireball shot from the heavens. It landed in the centre section of the roof, right above the throne room. Another followed and then another. It was as if the gods were hurling flaming meteors. Each burst on impact, sending more fire shooting forth.

The guardsmen had formed a human chain on the roof and were passing buckets of water along it. The fire was racing perilously close to where they worked. Soon they would be forced to retreat.

As Kumari gazed into the heart of the inferno, she thought she saw something. Narrowing her eyes, she focused harder. And then Mamma walked out of the flames. She stood, arms outstretched as if pleading.

'Mamma!' Kumari cried.

Beside her, Papa started. He, too, stared at the flaming roof.

'My love,' he murmured.

So Papa had seen her too. From her wrists hung those same chains Kumari had seen in her dream. The message was clear. Mamma was still in limbo, in bondage. A shuddering boom as another fireball struck the roof. When its sparks had died, Mamma was gone.

The Ancient Abbot touched Kumari's shoulder.

'The gods are angry,' he declared.

'Did you see her?' Kumari whispered, still staring at the roof in disbelief. 'Where has she gone? Where is she? Mamma, where are you?' She was shouting now but she did not care. She tried to run towards the roof, but the Abbot held her back. For an old man, his grip was surprisingly strong. He easily contained Kumari.

'Hush, child,' he murmured, his eyes infinitely compassionate.

'Did you see her?' Kumari asked. 'She was up there, on the roof.'

'I did,' said the Abbot. 'But that was not your Mamma, it was a mirage.'

'I tell you, it was her!' screamed Kumari. 'I saw her with my own eyes.'

'Kumari, you saw a vision. You saw what the gods wanted you to see. They were sending you a message, Kumari. They are missing one of their own. Your Mamma is still not with them on the Holy Mountain. You saw the chains on her wrists. She is still a prisoner to fate. All of this, it is a warning from the gods.' The Abbot's sweeping arm encompassed the burning roof and the fields beyond.

Through the ringing silence that filled her ears, Kumari heard the unmistakable sound of a sob. Horrified, she glanced at Papa, standing a few feet away beside the RHM, the king's Right Hand Man. Both their faces were lifted, gazing at the roof, their profiles silhouetted in ochre light. And then Papa turned to meet her gaze and she saw the tears streaming down his face.

'Your poor Mamma,' he said. 'We've let her down.'

'*I've* let her down,' said Kumari. 'It was up to me to destroy the Ayah in vengeance for murdering Mamma. And I thought I had when I sealed the labyrinth. Obviously, I've failed.'

She had been so sure when she trapped the evil Ayah and her cronies in the World Beyond that her mission was finally at an end. And yet Mamma was still caught in limbo, unable to ascend the Holy Mountain and take her rightful place there as a goddess. Each evening since she had brought the stone crashing down to seal the labyrinth which led to the Hidden Kingdom from the World Beyond, Kumari had prayed for a sign that Mamma was finally free. But it had never come and nor had Mamma, the many times she had tried to summon her up. Now she knew why. Somehow, Mamma's murderer must be still alive. And while the Ayah walked the earth, her Mamma would remain in limbo.

Suddenly it was all too much.

'What more do you want?' Kumari yelled, shaking a fist at the heavens. Her Mamma had been taken from her, and now it looked like she would lose her home and her Kingdom too.

'Hush, child.' The Ancient Abbot tried to comfort her but Kumari was having none of it.

'You want to test me, gods?' she shouted. 'Well, go on – try. I can't take any more. I've done my best. I thought the Ayah would be dead by now.'

A growl of thunder drowned out her words, so loud it sent an answering shudder through the ground. A blazing flash lit up the sky. Helplessly, she turned to the Ancient Abbot.

'Why are they doing this?' she pleaded. 'What do they want?'

'They want this finished,' said the Abbot. 'The longer your Mamma stays in limbo, the weaker she gets. Soon it will be too late to save her. The gods want her avenged now.'

So Kumari's instincts had been right. Somehow she must release Mamma from her chains. Kumari looked again at Papa. On his careworn face there was an expression Kumari had seen once before, the day Mamma was taken from them. Back then he had looked as if someone had torn his heart to pieces. Today it seemed they had ripped away what was left.

His lands were burning, along with his home and his memories. Unless a miracle happened, the Kingdom would be burned to dust. Distant cries from the town below were audible above the roar of the flames. The fire was out of control now, as unstoppable as the gods' ire.

At that moment, the RHM turned and met Kumari's stare, his face as inscrutable as ever. Impassively, he looked at her and then dipped his head. It was almost like a benediction. It was not just the smoke that caused her tears to flow unchecked now. For the first time in ages, Kumari had been truly happy here. The palace once more rang with the laughter of Kumari and her friends, Tenzin and Asha. Although the very walls

6

held memories of Mamma, they were loving memories that brought a smile to Kumari's face.

Mamma's portrait hung in the throne room above the dais where she had once sat beside Papa. Now and then Kumari would steal along in the evening to have a little chat with her Mamma. Of course, Mamma never answered back. Kumari knew it was just a portrait. But as she still could not summon her Mamma up, it was all Kumari had.

Now even that pleasure would be taken from her if the flames started to eat into the throne room. Kumari felt a surge of energy in her gut. She could not, would not let this happen. There had to be some bargain she could make with the gods, some way of appeasing their anger. A great cracking noise ripped through the air but this time it came from the building. Heart in mouth, Kumari stared at the great circular window in the throne room. From within, she could see an orange glow. The fire had taken hold inside.

The cracking was the sound of a roof beam breaking. Any moment now the flames would spread to the rest of the room, to Mamma's portrait. Forgetting any danger to herself, Kumari began to run, ignoring the Abbot's cry of protest. She could hear Papa shouting too and the shouts of guards pounding after her. Piercing through all of that, the plaintive cries of Badmash. For a second her heart lurched, but she had to keep going. Her Mamma's portrait was in there. It was all she had left.

She could feel the glow of anger ignite just like the flames, fuelling her courage. So the Ayah was still alive. She had to be, against all the odds. And the only way to free Mamma was to finish her off.

'I'll find her,' cried Kumari. 'Whatever it takes, I'll avenge Mamma. If I have to sacrifice my very soul, I will do it to set her free. You have my word. I promise. Just, please, give me a sign that you agree. Anything. Please, show me. But spare the Kingdom, spare the people. Tell me what you want me to do. I'm ready.'

She was gasping for breath as she ran, sobbing out her plea to the gods.

At that very moment, the heavens opened and rain poured down upon the palace. It pounded in torrents upon the roof, dousing the flames in gallons of water. It cascaded through the damaged throne-room ceiling, snuffing out the fire. Within a few minutes it was over. The palace stood, smouldering in the dawn. The rain stopped as quickly as it started, leaving Kumari soaked to the skin.

Speechless, she gaped at the throne-room door, singed but very much intact. She still had to get inside and rescue Mamma's portrait from the smoke and rain that could destroy it forever. The latch scorched her hand as she grasped it, but Kumari ignored the pain. Using the unique mechanism known to a very few, she unlocked the door within seconds. Flinging it wide, she thrust her way into the throne room and instantly had to clap her hand over her mouth and nose.

Smoke still swirled, opaque, making it hard to see. Once more she was reminded of her dream as she stumbled towards the dais. Behind her she heard a familiar squawk followed by a bout of coughing.

'Stay where you are, Badmash,' she called, her words muffled by the cloak she now held to her face. Even so, she could scarcely breathe. She dropped on to her belly and began to

8

crawl. There were a few inches of clearer air near the floor. The smoke was beginning to rise towards the ceiling. She caught a glimpse of the edge of the dais. A few more thrusts with elbows and knees and she could touch it.

Staggering up to her feet, Kumari thrust her way blindly up the steps and towards the thrones. She paused to wipe the tears from her eyes. When she opened them, the smoke had cleared.

'What the . . . ?'

Emblazoned across the wall in front of her, a message, stark white letters etched into the soot.

JUSTICE. REVENGE. DESTINY.

Kumari stared at it, silently mouthing the words. Justice – she understood. Revenge – that was obvious. But destiny? Why? What had fate to do with finding Mamma's killer?

'I don't know what to do,' wailed Kumari. 'I get it, but I don't get it. You want me to find the Ayah – fine, but I don't even know where to start.'

She gazed at the wall, not even sure what she was looking for. A clue, maybe. A sign. This, too, had to be a message from the gods. No mortal could have braved the inferno to etch this into the soot. It was inhuman, the work of the divine. Each letter was perfectly formed, spotless in the otherwise ravaged room. Kumari's eyes travelled down the wall. Mamma's portrait – where was it? No longer on the wall and not even a square to mark where it had hung. Suddenly frantic, she looked about. She spotted something behind Mamma's throne.

As her fingers grasped it, she could feel the frame give way. Carefully, gently she eased it out. Although the throne had shielded it from the worst of the fire, the portrait was charred beyond recognition. Where Mamma's face had gazed out, serene, there was now a blackened canvas. The careful brush-strokes had been burned away to reveal a thick undercoat of nothingness. A knot of pain twisted in Kumari's chest, so tight she could scarcely breathe. No more. Mamma's portrait was no more. Now she had lost just about everything.

'Why?' she howled to the heavens. 'Why take this? It was all I had.'

The tears fell unchecked, spattering the place where Mamma's face had once been.

'I said I'd do it,' muttered Kumari. 'I said I'd find the Ayah and avenge Mamma. I promised you, didn't I? So why do this? I don't understand. Is this supposed to be destiny?'

Fate. Destiny. Call it what you like. She had too often raged against it. The Ancient Abbot taught that all things were written, preordained. Kumari was not so sure.

'I'll make this happen,' she whispered. 'Whatever it takes, that's what I said. But I don't even know where to start.'

Through swollen eyes she gazed at the ruined portrait in her hands. All at once, she noticed something. Blinking away her tears, she looked again. There it was; the faintest out-line. Was this another hidden image in the portrait, just like the ones that had helped her save Papa? But those had existed alongside Mamma's likeness. This was something else entirely.

Try as she might, she could not make out any detail. It was time to try another tack. Gathering herself, Kumari gave it her goddess all, calling up Power No 2. Power 2, the Power of Extraordinary Sight, had served her well in the past. Now she needed it more than ever. Whatever was hidden within the portrait could be vital. However the gods chose to deliver their messages, they expected them to be received and understood, no matter how obscure the method. It was as if they were constantly testing Kumari, expecting more and more. She was, after all, a trainee goddess.

'DARA DARA DIRI DIRI . . .'

On and on she chanted.

She could feel it now, surging through her: the pure rush of Power. Opening her eyes, she looked at the portrait. The trick with her Powers was not to try too hard, to just let it happen. And it was appearing before her eyes, an image so clear it was luminescent. The shape was irregular. It looked almost like a large fish, with the right-hand side forming its tail. A memory stirred in the depths of Kumari's mind. Finally, it broke free and surfaced.

'America!' breathed Kumari. She had gazed at that very shape so often. In almost every geography lesson at Rita Moreno Middle School, she had studied maps of the vast terrain that made up the United States. The Ayah must be somewhere in America. First her dream and now this. There were no coincidences with the gods. She would follow their clues to find her destiny.

'Kumari! Are you in there?'

Papa's voice, calling from the door. Looking over her shoulder, she saw that smoke still swirled there, obscuring his view. It was only here on the dais that the air was clear. Just as the gods had intended. She could hear someone crashing towards her, the thud of a guardsman's boots. When she glanced at the damaged picture again, the map was gone. Gently, she touched the place where it had been. Beneath the marks her fingers made, she could see a glimmer of flesh-coloured paint.

11

Hardly daring to hope, Kumari rubbed at the soot, revealing more and more of Mamma's face. Miraculously, it appeared from beneath the layers of carbon and ash and at last Kumari stared once more into Mamma's dark eyes as she traced the gentle curve of her smile.

'Oh, thank you,' she whispered, her eyes filling with tears. 'Thank you for bringing Mamma back to me.'

She had her answer from the gods. Now it was up to her to keep her promise.

CHAPTER 2

'I tell you, she must be in the United States. I'd know the shape of the map anywhere. Then there was that dream I was having when you woke me up, the one about the Empire State. There are no coincidences with the gods. You taught me that yourself. In which case, it's obvious they're sending me a message. The Ayah is in America and very possibly New York.'

Papa sighed and patted Kumari's hair. She hated it when he did that. It made her feel as if she was still just a little kid when she knew she was halfway grown up.

'A dream is one thing, Kumari. A fact quite another.'

'Do you believe that, Papa?'

She stared into his eyes and watched as Papa's gaze shifted. Papa knew about the significance of dreams. He understood omens and portents. In which case, he had some other reason to dissuade her, one that was all too obvious. Papa did not really want to Kumari to go back to America. He wanted her to stay here and carry on her goddess studies. When he had allowed Theo to give her the pendant, he was agreeing to let her to spend time in the World Beyond. But Kumari knew that, in his heart, he was afraid. He had already lost her Mamma. He could not bear it if anything happened to his daughter too.

'If I may interrupt, your holy majesty . . .' The Ancient Abbot was hovering. The king nodded and the Abbot inclined his head. 'I think we should listen to Kumari.'

The king looked dubious, but the Abbot carried on. Sometimes Kumari admired his steadfastness. Her Papa might be a god-king but the Abbot had once been his teacher too.

'The gods are evidently angered,' continued the Abbot. 'And Kumari has told us she made them a promise. She swore to them she would avenge her Mamma, whatever it took. It was at that precise moment that the rains began to fall. I believe it was because the gods accepted her bargain. If they have accepted her bargain then Kumari must keep up her side of it. She must do whatever it takes to find the Ayah and that includes following the only clue that we have.'

For a moment, Kumari could imagine her Papa in the class-room, the Ancient Abbot drilling him in the metaphysical arts. Her Papa always treated the Ancient Abbot with respect and today was no exception.

'I understand what you are saying, Abbot, but these clues are hardly compelling. A shape appearing upon my dear wife's portrait. It could be interpreted in many ways.'

14

'And what about the words on the wall?' said Kumari. 'Justice. Revenge. Destiny.'

Her words seemed to hang in the air for a second and then the king brushed his hand across his eyes.

'Words, Kumari, just words. And where are they now?'

She had no answer. The words had disappeared along with the image. On the wall there was nothing save streaks of soot.

'I tell you,' Kumari insisted, 'they were there. I read them myself. Justice and revenge I understand. As for destiny, I just don't know. Was it Mamma's destiny to be murdered like that? Is it her destiny now to remain in limbo? I don't believe we have to simply submit to fate. I want to do what I can to change things.'

'Enough, Kumari!' roared the king. 'What you are saying is sacrilege. You know as well as I do that everything is pre-ordained. Not even we can alter the course of fate.'

Kumari flinched. It was so unlike Papa to raise his voice.

'Of course, Papa,' she mumbled.

'I am sorry, my child,' he said more gently. 'I still find it so hard to accept your Mamma's absence.'

Poor Papa, spending his nights thinking of her Mamma and his days dealing with the pain.

He gestured towards the portrait, lying in front of them on a table.

'That's all we have left of your mother and I thank you for saving this image. If it weren't for you, Kumari, we would not even have this to remind us. I wish with all my heart there *was* some kind of clue that would help to release her, but I am afraid I simply do not see it.'

'If I may, your holy majesty,' said the RHM. 'I do think Kumari has a point. She did, after all, clearly recognise the map of the United States. Surely it is worth the risk? If the Ayah is indeed alive then it is imperative we find her.'

Kumari watched her Papa's face as he gazed at the picture of her Mamma. She could see him wrestling with some inner conflict. Then, at last, he looked up and sighed.

'Very well, Kumari. You may undertake this mission.'

Before she could let out a whoop of triumph, the king added, 'But there are some conditions. You understand you have only one moon in the World Beyond. That is all your pendant will permit. You are to remain during this time in the company of the RHM. He has experience in the ways of the World Beyond. He knows this city and can keep you safe.'

The RHM dropped his head in a stately bow. 'I will guard Kumari's life as my own.'

'Thank you, RHM,' said the king. 'Secondly, Kumari, you must never reveal your goddess status. It would put you at even more danger in the World Beyond. You must remain circumspect.'

'Yes, Papa,' said Kumari, trying to forget the fact that one or two people knew already.

'And thirdly,' said her Papa. 'You must try to spread the message of Happiness. As I said only recently, we in the Kingdom have been selfish long enough. Wherever you can you must try to educate the people in the World Beyond in our ways. It is a sacred duty, Kumari.'

'And one I will help Kumari to uphold, your holy majesty,' said the RHM. 'Leave it to me to make the arrangements. We need to contact Kumari's friends in New York.

'Very well, that will be all,' said Papa, his eyes once more fixed on the portrait.

'Papa?' said Kumari as the Abbot and the RHM withdrew and the king stood lost in thought. 'Papa, are you all right?'

'Yes, of course, child,' said Papa and he smiled at her briefly. His smile, however, scarcely reached his eyes, which were infinitely sad.

'You miss her so much, don't you Papa?' said Kumari, laying her hand on his arm.

'I do, indeed. Almost unbearably. And I know you miss her as well.'

The look they shared was one of perfect empathy. No one else could truly know how they felt. Mamma had been the anchor of their little family. Without her, they were adrift. While they still had each another there was always a sense of something missing. Mamma's vibrant warmth had been extinguished, leaving nothing more than a void.

'I have to do this, Papa, for her.'

'I know, Kumari, I know. It's just . . .' Papa closed his eyes for a moment as if in pain. 'I could not continue if I lost you as well. The Kingdom could not continue, come to that. You are the heir to the throne. The trainee goddess.'

'Yes, Papa, but I am Mamma's daughter too. I have a duty there as well.'

'You are right, child. And I am proud of you. Go and do this for both of us.'

As Papa pulled her to him in an embrace, Kumari hugged him tightly back.

Ten days later the throne room had been restored and

Mamma's portrait once more hung in its rightful place. Workmen had toiled day and night to mend the roof and clear every trace of fire damage. Palace School, suspended while work went on, was back in full swing. They were in the middle of a spectacularly dull trigonometry class when the RHM interrupted proceedings.

'Wonder what he wants,' muttered Kumari to Asha.

As it turned out, he wanted a private word with her in his office.

'I have had word from the World Beyond,' said the RHM, gesturing to Kumari to sit before his desk. 'Ms Martin's father has organised a plane. You and I will leave the day after tomorrow. I suggest you prepare plenty of schoolwork to bring along. This mission may be important, Kumari, but so are your goddess studies.'

'Yes, RHM,' said Kumari, her heart leaping at the prospect. The World Beyond. Her friends. Chico. Then again, there was the Ayah to face too.

'RHM,' said Kumari, 'how do you think we're going to find the Ayah? America is a huge country. She could be any-where.'

'She could, indeed, Kumari. That is our main problem. To be frank, we have very little to go on apart from your dream and the map you say you saw.'

Before Kumari could protest again, the RHM held up his hand for silence.

'It's all right, Kumari. I happen to think this is a line of enquiry worth pursuing. It is likely that Mr Razzle, at least, made it back to his homeland. I suggest we start our search with him.'

The crazed cosmetic surgeon. Kumari shivered at the sound of her old enemy's name.

'Do you think he knows where the Ayah is?'

'He is our best hope, Kumari. They were, after all, working together when they tried to abduct you again. Mr Razzle is not subject to the strictures of Time that affect the Ayah. There is no reason for him to have perished.'

'But that's what I don't understand, RHM. How come *she's* still alive? I mean, she has only a year and a day to live outside the Kingdom like the rest of us. She should have succumbed to Time by now.'

'That I do not pretend to understand, Kumari. No doubt the answers are out there. We need to take it one step at a time. Find Mr Razzle first.'

'And how do you suggest we do that? Simply go and knock on his door?'

The RHM let out an exasperated snort.

'That would be a start.'

It was possible that Simon Razzle had gone back to his old life. Possible but unlikely. For one thing, Theo and Ma had alerted the authorities in the World Beyond to his criminal activities. Kidnapping was a federal crime. And not once but twice now he had kidnapped Kumari, although only the first had taken place on American soil. Kumari still shuddered at the memory of Razzle's clinic, the stark white room in which he had imprisoned her.

'But what if he's not there?'

'Then we have a problem.'

'I know,' said Kumari. 'Why don't we try and flush him out? I bet if he knew I was back in the World Beyond, he'd try to snatch me again. The one thing Razzle loves is money and I'm worth billions to him. From me he can extract the secret of eternal youth and sell it to the world, or so he thinks. Believe me, that is priceless. '

'Don't be ridiculous, Kumari,' snapped the RHM. 'Your father would never countenance it.'

'Papa doesn't need to know.'

'Kumari, this conversation is over.'

'I know it would work,' Kumari was still muttering under her breath as she returned to her desk.

'What did you say?' whispered Asha.

'Uh, nothing. It's not important.'

But it was, vitally important. And the more Kumari thought about it, the more her stomach churned. It would be wonderful to see the World Beyond again. Wonderful and frightening. The first time she had been taken there by force, snatched by her kidnappers. This time she was going by choice. She had much to gain and a lot to lose. On the one hand, she had friends here now, at the palace. Asha and Tenzin were her stalwart buddies and she had got to know the other kids better too. Out in the World Beyond she also had friends, the first she had ever made. Back in the kingdom, she missed them, although not as terribly as she had at first.

Now she was going to miss her friends here in turn as she ventured out on her dangerous mission. Added to that the prospect of tracking the Ayah down and her feelings were decidedly mixed. Why *not* use herself as bait to entice Simon Razzle? Tenzin was a fisherman. He would understand her tactics. But when she casually threw the idea into conversation later, Tenzin looked at her as if she were mad.

'Use yourself as some kind of human lure? Kumari, are you crazy? This is the guy who tried to cut you up. The one who was going to hand you over to the Ayah.'

'Yes, I know, but now he could lead us to her. He knows what happened after I blocked the labyrinth. At least, it's worth a shot. I have to avenge Mamma once and for all. Look what happened to the palace. I promised the gods I'd do whatever it takes. Heaven only knows what they might do next.'

Kumari glanced up at the roof as she spoke. The patches where it had been mended were hardly visible. They were standing in the classroom courtyard during their break, huddled together near the mango tree. From its branches, they could hear a sudden rustling and then a beak poked out from within. Two sleepy eyes blinked as Badmash yawned and stretched.

'Have you told him about Razzle?' asked Asha.

Instantly, Badmash was on full alert. He fluffed his feathers out so he appeared twice his already considerable size. A vicious hissing sound emerged from his throat. He hated the very sound of Razzle or the Ayah's names.

'It's OK, Badmash,' Kumari soothed. 'They're not here, remember? They can't come back.'

Instead, she was going after them. And Badmash would have to come with her. There was no way he would stay in the Kingdom by himself. He would pine away or try to follow. Rather than have him attempt to fly across half the world again, it was safer to simply take him along. Besides, out in the World Beyond was a steady supply of the one thing Badmash loved most in the world besides Kumari. She could deny him

21

some things for his health, but she would never deprive him of doughnuts.

'I still think it's a bad idea,' insisted Tenzin. 'Why not just stay here? Why go to the World Beyond at all?'

'You know why,' said Kumari.

'And I support you,' said Asha.

The two girls exchanged a look. This was one thing they shared, the loss of a mother. At least Kumari had a chance to avenge hers. Asha's mother had disappeared, never to be seen again.

'Thanks,' smiled Kumari. 'It's nice to know someone believes in me.'

'I believe in you,' said Tenzin hotly, 'I just don't want you to get hurt.'

'Well, I won't,' said Kumari. 'I have gained more Powers now. I can look after myself.'

'That's debatable,' said Asha, earning herself a playful clout around the head.

'Anyway, I'm going and that's that. We leave in two days' time, on the New Moon. That's a good time to be starting something major like this. Ms Martin's father has organised a plane.'

A sudden silence fell between them. Looking at their faces, Kumari could have kicked herself. Her friends had never been on a plane and, in all likelihood, never would. It was one more thing that set her apart, and just when they had been getting along so easily.

'That sounds exciting,' said Asha, sounding unconvinced.

'You think so?' Tenzin pouted. 'Me, I don't need a plane. I've got two legs and that's enough.'

'Of course it is,' said Kumari. 'But it would take an awfully long time to walk to New York. And I need to find the Ayah soon or goodness knows what the gods will do.'

'You don't even know she's there,' said Tenzin.

They were back to the beginning of their argument.

'Ignore him,' said Asha as they watched Tenzin stride off in exasperation. 'He's jealous, that's all.'

'There's nothing so great about going to New York,' said Kumari. It was, after all, only a little lie.

'Not about that, silly. About him, that other guy.'

'What other guy? You mean Chico?' Kumari gaped at Asha. It had not even crossed her mind that might be the issue. She and Tenzin were just friends. Besides, she knew Asha liked him.

'Come on, Kumari,' said Asha impatiently. 'You can see the way he looks at you. I can hope and wish all I like but he's never going to look at me like that.'

'But that's not true,' cried Kumari.

'Oh yes it is and you know it. Don't worry about it, I don't blame you. How could I ever compete with the girl-goddess?'

The hurt in Asha's voice was evident, no matter how hard she tried to mask it. With her brave smile she might feign indifference, but Kumari knew better.

'There is no competition,' said Kumari.

'You've said that before and it wasn't true then. It's all right, Kumari. I value our friendship too much to let it come between us. I mean, he's only a boy, right?'

Kumari answered Asha's grin with one of her own. 'He is only a boy.'

And, linking arms, they burst out laughing. Whatever happened with Tenzin, they would never let him come between them. They were friends. And that was far more important.

From a second-floor window above the courtyard, the RHM looked down on Kumari. She was chattering with Asha, throwing her head back and laughing giddily. Although she had made considerable progress with her Powers, there was still some way to go before she became a full goddess. At this rate, many moons would pass before she was ready to take on her responsibilities.

Given her Mamma's death, the RHM had hoped for greater focus. But Kumari seemed happy to take her time, a state of mind supported by his holy majesty.

'Let her enjoy her freedom while she can,' the king had said. 'There is plenty of time for the affairs of state.'

While his holy majesty might be sanguine, the RHM wanted results. The trip to the World Beyond might prove a blessing, requiring as it did intense effort on Kumari's part. He knew she would do anything she could to find the Ayah, including acquiring and utilising her Powers. They must make sure they took the Sacred Sword with them – that way Kumari could attempt Power No 1 if necessary. Power No 1: the greatest of them all. But did Kumari understand the implications?

Acquire and use Power No 1 and Kumari would instantly become a full goddess. Naturally, all the other Powers must already be accomplished, but it was not beyond the bounds of possibility. Necessity had a way of forcing the best out of people. Place Kumari in a position where she had no choice and she might well do them all proud. The RHM watched her for a moment longer. She really would make a fine goddess-queen. With a sigh, he turned away from the window. There was so much he needed to do first. So much Kumari needed to achieve.

KUMARI'S JOURNAL
(TOP SECRET. FOR MY EYES ONLY.
EVERYONE ELSE KEEP OUT!)
THIS MEANS YOU!

My bedroom

The night before our journey back to the WB

This pendant Theo made me is so small. Can it really keep me alive in the World Beyond? I know Theo is a brilliant scientist and everything, but I can't believe it really works. And the smoke that comes from it is absolutely invisible. How will I even know that it's working? I guess the only way to find out is to test it – and that I can only do by stepping out there. Oof. What an idea. It scares me. A whole lot.

  If it doesn't work then that will be the end of me. I will die within minutes. But I don't have a choice, do I? The gods have made that very clear. This time, they saved the palace. Next time we might not be so lucky.

What I don't understand is how the Ayah can be alive. By all the laws, it should be impossible. Everyone in the Kingdom can only live a year and a day outside its borders in the World Beyond. Everyone except the RHM, of course, seeing as he was born there. But I trust my dreams and I trust the messages from the gods. Somehow, the Ayah's still out there.

Avenging Mamma has to be my number one priority, even if the RHM thinks otherwise. I mean, I know he supports me in this mission, but I also know he's not too happy with my progress. He had another of his 'little chats' with me tonight and it was the same old, same old: I need to acquire my other Powers. I must work harder at becoming a full goddess. He even lent me this manual, some old book he keeps on one of his musty shelves. He said I can bring it on our journey – that I will find it 'enlightening'.

I don't know what can be so enlightening about stuff I have known backwards since the day I was born. I grow up, I become a goddess. One day. In my own time. OK, so there are a few Powers to acquire, but I think I'm doing pretty well considering. How many other girl-goddesses have to cope with being kidnapped – not once, but twice – and have to deal with people as crazy as the Ayah and Simon Razzle? And how many have had their Mamma taken from them by some evil murderer and then had to track down the killer and avenge them? OK, so I don't know any other girl-goddesses, but I bet the answer is a big, fat zero. I am the only girl-goddess in this position and that's something no book can help me with.

Anyway, I'll put it in my bag. The RHM will only be on my case if I don't. I don't exactly have a lot to pack apart from my iPod and the copy of Mamma's portrait. I'll have to get some clothes once I've arrived. There is certainly no way I am walking round New York City in this outfit. Hannah and Charley would have hysterics! I wonder what Chico would think? Part of me thinks he might quite like it. He always did say he likes that exotic, mysterious side of me. Ha! Me, exotic and mysterious!

It is hard to imagine seeing my friends again. I bet they've changed. I know I have. I just hope they haven't changed so much that they don't like me any more. I think that would really break my heart. The Abbot says that everything and everyone must change and that we live in a constant state of flow. He explained it's just like water, always moving, otherwise it gets stagnant. He said it was the same with people and that therefore it was a mistake to try to keep things the same.

Life has to change or it grows stale. I know that, but sometimes it's hard. Some changes are not so good – like Mamma's death, for instance. The Abbot also says there is a reason for everything and that all change helps us grow, but I'm not sure I agree with him. What possible reason could there be for Mamma's death that makes sense? She never harmed a single person. I don't feel like it helped me grow. In fact, it made me feel like someone had sliced half of me away. And if my friends in the World Beyond are no longer my friends, I will feel like another part of me has been stolen.

CHAPTER 3

Two days later, Kumari hugged Papa goodbye.

'Don't worry, Papa,' she whispered. 'I'll be back before you know it.'

In response, Papa clutched her to his heart.

'I will guard her with my life, your holy majesty,' said the RHM. 'You can depend upon that. You have my word.'

'I know – and thank you,' said the king, finally letting Kumari go. He and the Abbot stood back and bowed formally.

'Blessings upon you,' said the Abbot. 'May the gods guide and guard you at all times.'

Kumari hugged them both one more time, briefly, and then turned resolutely to follow the RHM. Soaring above them was the petrified waterfall formed from mountain rivers long run dry, a protective carapace between them and the World Beyond. It marked the eastern border of the

Hidden Kingdom, its outer wall hidden within forested slopes that gave way to open mountainside. Once more, Kumari was leaving her idyllic cocoon, although this time by choice. The RHM had already disappeared ahead along the hidden walkway but Kumari still turned to look over her shoulder. Papa and the Abbot suddenly looked so small and already so very far away.

'Goodbye,' she murmured. 'I'll see you soon. I love you.'

Perched on her shoulder, Badmash softly cooed as if echoing her sentiments. With an effort, she wrenched her gaze away, setting one foot in front of the other. Each step felt like she was treading over shards of glass, the pain shooting through her heart. Was this an omen or just the wrench of leaving those she loved behind? It was hard to tell.

When she and the RHM emerged from the protective canopy of the forest on to the open mountainside, the freezing air hit them full blast. It was blowing a blizzard, the wind whipping stinging snowflakes into their eyes. Kumari held her gloved hand out at arm's length and could no longer see it beyond her wrist. There was no way they would get down the mountain through a snowstorm of this magnitude. Kumari could hear Badmash whimpering as he tried to crawl inside her hood.

'We must retreat,' said the RHM, pulling Kumari back into the shelter of the trees.

'Go back? No way,' said Kumari. She had made her decision. Besides, she could not bear to go through another farewell with Papa or to prolong the anticipation of testing her pendant. She took one tentative step out from under the trees. Her foot sank into soft snow. She held her breath, but there appeared to be no ill effects. The haze from the pendant was acting like a protective bubble. Theo had designed it to act as a miniature fire of Happiness, providing Kumari with the enchanted air that kept her alive.

Without it, she would swiftly succumb to the effects of Time, crumbling into the dust that was the curse of mortality. She had already used up her year and a day in the World Beyond. Now there was nothing to stop its lethal impact on her save the pendant. It was like having her own personal scuba system underwater, allowing her access to an environment that was thoroughly alien.

And that system seemed to be working. She took two more steps and stood still. She was just a metre from the tree-line that marked the edge of the Kingdom's protective influence, but she might as well have been on the moon. Safe within the shelter of the trees, Badmash let out a squawk of fear. She waved a hand, telling him not to worry. She had her own source of sustenance and it seemed to be working. Just like an astronaut, she was free to explore. She wanted to dance in exhilaration. She began to spin round and round, a whirling dervish amid the snowflakes. As she did so, she could feel her Power rising.

She was calling on Power No 8, the Power to have Command over the Elements.

'OM BANZEN TARE SARVA
SHINDHAM KURU SOHA . . .'

From somewhere behind her in the forest, she could feel the RHM's approving gaze. *Concentrate, Kumari. It's not about him. You need to bend the elements to your will. You can feel it. It's happening!*

Her whirling slowed to a gentle spin. The snowflakes no longer stung her eyes and cheeks. She was staring down the mountain. A clear passage ran through the snowstorm just as if someone had blown a tunnel through it. On either side, the wind still blasted a furious flurry of flakes, but the sky above the passage was clear. She had carved them a path through the snowstorm that would hold as long as she sustained her Power. Beckoning to the RHM, Kumari began to descend the mountain and heard a whoosh of wings as Badmash flew past to lead the way.

It was hard to sustain a Power while scrambling down over compacted snow and jutting rocks. Kumari had taken the precaution of wearing her stoutest boots, but still they slipped now and then. Whenever that happened, she would once more begin to chant, focusing all her concentration on her belly, seat of her Powers. All the while, the RHM never said a word and she was grateful to him for that. As her teacher, he knew just how hard she was working to keep them safe. This was the longest she had ever managed to keep a Power going. It could simply switch off at any minute.

Somehow, though, she did it. The passage held all the way down the mountain. At last they trudged into the village on a plateau far below, the snow once more whirling at their backs. Kumari's Power was all but spent and she felt infinitely weary. The RHM laid a hand on her shoulder.

'Well done, Kumari,' he murmured as their Sherpa guide rushed to meet them.

A grateful Kumari handed her baggage to their guide and they were led the rest of the way to the airfield. A small plane sat on the airstrip. Kumari's heart began to beat faster.

31

Suddenly it all seemed real. She was going back to the World Beyond. Back to the people who held a special place in her heart. Back to destroy her mortal enemy. She could hear Badmash cooing in excitement.

Strapped in her seat, Kumari gazed out, staring sightlessly at the snow banked up beside the makeshift runway. They would be making a short hop on this tiny aircraft before changing to the private jet sent by Ms Martin's father. As the plane took off her stomach lurched – and not just because of the air currents. To distract herself, she pulled out the manual the RHM had pressed upon her. Picking a chapter at random, Kumari began to read.

The book was so boring that she soon had to stifle a yawn. Badmash was already snoring softly in her lap. He, too, was exhausted by their trek. The temptation to shut her eyes was overwhelming, but Kumari fought it. In little more than an hour they would be changing planes. It made sense to stay awake. She did her best to focus on the page, but the words seemed to swim before her. All at once, a sentence coalesced. Kumari sat up in her seat.

She read it twice over to make sure then simply stared at it, her mind racing.

Once full god or goddess status is attained, the new god or goddess must remain within the confines of the Hidden Kingdom until such time as they are called upon to ascend the Holy Mountain.

Kumari felt the hairs prickle on the back of her neck. A cold shiver rippled down her spine. There could be no mistake. It was written in black and white. Put in plain terms, it meant that full goddess equalled *finito* to her freedom. No more trips to the World Beyond. She would be effectively trapped. But why had no one told her this before?

She glanced surreptitiously at the RHM. He was sitting across the aisle, perfectly upright with his eyes closed. He must have known what the book said. Maybe he had given it to her so she could find out. Or maybe he had assumed she had always known. Her goddess education, after all, was a shared affair, divided between the Ancient Abbot and himself. Papa, too, would have been well aware of the strictures placed upon a full goddess. But not one of them had thought to tell Kumari. And that really hurt.

Of course she wanted to become a full goddess. One day. At the right time. But there was so much she wanted to do first, and some of it in the World Beyond. She had friendships to pursue, places to see and things to learn. She wanted to hang out with Charley and Hannah at the mall. To dance under the stars with Chico. Unconsciously, Kumari touched the necklace he had given her the last time they had parted. It hung alongside her life-giving pendant and was every bit as precious. OK, so they were young, but there was something between them that was very special. Chico was much more than just some boy. He was her very best friend.

That wasn't to negate her other friendships. She valued each and every one. She had shared so much with them all in different ways. Each one of them accepted her. But Chico, he was different. She liked the way he looked at the world. Sometimes it seemed he had lived a thousand lifetimes, and at others that he saw everything anew. Chico was an original and she loved him for it. He made her feel good just by being there. She would lose that if she became a full goddess.

Confused, Kumari stared out of the window once more. She had no idea what to do. Best thing was to say nothing and pretend she hadn't even read that particular chapter. The RHM was keen for her to study hard and gain her Powers sooner rather than later. It wouldn't be too difficult to pretend to make an effort while continually failing to get it right. That was, after all, what she had done for ages without even trying. Even now, she could only manage five Powers. Today was the longest she had ever managed to sustain one.

If she stayed quiet about what she knew, she could keep this up forever if necessary. The grown-ups might think they held the reins, but Kumari knew differently. Knowledge was power and now she had it she would hold it tight. She slid another glance at the RHM, still snoozing in his seat. A lurch of the plane downwards signalled that they were beginning their descent. In her lap, Badmash stirred. She would wake him in a minute.

'Time to change planes, Kumari.' The RHM must have felt it too.

'Yes, RHM,' she smiled.

She would act as if she'd never read that particular passage in the book, at least until she worked out what to do about it.

CHAPTER 4

Another set of ground lights rushed up to meet them. A thud as the private jet hit the ground and bounced once before settling. The engines screeched as the pilot slammed on the brakes, the backward thrust pinning Kumari to her seat. JFK Airport: they were back in New York City at last. Eagerly, she gazed out at the bright lights and the airport buildings. It looked at once strange and familiar.

She had been away for nearly eight months yet it felt like yesterday. As the plane taxied to a halt, she could vividly recall saying goodbye to all her friends right here. She half wished they could be there to greet her now, but it was unlikely, given the need for discretion. Perhaps Ms Martin would come or maybe Theo. Possibly even Ma. As the plane door swung open, the sultry night air filled the cabin. Dressed for the year-round snows of the mountains, Kumari felt uncomfortably hot.

The Hidden Kingdom was always temperate; neither too hot nor too cold. Here, the summer heat was stifling, even at night. It brought back memories of last summer, days spent at the beach with CeeCee and LeeLee or hanging out on the stoop with her friends, ice cream and sodas at hand. Flinging aside her winter cloak, Kumari scrambled to look out the door. The steps were already in place, but she could see no one waiting to meet them.

Swallowing her disappointment, she called to Badmash to come and take a look.

'See, we're back in America,' she said. 'You remember – the land of doughnuts.'

Instantly, Badmash was on red alert, beadily scanning the ground just in case one might magically appear.

'Later, Badmash. There's nothing there,' sighed Kumari.

Just then, two long, black cars swept up to the bottom of the steps. From the first, a distinguished figure emerged as a flunkey held the car door open. Several large men in suits disgorged from the car behind and stood in a silent, protective arc.

'Jack Raider!' exclaimed Kumari.

The Mayor of New York City himself. She might have helped him win his campaign, but he was the last person she expected.

Raider flung his arms wide and, with a beaming smile, bounded up the steps towards them. 'Kumari, my dear, it is so good to see you.'

'Uh, hello Mr Raider.'

He hadn't changed a bit. Same old back-slapping cheesey manner coupled with a sharp suit and sharper haircut. Jack Raider: man of the people. She had never quite bought into it.

'RHM. We meet again.'

'Indeed we do,' said the RHM as Raider pumped his hand. The RHM's face, usually so stern, was a picture as he struggled to mask his astonishment.

'When the kids told me you were expected,' said Raider, 'I just had to come meet you both myself.'

'I see,' said the RHM. 'Well, that is very kind of you.' His eyes were narrowed in suspicion.

'Not at all,' beamed Raider. 'You are our honoured guests.'

'The kids?' said Kumari. Curiouser and curiouser.

'A couple of your friends at Rita Moreno. You know I sponsor the school and I like to take a hands-on approach. I was in there just the other day, opening the new Jack Raider Library.'

'Uh, right,' said Kumari. Of course Ms Martin had known exactly when she was coming. Maybe she'd told a couple of Kumari's friends. It was unlike her, though, to break a confidence. Kumari's arrival was supposed to be kept quiet. Maybe she could not help herself. Perhaps she was excited as Kumari. In which case, why was she not here to greet them? It was all very odd.

'Why don't you both come with me?' said Raider, ushering them down the steps. 'Someone will see to your bags.'

The chauffeur sprang to open the car door. The RHM hesitated and looked at Raider.

'I'm not sure —' he began, but Raider broke him off.

'Relax,' he said with a smile. 'We all agreed it was best I come and meet you folks. I can offer the best security, after all.'

'Well, that is true . . .' said the RHM.

'And I can absolutely assure you of discretion. No one

knows that I am even here and, if they did, we'd keep them quiet.'

'I have no doubt of that,' said the RHM. 'Kumari, are you happy with this arrangement?'

'I . . . guess so,' said Kumari. Raider had always been totally overbearing. But it seemed her friends had agreed with this plan so she might as well go along with it and see how things played out.

'Gracie Mansion,' said Raider to his chauffeur, once they were settled in the first limo. The interior smelled of butter-soft leather and something else: a heady mix of money and power. As they headed in over the Brooklyn Bridge, Kumari caught her first glimpse of Manhattan, its skyscrapers gleaming in the late-afternoon sunlight, the island a magical citadel.

'Are we not going to Ma's?' asked Kumari. She was dying for one of Ma's reassuring hugs. OK, so Ma might not have come to the airport, but there had to be a good reason.

'I thought you would like to settle into your accommodation first,' said Raider smoothly. 'I felt it best you stay with me. My official residence is a little more . . . spacious than Ms Hernandez's apartment and there are, after all, two of you.'

He had a good point, but Kumari's disappointment only deepened. She had wanted so much to live again those heady days when she had stayed with Ma the first time she came to New York. Yes, it had been fraught and often terrifying, but the good times outweighed the bad. It was there she had discovered friendship along with the rough and tumble of family life. It was also where she had picked up all the best English phrases from the TV and found out just how good junk food could taste. More importantly, it was where she had rediscovered hope when a return home had seemed impossible. Ma's apartment represented far more to her than she could ever express. It was there that she felt safe.

Still, she did not seem to have any choice in the matter. Ma must have agreed to Raider's plan. Perhaps she, too, thought it would be better they stayed with Raider, although Kumari had her doubts. Even so, when the limo purred to a halt in front of Gracie Mansion, Kumari could not help but be impressed. The official residence of the Mayor of New York City was smaller than she had expected, but no less exquisite for that. Even Badmash fell silent as they gazed at the classic, yellow mansion, graceful columns supporting the wide veranda that stretched the entire length of the ground floor.

Leading them through a grand foyer, Raider preceded them up a sweeping staircase to a first-floor reception room.

'Your bedrooms are upstairs,' he announced. House-keeping will take care of your unpacking. Now, may I offer you something to drink? Dinner will be at seven.'

It was just like being back at the palace. Kumari looked about appreciatively. The room in which they were seated awaiting refreshments was painted a golden yellow, its antique furniture grouped in graceful arrangements around an imposing white fireplace. Kumari was perched on a sofa upholstered in a gold fabric that reflected the colour of the walls while the RHM sat opposite in a sage-green wing chair. A green and gold carpet matched the heavy draperies at the windows. It was a room worthy of a mayor and Jack Raider clearly gloried in it.

'So, how are things at the school?' Kumari asked politely.

She was dying to fire off questions, but restrained herself under the RHM's watchful eye.

'Things are good,' said Jack Raider, 'but they could be even better. In fact, I have some plans I want to talk over with you. Once you've had a chance to settle in, of course.'

'Of course,' said Kumari. She might have known he had some kind of scheme in mind. 'So when can I see my friends?' she added.

'All in good time.'

'Kumari.' The RHM shot her a warning glance. 'Mr Raider has been very kind. Remember our main purpose in coming here was not to see your friends.'

'No, of course not, RHM,' muttered Kumari.

'So what is your main purpose?' said Raider affably as another flunkey silently entered the room. He waited while the man placed a tray upon the coffee table before smiling expectantly at the RHM.

As Kumari, too, glanced at the RHM she realised she was digging her nails into her palms. *Don't say too much*, she begged silently. *Raider is not to be trusted. Whatever he says or does, there has to be something in it for him.*

The RHM was no fool and he met Raider's smile with an equally bland expression. 'We have some business to take care of,' he murmured before taking a sip from his cup of tea.

'Anything I can help you with?' said Raider. 'My contacts are among the best.'

'I . . . am not sure,' said the RHM. 'This business is of a personal nature.'

'I see,' said Raider. 'Well, you just shout out if you need anything.'

'We will, thank you,' said the RHM. Kumari could see his mind working overtime. He seemed to be weighing something up, calculating the pros and cons. After a moment, he placed his cup and saucer on the table. He appeared to have reached some sort of decision.

'You see, this matter is rather delicate,' said the RHM. 'It concerns Simon Razzle, the cosmetic surgeon who attacked Kumari at Madison Square Garden. I am sure you remember. You were there.'

'Absolutely,' said Raider, looking serious. It had been part of his finest hour. His concert to win the youth vote had culminated in a finale he could not have dreamed up if he tried. Folks still talked about the flying lion and the fight. They thought it was all down to special effects. Raider, however, knew different. He knew it was thanks to Kumari pulling some goddess strings. He had no idea how she had done it, but he wanted more of whatever it was. It had ensured his success.

'We intend to find out where Simon Razzle is,' said the RHM.

So no mention of the Ayah. *Very wise,* thought Kumari. *Better not to tell Raider everything.*

Raider refocused on the RHM. 'Why? Do you think he might try another stunt?'

'We just like to keep our enemies in our sights.'

'I'd like to do what I can to help.'

'Thank you,' said the RHM. 'Your help will be much appreciated.'

The two men smiled innocuously at one another. So the RHM had accepted Raider's offer of help. Perhaps he realised they needed it. They had little chance of finding Razzle alone.

Kumari slowly exhaled. She was not altogether sure why she distrusted Raider quite so much. Something about his smile, maybe. It was at odds with his shrewd eyes. Even when she had helped Raider out with his campaign she had known he had that in him: a calculating eye hidden under a veneer of charm. It had won him the mayoral race and would probably take him further. Raider wore his ambition lightly, but he did not deceive Kumari for an instant.

They sat and sipped their drinks as Raider made small talk. All the while, Kumari longed to be somewhere else. Ma's place, preferably. A tentative tap at the door interrupted Raider's discourse on his mayoral duties. A second, louder one elicited a tetchy 'Enter' from Raider. He did not like to be interrupted.

'Excuse me, sir,' said the man who had delivered the tray earlier. 'But there are some people downstairs who say they're here for Miss Kumari and they're insisting on coming up.'

At that moment, the panelled door to the room was flung back. Kumari could hear raised voices coming from the hall outside. And then someone burst in with a security guard in hot pursuit.

'Kumari!'

'LeeLee!' Ma's daughter, her pretty face alight with anger. Taller than Ma and slender, she looked older than her eighteen years.

'I kept telling these people to just let us up. But would they listen? Hell, no. Can you see now I was telling the truth?'

As LeeLee glared at the security guard, more familiar faces

42

began to appear. First LeeLee's twin sister, CeeCee. Then Ms Martin and Theo, towering over them all. Kumari gaped at them, bewildered. Here they were at last, her friends; Ms Martin dressed in her customary A-line skirt and blouse. As ever, she sported a pair of dangly earrings that defied her preppy look. Today it was a set of yellow sunflowers. Beside her, stood Theo, smiling. They made such a great couple. Last time Kumari had seen Theo it had been in the Kingdom. She touched her pendant and grinned. Theo was responsible for her being here, in the World Beyond. The pendant was his invention. He might look like a slightly-scatty-if-handsome scientist, but Theo was one clever dude.

Then there was Hannah, the taller, darker half of Kumari's best buddies, the Deadly Duo. At least, she and Charley had a killer attitude to shopping. Together with Kumari, they made up the Retail Trio. Even as she flung her arms around Hannah, Kumari wondered where Charley was. Still, there would be time for questions later. Right now, she was just so glad to see her friends.

'It's all right,' said Raider to the guard. 'You can let these people stay.'

'Welcome back, Kumari,' said Ms Martin. 'We were so worried about you. When we got to the airport and found you gone, we didn't know where to look. And then someone said they'd seen you head off in the mayor's limo. That's when we got round here as fast as we could.'

She shot a frosty look at Jack Raider.

'You could have told us you were picking them up,' she added.

'I had no idea you had plans.'

Although Raider's tone was smoothly placatory, Kumari detected a combatant gleam in his eye. So he had lied at the airport. What exactly was Raider up to?

'Well, all's well that ends well,' said the RHM as he rose to shake hands with Theo. Badmash was already bouncing with delight from Ms Martin to CeeCee, cooing with love and anticipatory greed.

'Here you go, Badmash,' said Theo, extracting a squashed doughnut from his pocket. The vulture fell upon it with cries of ecstasy and gobbled it within seconds. Raider glanced with distaste at the pile of crumbs on the carpet, but refrained from comment.

'Hello, Kumari,' said CeeCee, stepping forward to hug her. 'It is wonderful to have you back.'

'It's great to be here,' said Kumari. 'I mean, in New York. Not,' she added hastily, 'that it's not good to be here at Gracie Mansion.'

'Not where we expected to see you, though,' said Theo, taking his turn for a hug. He, too, threw Raider a speculative glance.

'Well, what are we waiting for?' said LeeLee. 'There's a cab downstairs waiting. Ma's back at the apartment and I'm sure she can't wait to see you.'

There was something in her tone that alerted Kumari, a slight hesitation that made her wonder if all was quite well. LeeLee was already tugging Kumari out through the door. When she was like this she reminded Kumari of Ma: implacable, determined. Raider and the RHM scurried after them in hot pursuit down the stairs and out of the front door of Gracie Mansion. In front of the steps sat a yellow cab, its bored driver staring steadfastly into space, ignoring the security guard tapping on his window, ordering him to move on.

They piled into the cab with lanky Theo taking the front seat. The driver took one look at Badmash and pulled a face.

'I don't take no birds,' he announced.

Theo hastily slipped him a few notes and the driver capitulated. Kumari glanced out of the window and saw Raider summoning up his official car. For a second she felt a stab of guilt. The RHM was her appointed guardian, after all. But there was no room for him and Raider in the cab. She could hardly imagine the RHM squashed up on the back seat or, worse, sitting in someone's lap.

Then they were swooping down the drive and out of the gates and the RHM was forgotten. The motion of the vehicle brought back vivid memories of waking up in the back of another cab, the first time she had come to New York. Back then she had been blindfolded and surrounded by the kidnappers who had taken her from her beloved Kingdom. The same queasiness that had saved her then now boiled in the base of her stomach. Up and down the cab bounced, heading for Ma's home in the Bronx.

She glanced at CeeCee, squished up next to her on her right. Impulsively, Kumari seized her hand.

'Is something wrong with Ma?' Kumari asked.

CeeCee looked at LeeLee, who said nothing.

'There is, isn't there?' Kumari persisted. Her grip on CeeCee's hand intensified. CeeCee squeezed her hand back, but stayed silent. It was as if she could not speak.

'All in good time, Kumari,' said Ms Martin, bestowing a soothing smile upon her. It only made Kumari all the more anxious. Something was definitely wrong. There was no way Ma would have stayed back home unless she was physically unable to leave her apartment. Ma would have been the first in line to greet her, to welcome her back. Unnerved, Kumari sat, staring sightlessly at the buildings swishing by as they turned on to First Avenue, heading for the Bronx. An icy dread clutched her heart.

What on earth was going on?

CHAPTER 5

The instant Kumari stepped into Ma's apartment, she could feel something was different. And then she realised what it was. The silence was deafening. The TV sat in the corner of the lounge exuding a glassy emptiness. Normally it blared at a constant full volume. Now it was turned firmly off. Curled into a tight ball on the sofa, a wizened figure remained motionless as they entered. Kumari had to look twice before she realised this was Ma. Beside her sat Mrs Brinkman, knitting.

'There you are!' said Mrs Brinkman brightly, rising to drop a kiss on Kumari's cheek. Kumari, however, barely felt it. Her eyes were locked on Ma. How could someone have shrunk so swiftly and comprehensively? Not a few months before in the Hidden Kingdom, Ma had been her old self. The woman on the couch bore no resemblance to the loud, colourful Ma who held such a special place in Kumari's heart.

'Ma?' Kumari murmured, reaching out to touch her shoulder. Even Ma's hair hung lifeless from her scalp. Once it had been her pride and joy. She could feel Ma's bones underneath her ill-fitting clothes. That, too, was startling. The old Ma had filled her colourful outfits with glorious flesh. She had been curvaceous and proud of it.

Seeing Ma, Badmash let out a cry and hopped up to sit beside her. He reached up with one wing to caress her cheek. There was nothing. No reaction.

'What happened?' Kumari demanded, looking up at CeeCee and LeeLee.

'Sonny died the month before last,' said LeeLee. At the mention of her son's name, Ma stirred. A tiny moan escaped her lips.

'How? Why?' gasped Kumari.

'He was killed,' said CeeCee, her eyes filling up with tears.

'B-by whom?' asked Kumari, not wanting to hear the answer.

'We have no idea. You know Sonny. He probably got in way too deep.'

Of course he did, thought Kumari. He had too many fingers in illegal pies, including a stint serving Simon Razzle. Had he outlived his usefulness there? Razzle was certainly ruthless enough to dispose of Sonny without a second thought. Look what he had already done to her. What he and the Ayah would still love to do to her, if her suspicions were correct.

'Why didn't you tell me?' said Kumari.

'We did. We wrote you many times.'

Kumari stared at LeeLee, horrified. 'I didn't get any letters.'

'Then how come you're here?'

It was LeeLee and CeeCee's turn to look confused.

'I–I came on a mission,' said Kumari. Right now did not seem the best time to explain things. Where to begin? It was all so complicated. Besides, right now she needed to concentrate on Ma. She glanced at her curled up on the sofa, looking completely broken. Kumari could feel Ma's pain echoed in her own heart. It was the dull ache of loss.

'Well, at least you're here now,' said Ms Martin, putting a gentle hand on Kumari's arm.

'All thanks to you,' said Kumari.

'Not at all. I was pleased to help when the RHM got in touch. Anything that will bring you back to us, Kumari. We have all missed you a great deal. None more so than Ma. Isn't that right, girls?'

'You bet,' said CeeCee. 'Ma, she asks for you all the time. Seems like you're the only one she thinks can help her.'

'That's why we tried so hard to reach you,' said LeeLee. The two sisters looked at one another. As twins, they were more attuned to one another than most and their faces bore an identical expression: the exhaustion of long nights of despair mingled with a faint gleam of hope.

'But I don't know how I can help,' said Kumari. 'She doesn't even seem to know I'm here.'

'You're supposed to be a goddess,' said CeeCee. 'There must be something you can do.'

'How about you try one of your Powers?' interjected Theo. 'It can't hurt, can it, Kumari?'

When even Theo the scientist was urging her inner goddess on, Kumari knew she had no choice. But which Power to use? She ran through them in her head. None of the ones she had acquired so far would suffice. Which meant she would have to try to gain a new one and take herself one step closer to becoming a full goddess in the process. Kumari hesitated for a fraction of a second, remembering the paragraph in the book. But there was no choice when it came down to it. She would do anything for Ma and that included taking this risk.

Power No 5 ought to do it: the Power of Rejuvenation. That would cover a host of stuff, including revitalisation of the soul. Gently, Kumari's took Ma's hand.

'I'm going to make you better,' she said softly.

Then she closed her eyes and tried to concentrate, shutting out everything but the task in hand. Forcing her focus on the pit of her stomach, Kumari felt the energy begin to stir. *Please let me get this right,* she begged silently. *Ma needs me. I need her.* It was growing now, surging through her, like lava through a volcano. Kumari threw her head back and began to chant, unleashing Power No 5.

'OM TARE TUTTARE

BRAYA AYU SHAY SOHA . . .'

All the while, she held Ma's hand, determined to infuse her with new life. They were crammed into the tiny living room, squeezed tight around the sofa, everyone willing her on, Kumari doing her best. Finally, she felt a tiny flicker of movement. Opening her eyes, she gazed at Ma. Two black eyes stared back at her and in them was an unmistakable spark. Squeezing Ma's hand tighter, Kumari carried on until she saw the ghost of a smile flit across her face.

'Kumari?' whispered Ma. 'Is that really you sitting there?'

'It's me,' smiled Kumari. 'Badmash is here as well.'

At the mention of his name, Badmash let out a squawk and snuggled closer into Ma's lap. It was as if he was determined to warm her back to life with the heat from his plump little body.

'LeeLee, CeeCee, Kumari is here.' Ma was gazing at them all in wonder.

'She's come to see you,' said LeeLee. 'Everyone, they're here because they love you.' Beside her, CeeCee choked back a sob. Kumari could feel her own throat tightening.

'We'd better be getting along,' said Ms Martin. 'I'm sure you all have plenty to talk about. We'll stop by tomorrow to see you both, won't we, Theo?'

There were a lot of 'we's in that little speech, Kumari noted, not that Theo was objecting. He and Ms Martin fitted well together, a bit like she and Chico had. *Chico.* She pushed the very thought of him from her mind. Time enough for that later. Right now, she had to focus on Ma. And focus she did as they sat companionably together on the couch. As time went by, Ma unfurled from her foetal position until she was once more upright. Once or twice she even laughed as the banter flowed between them. Still, Kumari could see she was tiring fast. Perhaps it was time to go.

Except she didn't want to go. Not back to Gracie Mansion at any rate. She wanted to stay here, at Ma's side, among the people who were her friends.

Just then, there came a loud rapping at the door. CeeCee sprang to open it. She returned with an icily polite RHM in tow. Hard on his heels, a furious Raider.

'Well, you took some finding,' said Raider. 'Darn fool driver took us round and round in circles.'

'Come, Kumari,' said the RHM. 'It's time to leave. We were informed dinner was to be at seven.' Icicles dripped from every word. He scarcely acknowledged the others in the room.

Kumari glanced at the clock on the wall, suppressing a shudder as she did so. It was already nearly eight o'clock. Time had flown by.

'I am very sorry to have put you to such trouble,' she said. 'But I can't leave Ma now. Not tonight. She's only just getting better.'

'You shoulda been here,' butted in Mrs Brinkman. 'I tell you, it was a miracle. One minute Ma is there, half dead on the couch. The next, Kumari does her fancy schmancy stuff. Upon my life, I have never seen anything like it. Ai, ai, ai, I am so happy!' And with that she performed a little jig of joy.

The RHM stared at her in astonishment. His gaze shifted to Ma, propped up on the couch, Badmash nestled in her lap. Kumari noticed his look of surprise as he observed the change in her.

'It is good to see you again, Ma,' he said, inclining his head in formal fashion.

'And you too,' said Ma, but her voice lacked warmth. The two of them had never been bosom buddies.

The RHM's eyes flicked to Kumari. He seemed to be making one of his mental calculations.

'Perhaps it would be better if Kumari stayed with Ma tonight,' he said. 'She appears to have done good work here.'

'You bet she has,' said Mrs Brinkman. 'She brought happiness back to this place.'

'Thank you, RHM,' said Kumari, feeling relief flood through her. She noticed Raider's gaze upon her now. In his eyes, too, a speculative look.

'Of course you must stay, Kumari,' he said in a honeyed tone. 'It seems you have truly wrought a miracle. It's what I always say to my electorate. You never appreciate Happiness until it's gone.'

'Shouldn't that be "health" you never appreciate?' demanded LeeLee. She had always been a stickler for accuracy.

'Health, Happiness – they are one and the same. It is what I have always promoted through HUNK.'

Ah yes, HUNK. Raider's erstwhile campaign on which he had ridden to mayoral victory. HUNK stood for: Happiness, the Ultimate New Knowledge. Raider fancied himself a guru on the subject. Except that, like most gurus, he was nothing more than a fake. What Raider knew about happiness could be fitted on the back of Kumari's little fingernail. Yet again she wondered about his real agenda. First the airport pick up that turned out to be more hijack and now the look of avarice in his eyes.

If there was one thing Kumari recognised, it was a profit motive. She had learned that one from Razzle and the Ayah. Now it seemed she was to get a refresher course. *If that's the way it's to be,* thought Kumari, *then I'll use you as much as you use me. No more Miss Nice as Pie.* This was the way the World Beyond worked. Even as she thought it, Kumari could feel herself slipping down the Happiness scale. Hastily, she inhaled deeply from her pendant. This was going to be a hard balancing act to maintain.

On the one hand, she had to be true to herself. On the other, she had to succeed in her mission. There was no one more well connected than Jack Raider and she needed his help to track Razzle down. Razzle was her one link to the Ayah and therefore the only means of avenging Mamma. Oh, why did things have to be so complicated? For a second, she regretted she'd ever come back to the World Beyond. One glimpse of Ma's face, though, and Kumari knew she had done the right thing. What was it Papa had said not so long ago? That they'd been selfish in the Hidden Kingdom long enough. As well as tracking down the Ayah she also had a sacred duty to spread Happiness. She might play by the rules of the World Beyond but ultimately she had to live by the kingdom's tenets. Ma was just beginning to recover thanks to Power 5. Sometimes it was good being a girl-goddess.

So much better did Ma feel, in fact, that she insisted on seeing the RHM and Raider out. Kumari half suspected it was so she could deliver her parting shot: 'Y'all just holler if you get lost.'

Not long after they left, Mrs Brinkman retired to her apartment a few streets over. CeeCee and LeeLee staggered off to bed soon after and then it was just her and Ma.

'Well,' said Ma softly as soon as they were alone. 'Looks like you saved me, girl. I am never going to forget that, Kumari. You're more special to me now than ever, if that were possible.' She took Kumari's hand in both of hers. The two of them looked at one another.

'Don't be silly,' said Kumari. 'You would have done the

same for me, I know that.'

She glanced at Badmash, snoring on a cushion. Ma was a surrogate parent to them both.

'I'd do anything for you, sweetie, but I ain't no goddess now, am I?'

'And nor am I,' said Kumari. 'At least not yet. I'm still a trainee.'

There must have been something in her voice that alerted Ma because suddenly she was all ears.

'Is something bothering you, Kumari?' she asked.

'I . . . it's just . . . I read something in a book the RHM gave me. It said once I became a full goddess I couldn't leave the Kingdom. Like, never again. Not ever. I'd be stuck there for the rest of my life. I'd never be able to come back here, to the World Beyond.'

Miserably, she looked at Ma. She hadn't meant to say all that. But this was Ma she was talking to, the person who knew her almost better than anyone.

'I see,' said Ma and she exhaled slowly. 'That ain't so good, is it, Kumari? So how come they never told you this before? Or did they just kinda imagine you knew?'

'I don't know,' said Kumari. 'I don't understand. I thought maybe that was why the RHM gave me the book. But whatever, I'm not going to do it. They can't force me to acquire my Powers.'

At this, Ma looked shocked for a moment and then let out a deep, guttural laugh.

'Kumari, honey, you are one of a kind, girl. How you going to keep from becoming a goddess?'

'Easy – I'll carry on failing like I used to. Remember, I am very good at being a klutz.'

'That was then. This is now, Kumari. Your Pops said you'd make a fine goddess.'

'Are you telling me that you're on their side?' Indignation swelled in her throat.

'Nope. I'm just pointing out some things are inevitable. Kumari, you were born to be a goddess. We all have to grow up and into ourselves. That's what life is all about.'

'Yeah, well, things can change. *I* can change. I already have.'

'Kumari, honey, don't get so worked up. I'll support you whatever you do.'

They looked at one another and the silence hung heavy, pregnant with things unsaid. At that moment, Kumari heard a soft tapping. Someone was at the front door.

'Now, who in the world can that be at this time?'

Ma heaved herself to her feet. Kumari took her arm to steady her. Ma peered through the peephole then grunted in surprise. The door swung open and there stood Chico, his mouth quirked in a tentative smile. He looked just the same and yet different, a little taller and more muscled. His dark hair was shorter, hugging the nape of his neck, his lips still full, curving perfectly. Absolutely kissable.

'Well, better late than never,' quipped Ma. 'Son, do you have any idea what time it is?'

Kumari tried to think of something to say, but she seemed to have lost the power of speech. Chico, too, appeared thunderstruck. At least, he wasn't saying anything. He was looking at her, though, and those gloriously familiar eyes were alight with emotion. What it was, though, she could not precisely tell. It was hard to be perceptive when your stomach was doing back-flips.

'I guess I'll leave you two to it. Looks like you have a lot to say to one another.' And with that, Ma closed the door behind Chico and slipped quietly to her room.

'Uh . . . come in. Sit down,' said Kumari. Why couldn't she think of something more profound to say? Something like how much she had missed him and how incredible it was to see him. She glanced down. Oh my god, she was still wearing her robes. There had been no time to find something more in keeping with the World Beyond. Instead, she was covered frumpily from head to toe. Amazingly, Chico did not appear to notice. He was too busy staring into her eyes.

'Actually,' said Chico, 'do you mind if I don't? There is something I want to show you upstairs.'

Upstairs? How bizarre.

'Oh yeah?'

'Yeah. So what say you come along with me?'

She took his outstretched hand without a murmur, their fingers slotting together. He eased open the door once more and led her out into the corridor. From there they took the stairs, climbing silently in unison, Kumari bunching her robes in her free hand so she wouldn't trip.

Four storeys up, there was a service door that gave on to the roof. When Chico pushed it, it swung open. They stepped out into the open air.

A low stone parapet ran round the edge of the building, shielding them from the drop to the street below. The sulphurous glow from the street lamps lit up the tableau before her. Someone had arranged a couple of packing crates so they formed a rickety table. On the table, candles set in jars flickered, illuminating the bunch of daisies arranged in the middle. Two places were set opposite one another, the seats being formed from two more packing crates.

'You did this,' said Kumari. She could feel her eyes brimming.

'You don't like it?' asked Chico, suddenly all concern.

'I love it. It's perfect.'

He led her over to the makeshift table and pulled her packing crate out with a mock bow.

'Ma'am . . .'

'Why, thank you, sir . . .'

With their easy laughter, the ice was broken. Well, maybe not broken exactly, but definitely cracking in places. She had waited so long for this moment and now it had come she had no idea what to think. The gulf of months spent apart yawned between them. She looked at Chico, the same but different. She wondered if she seemed that way to him.

'You're wearing it,' he said, leaning forward to touch her necklace. It was the one that he had given her when she left the World Beyond some eight months before with their initials intertwined.

'I never take it off,' she said, almost flinching as his fingers gently grazed her throat. It was not that it was unwelcome. The opposite, in fact. His fingertips sent a thrill through her that was at once wonderful and terrifying. How could one person have such an effect?

'But what's this?' he asked, weighing her pendant in his hand. It hung heavy next to the necklace, emanating its invisible fumes.

'That . . . oh, that's nothing.'

'Come on, Kumari. This is me, Chico, remember? Now what's with this weird pendant?'

'Theo made it for me back in the Kingdom. It's what keeps me alive out here. It's a miniature fire of Happiness. If I lost it, I would die.'

For a moment, he looked stricken. 'I couldn't bear that,' he murmured. 'Hey, good old Theo, coming up with that.' His tone was forced and falsely cheery.

An awkward silence fell between them, laden with possibility. *He can't deal with it,* thought Kumari. *He can't deal with the fact I am so different. He likes the Kumari he knows, the one he met at Middle School. I thought the goddess stuff didn't freak him out, but it does. It really does.*

It was in that moment that Kumari made her decision. She absolutely must not tell him about the full goddess thing. It would be the end of them, she knew that. If Chico knew the truth, then why on earth would he hang around? Why when he had his own life to live and she could disappear from it at any moment? OK, so they were really young, but somehow Kumari knew in her heart and soul that he was the one.

All of this whirled through her mind as they sat, gazing at their plates. Finally Chico cleared his throat.

'I'm sorry I didn't come earlier,' he said. 'But I wanted to see you for the first time again on my own.'

'I understand,' said Kumari. His eyes were molten in the light. *I need to remember this moment,* she thought. *It might have to last me forever.*

'Great outfit, by the way,' he teased her.

'Thanks.' She raised a smile.

'No, really, I love it. It suits you.'

'OK, OK. Enough. I know I look strange.' She could feel herself begin to relax once more.

'Exotic, I would say. And what's wrong with strange? It's never stopped you before.'

'I love you too.'

She hadn't meant to say that, it had just slipped out in a sarcastic way. But now she had it lay between them like a sleeping serpent, something neither of them wanted to touch, but both knew was there. During the awkward pause that ensued they both dropped their eyes and stared once more at the makeshift table. After an excruciating moment, it was Chico who finally spoke.

'Anyways,' he went on. 'I figured you might want something to eat. This is your favourite, right?'

He indicated the pizza carton on the table. Emblazoned across it in curly letters: *Giovanni's – Pizza Fit for Kings.*

'Think they cater for goddesses too?' said Chico.

'I think they might just include us on the menu.'

'Double cheese feast with chilli?'

'You remembered,' she smiled. Unbelievable that he should, but then, that was Chico all over. He was Mr Thoughtful to the max. She could feel the ice thawing to a slush.

'And,' Chico added, flourishing a can, 'Coca Cola for the lady.'

Her favourite-ever meal. He had got it exactly right.

All of a sudden, though, Kumari did not feel like eating. There was something about Chico's proximity that had all but killed her appetite. But he had gone to such trouble that she had to at least take a nibble.

'Mmm, that is heavenly.'

'High praise from a goddess.'

He grinned at her and raised his can, clinking it against hers in a toast. *Maybe he's OK with it,* she thought. *No, don't take any chances, Kumari.*

'To you,' he said, then added, so softly she almost missed it, 'To us.'

To us. Oh my goodness. He had said 'To us'. Or maybe he hadn't.

'What did you say?' she asked, then immediately wished she hadn't.

'I said "To us". I mean, I hope there is an "us". We're still friends, aren't we, Kumari?'

Friends. What does he mean by 'friends'?

'Uh, sure. Of course we are.'

He looked a little crestfallen, as if she had said something wrong. But she had said they were friends, hadn't she? Boy, this was triple confusing.

He leaned across the makeshift table and took her hand. A thousand volts thrilled through her. He might as well have lit a match and held it to her palm. She could feel that heat spreading to her face, extending across her cheeks in a telltale flush. Thank goodness for the dim glow from the street lights. Puce was never a good look.

'I missed you,' he said.

'I missed you too,' she said. Why had her brain gone into jelly mode? There were a million things she wanted to say, all of them snappier than that. But somehow all she could think of was that he was here, holding her hand and she never wanted it to stop. It flashed through her head, the sentence

61

she had read in the RHM's musty manual: *Once full god or goddess status is attained, the new god or goddess must remain within the confines of the Hidden Kingdom . . .*

No, she could never, ever tell him about the sword poised above both their heads. An actual sword; the Sacred Sword, to be precise. The moment she wielded it with intent, she would become a full goddess and their love would be over forever. There was no going back once that happened; she would be confined to the kingdom, a divine creature. Destined to live as an eternally youthful being until her time came to ascend the Holy Mountain.

Somewhere in her gut she had always known it, but for the first time Kumari faced the truth. She and Chico could never be – and yet she wanted him with all her heart. Love. Another thing she had acknowledged.

The price for which was always pain.

At least, in her experience.

CHAPTER 6

Chico collected Kumari the next morning in a cab.
'I still think you're crazy,' he said. 'Why do you want to
go back there, of all places?'

They looked at one another, sharing the unspoken memory
of Razzle's clinic on Park Avenue. It had been from there that
Chico had rescued her, half dead, hallucinating thanks to the
cocktail of drugs Razzle had pumped through her veins. The
same veins he had intended to slit open in his search for
the secret of eternal youth.

'Because there might just be some kind of clue as to where
he is now. Find him, I find the Ayah. OK, it's a long shot, but
it's worth it. Where else would I start?'

They headed south, towards Park Avenue. As they rode,
the buildings became progressively smarter, the streets more
salubrious. Kumari knew for a fact Razzle was no longer

there. Raider's 'people' had confirmed it, although so far that was the only information they had come up with. Their search continued, but far too slowly for Kumari's liking. Simon Razzle had gone to ground and she needed to flush him out to find the Ayah. One thing on her side was the surprise factor: they would never expect her to come after them. As far as they knew, Kumari could not leave the Kingdom. Well, she *had* left the Kingdom, thanks to Theo's pendant, and she was hot on the trail of revenge. But as they drew up outside the building, Kumari had to brace herself.

'OK?' asked Chico softly.

'OK,' said Kumari. Last time she had arrived here it had been in Sonny's clutches. This time, it was under her own steam. Even so, she took a deep breath before she raised her eyes to look at the entrance. So many bad memories . . . but the place looked benign enough. It was a typical imposing midtown building, complete with doorman and covered walkway. She barely glanced at the doorman as they passed, heading for the elevator.

'It was on the sixth floor,' said Kumari. 'But there's no nameplate here now.'

Kumari had little memory of being taken to the clinic and only the haziest recollection of Chico's rescue. One thing that would forever stick in her mind, however, was seeing the number six on the wall beside the elevator that would take her to freedom. Those days incarcerated at Razzle's mercy were some of the darkest of her life.

As they emerged from the elevator, Kumari automatically turned left. They were looking for suite 606 but she didn't need a number to find it. The moment she stood outside the door, it all came flooding back. She half expected to open it and find the same hushed waiting room occupied by a couple of elegant Park Avenue ladies. In fact, the ladies looked much the same, but they were evidently there for a different purpose. Instead of Razzle's softly-lit photographs depicting cosmetic perfection, there were now orthodontic charts on the walls.

'Can I help you?' A severe-looking woman peered over her spectacles. Razzle's carefully enhanced receptionist had been replaced by an altogether more realistic specimen.

'I . . . uh . . .'

Overwhelmed by the waves of nausea that suddenly attacked her, Kumari struggled to speak. This was the place she had nearly lost her face; the clinic where Razzle had wanted to carve her up.

'I need to sit down,' she stuttered, collapsing on to a seat next to a well-coiffed woman. The woman threw Kumari a frosty look and moved up a space.

'Do you have an appointment?' demanded the receptionist.

'Hey lady, can't you see she's not well?' said Chico. 'Do you have any water? Come on, Kumari, you hold on tight. I said, she needs a glass of water.'

Way to go, Chico, thought Kumari as she stuck her head between her knees. Sometimes it paid to give as good as you got. This was no time for social niceties.

'All right already,' said the receptionist. 'The water fountain is over there.'

Kumari raised her head. 'I'm OK,' she mumbled.

Her head was once more whirling, but this time with bizarre visions. It seemed Power 2, the Power of Extraordinary Sight, had come upon her without her even having to summon it up. Was this another sign that she was hurtling towards becoming a full goddess? Kumari sincerely hoped not. In her head, she could see Razzle, only it was not Razzle. Or at least, this Razzle was different. In her vision, his face did not look exactly the same, but she could not quite put her finger on what it was. And the hair – that was definitely something else. The Razzle she knew had short, brown hair, but this Razzle sported a shock of bleached tresses that fell in a fringe over his forehead. The eyes, though, were unmistakable, still as marble cold as ever. Try as she might, she could not see beyond Razzle's head and shoulders. There was no clue to his surroundings, nothing that might help lead her to him. As Power 2 drained away, Kumari sat slumped on the waiting-room chair. It looked like they had reached a dead end. They would have to try another way.

'Let's go,' she said to Chico, staggering shakily to her feet.

She had to get out of there before the evil in the air choked her.

'She's been to Park Avenue,' said the voice on the phone. 'She came with some young dude who was all protective.'

'I trust the doorman did not say anything to them?' asked Razzle.

'Of course not. We paid him well.'

'How long did she stay?'

'A few minutes at the most. The receptionist said she acted kind of dizzy, like she was feeling sick or something.'

'I see. But nothing else? She didn't do anything out of the ordinary?'

'Whaddya mean "out of the ordinary"?'

'You know – anything strange or unusual.'

'Like I said, she got a bit dizzy.'

'And the young guy – did he say or do anything?'

'He was concerned about the girl, that was all.'

'Are they still staying at Gracie Mansion?'

'That older foreign guy is, but she's moved out.'

A sudden, frosty silence that throbbed across the airwaves.

'What do you mean she's moved out? Where exactly is she staying?'

'At the apartment in the Bronx. The one that kid used to live at. You know – Sonny, Ratboy, whatsisname . . .'

'Enough. This line may not be secure.'

'Hey, I'm scrambling the signal. I know my job, mister.'

'You know your job, so get on with it – and this time keep me fully informed. If that girl so much as sneezes I want to know about it. Kumari is your number one priority.'

'Mister, I'm on the job twenty-four/seven.'

'Make sure you are or I'll know about it.'

And with that, the connection was abruptly cut off, leaving the man staring at his cell phone.

'Jeez,' he muttered. 'You sure want this kid.'

Something about this job was beginning to bug him a great deal.

CHAPTER 7

'I think it's time to get my sorry ass to the salon,' said Ma. 'Find out what Lola has been up to.'

It was seven o'clock in the morning. Kumari opened one reluctant eye. She was back in the bedroom she'd occupied when she first lived with Ma although 'bedroom' was a generous description. The room was so small she could sit on the bed and touch both walls at the same time. Kumari loved it, nonetheless.

'Are you sure that's wise?' asked Kumari, wearily propping herself up on one elbow. From the extra pillow beside hers, a snuffled protest sounded. Badmash had never been a morning bird.

They had only been at Ma's apartment a couple of days. A visit to the salon seemed a little premature. Then again, Ma's regular blast of Power 5 was beginning to really work. A hint of the old bounce had returned and there was that glimmer of hope in Ma's eye. She was still, however, a shadow of the woman who had single-handedly strutted the cause of purple leggings. There was a long way to go before Ma was restored to pink-tipped glory.

'Wise? You bet it's wise! Lord only knows what Lola's been doing. Don't get me wrong – I appreciate her help and all. But that place needs my special touch.'

It certainly needs something, thought Kumari as they turned up at Hoodoo Hair an hour later, Badmash still protesting in her ear. The salon looked forlorn, as if it had been missing its owner. The orange walls appeared somewhat faded; the silver fittings tired. There was no jar of candy on the front desk. Even the snake that curled across the sign looked limp. Hoodoo Hair had lost its mojo in much the same way as Ma.

'Nothing we can't fix,' said Ma as she surveyed it, although Kumari could hear the tremor in her voice. Rolling up her sleeves, Ma set to, putting the place to rights. Kumari worked quietly beside her, fetching and carrying as directed, occasionally passing an object to Badmash so he could polish carefully with one wing. Soon the towels were arranged just so and fresh flowers adorned the desk. By the time Lola appeared to open up, even the candies were sparkling in their jar. She fell on Ma with a cry of delight.

'I heard you were better, honey. Oh my goodness, but look at you, girl!'

'I was aiming for size zero,' said Ma. 'But then I figured it was a waste of time. Who wants to be a *nothing*, anyway? I like my numbers, like my shoes, in pairs.'

As Lola shrieked with laughter, Kumari glanced at Ma's feet. Less bleary-eyed now, she noticed what Ma was sporting: silver running shoes with sparkly pink streaks. It reminded her of the way Ma's hair had been the last time she had seen her, in the Kingdom. Only a few months ago, Ma had been happy and complete.

While Lola smothered Kumari in kisses, an idea began to germinate.

'Hey, Lola,' said Kumari, emerging breathless. 'How about you do something with Ma's hair?'

At this, Ma visibly bridled.

'I can do my own hair, thank you.'

'Come on, *chica*. What is it – you don't trust me?'

Ma eyed Lola's own dubious coiffure. Her locks, dyed an improbable burgundy, cascaded from her scalp in tight ringlets. Coupled with kohl-rimmed eyes and Lola's love of scarlet lipstick, the effect was unflattering at best. Somehow, though, Kumari liked Lola's style. She preferred to age disgracefully. There was something about her defiance that was heartening. Why should the effects of Time stop a person having fun?

With a sigh, Ma capitulated. Soon, Lola was a flurry of hair dye and pins. By the time the first customers appeared at the salon, Ma was ready. She looked like a Medusa who had had an accident with a palette. All the colours of the rainbow corkscrewed through curls that sprang at haphazard angles from Ma's head. The *pièce de résistance* was the bow that hung drunkenly over one temple. While Lola clapped her hands in delight, Ma gazed at herself in the mirror in disbelief. To Kumari's horror, her shoulders began to heave as tears streamed down her face.

'Ma, are you OK? Ma, it's not that bad.'

The other ladies were crowding round. Motherly Mrs Martinez pulled a handkerchief from her purse, but Ma managed to wave it away. A sound emerged from her throat amid the soundless wheezing and gasping.

'Heeee heeee heeee,' Ma guffawed. 'Ha, ha, ha. Oh my Lord . . . yeee hooo . . .'

All of a sudden, she was on her feet and dancing, waving her hair around. Occasionally she would stop and glance in the mirror before the giggles overtook her once more.

'Lola, that is the worst hairstyle I ever seen. I love it. I love you. It's *horrible!*'

Dumbstruck, the ladies looked on until Lola, too, began to chortle. Soon, tears were streaming down all their faces, a mixture of laughter and relief. Their beloved Ma was back with them and so were Kumari and Badmash, who was taking advantage of their distraction to help himself to the jar of candies.

'Hey, look at that,' called out Lola all of a sudden. She was pointing through the salon window across the street. 'That man, he's back,' she added. 'The guy who's been keeping a watch on the place.'

The merriment ceased as abruptly as if someone had thrown a switch. They crowded round Lola, still pointing, but of course the man had gone.

'We've seen him a few times now,' piped up Mrs Martinez.

'I'd like to get my hands on the schmuck,' said Mrs Brinkman.

All at once, the troubled look was back on Ma's face.

'How long has this been going on?'

'Just the past few days,' said Lola. 'We got no idea what he wants. Reminds me of when Kumari was last here and the place was being staked out.'

Kumari looked at their anxious faces. Oh no, it was starting again. She had only been back in the World Beyond a couple of days and already paranoia was setting in. If the salon was being staked out then she was most probably the target. And who would want to know her movements but someone who wished her ill?

Over a hundred blocks away, on the Upper East Side of Manhattan, the RHM was rummaging under his bed. His fingers closed around a scabbard and he pulled it out, laying it carefully on the coverlet. Kumari had been given the State Bedroom across the hall, as befitted her status, but his was equally comfortable. With the utmost care, he withdrew the Sacred Sword from its silver sheath and held it up to the light. Carved along its deadly arc, prayers to the gods demanded justice and divine might.

This was a scimitar like no other; the ultimate weapon of a living god or goddess. The moment Kumari seized hold of this, she, too, would join their ranks. The RHM shut his eyes for a moment and tried to picture her holding it. She was slight but very strong, honed by years of Karali instruction. The lethal martial art had given Kumari a poise and balance worthy of her station. He could almost imagine her wielding the sword with supreme accuracy. Almost, but not quite.

Emitting a soft sigh of frustration, the RHM slid the sword back inside its tooled scabbard. She was so near and yet still so far. Kumari needed to progress with her Powers. It was indeed marvellous that she had acquired Power 5 and impressive to see the results, but it was a big leap from there to full living goddess status. He was not even sure she wanted to make the jump.

Naturally, the prospect of becoming a full goddess might seem rather daunting, but Kumari was a brave girl. He had witnessed that many times now, not least when she had run into the burning palace to save her mother's portrait. Of course, her current lifestyle would be curtailed somewhat once she achieved her rightful status, but the rewards would more than make up for it – especially, he was sure, once he had shared his vision for the future with Kumari. Besides, she had always known that the position was her birthright; that the Kingdom needed its female figurehead. Kumari would come through. She might just need a little persuasion.

SECRET CHAPTER

Some years before . . .

The young woman stood in the forest glade, listening to all the familiar sounds. She could hear the chattering of the monkeys in the trees. The rush of water over rock. The sweet song of the birds flitting from branch to branch. The melody of remembered laughter. With a sigh, she looked at the basket in her hand. She was here to gather flowers and herbs for her mother. She had better get on with her task and forget all about her friend. It was obvious she was not able to come.

She should have expected it, of course. Once you became a royal, you forsook friends and close family. That was the unshakable rule of the Kingdom. And yet it was a rule that seemed so unfair in a place where Maximum National Happiness was paramount. As children, they had played here. But now her friend was goddess-queen and her life was restricted to the palace. It was a double shame now they both had daughters of their own. It would have been wonderful to see them play together.

Kumari and Asha were almost the same age; they had been born three months apart. When the goddess-queen gave birth the whole Kingdom rejoiced. Asha's arrival was a more muted affair. And yet she bore no envy or malice towards her friend. How could she, when the goddess-queen had sacrificed so much? She existed in a gilded cage. Divinity was a blessing and a curse.

Despite everything, though, they had managed the odd assignation over the years, especially since Kumari's birth. It helped that the goddess-queen's sister now worked as Ayah to Kumari, although that, too, was a secret. Everyone thought that the Ayah was some distant cousin. She would not have been allowed into the palace otherwise. No friends or close family – what a stupid rule. Sadly, the young woman shook her head.

She knew her message must have got through. She had handed it to the Ayah herself. There was something about the woman she had never trusted, but she was the only conduit she had. In spite of her obvious jealousy towards her sister, the Ayah had proved reliable in the past. In which case, the goddess-queen must have been detained on some palace business. It was the way that things were now.

Spying a particular flower in the grass, the young woman bent to pluck it. Her mother wanted this to add to her medicinal tincture as well as the leaves that grew up high. A sharp crack brought her head up. Could her friend have come after all?

'Hello? Are you there?' she called out in a hushed voice. Even here, you had to be careful.

There was no answering call from the forest. The birds had ceased to sing. Sighing, she bent once more to her task. It was then she heard it, an odd swishing sound. Before she could cry out, something hit her hard on the head. It brought her crashing to the ground. Scrabbling to her knees, she tried to stumble away. Whatever it was, it came after her.

Throwing one arm up to fend it off, she twisted around so that she could see.

'You!' she gasped. 'Why . . . what . . .?'

She could say no more. He was dragging her now towards the depths of the forest. *He's going to leave me here, she thought. Somewhere I will never be found. I'll never see my daughter grow up. I'll never know what Asha becomes.* She wanted to scream, but she no longer had breath to; she wanted to weep, but there were no tears left.

Somehow this man had known she was going to be here. He must have found out about her meeting. Which meant that her friend, the goddess-queen, was also in danger. It was obvious the man was ruthless. He had stopped now, throwing her aside as if she were no more than a bundle of rags. He bent low and spoke so he was sure she could hear: 'So you thought you'd break the rules of the Kingdom,' he murmured. Somewhere above her she could see the sky through eyelids that were almost closed. She could feel herself slipping away. It was no good, she could not fight.

'No one breaks the rules,' said the man. 'I have a vision for this place, a plan. It's people like you who would destroy that. And that is why I cannot let you live.'

The last thing she heard was bird song. It was as sweet as her daughter's laughter. *I love you my child,* she thought. *Be strong and remember me, Asha. Grow up and look after Kumari.*

CHAPTER 8

Balloons and banners bedecked the tiny living room. Even the TV had once more been turned off in Kumari's honour. A table outside the kitchen groaned with her favourite treats: Twinkies, Cheetoes and cans of Coke alongside pizza from Giovanni's. The ladies from Ma's salon were there, bags bulging with yet more goodies. Mrs Brinkman dispensed gobbets of wisdom in one cramped corner while Lola danced with Theo in another, craning her neck to look flirtatiously up at his face.

Giddy with joy, Kumari spun from one person to another, one moment giggling with CeeCee and LeeLee, the next exchanging smiles with Ms Martin. Dressed in an old, cut-down pair of LeeLee's jeans and a strappy red top of CeeCee's, she felt freer now to be her New York self. She was light-headed with exhaustion; running on empty. Far too excited to eat and, besides, too busy talking. But still, she felt she could party on forever if it meant being with her friends. There was just one nagging ache, however, that threatened to overshadow her glow of happiness, a noticeable absence that she could not manage to ignore.

She had not seen Chico since that evening on the roof and that was four days ago. She had thought they had re-established something special that night. So how come she hadn't heard from him since? They had come up with the idea of a party the day before, in the salon. It was mostly to welcome Kumari back but also to celebrate Ma's recovery. Everyone was invited: all Kumari's friends from school and beyond. *So what if he's not here,* thought Kumari. So a lot, that was what.

Her eyes slid past the RHM, standing uncomfortably near the door. The RHM was cross she had changed out of her imperial robes, but there was little he could do save purse his lips. Kumari forced herself to look away even as she glanced yet again at the doorbell. If only it would ring to signal his arrival. Maybe he was just late. Or maybe he wasn't coming at all. And if he wasn't coming, then what could have happened? Some kind of crisis or, worse, no crisis. *Come on, Kumari, don't be selfish.*

There was someone else missing. Kumari sidled over to Hannah. Her friend was looking gorgeous in boho blue, her cloud of dark hair framing her pretty, intelligent face.

'Where's Charley?' Kumari asked.

Hannah's face darkened. 'We don't hang out together any more,' she said.

'Why not?' Kumari demanded.

'Charley's kind of hanging with a different crowd.' It was

clear from Hannah's tone of voice that she did not approve of Charley's new friends.

'You don't like them?' asked Kumari.

'No one likes them. They're scumbags.'

To Kumari's horror, Hannah's eyes began to fill with tears.

'Hey, don't cry,' she murmured, pulling Hannah close for a hug.

'I'm sorry,' mumbled Hannah. 'I didn't want to lay this on you at your party. I guess that was kind of stupid. You were bound to notice she wasn't here.'

'Yeah, well,' said Kumari, 'you're here and that's all that matters. We can talk about Charley later. Right now, let's have a good time.'

It took all she had not to mention Chico, but her friends had thrown her this party and she would do her best to enjoy it. She glanced up to see Ms Martin squeezing through the throng, diamante earrings bobbing, skirt more festive than usual.

'Kumari.'

'Hey, Ms Martin.'

'We haven't really had time for a chat. So much has happened. Theo told me a lot, but I'd like to hear about it from you.'

Kumari looked at her old teacher. Ms Martin was something special. She was one of the few who had believed in Kumari in those early dark days at Rita Moreno. Theo was one lucky man to have her. Actually, they were lucky to have one another. Theo had been great back in the Kingdom. Kumari still regretted how she had suspected him of being up to no good. She could see him now, dancing with tiny Mrs Martinez, hunching his shoulders and gallantly attempting to salsa. Never mind that the music was reggae. Salsa was all Mrs Martinez liked to do.

'It was crazy,' said Kumari. 'The Ayah and Razzle cooked up this plot to kidnap me. They were working with the warlords who roam the borderlands. They have always wanted to invade our Kingdom.'

'Theo said they tried to steal some Secrets,' said Ms Martin.

'They did but we got them back. The Ayah tried to force me into the World Beyond, her and her little gang. She knew I would die almost instantly. She tied poor Badmash to a tree and then taunted me, trying to make me rescue him. I only got out of it by using some Powers and shutting them out of the Kingdom. Being a trainee goddess comes in handy sometimes.'

'I'll bet,' said Ms Martin. 'But it sounds awful for you. How are you doing with the goddess thing?'

Kumari dropped her eyes. 'Let's just say I'm trying to avoid it. The thing is, I think the Ayah is still alive. That's why I'm here, to track her down – only you mustn't tell anyone as it's a secret. You see, as long as she lives, Mamma is not avenged and is still stuck in limbo. I know it sounds weird, but the gods have sent a warning and I made a bargain with them.'

'It doesn't sound weird at all,' smiled Ms Martin. 'Not coming from you, at any rate. But how are you going to track the Ayah down? The world is a big place.'

'I know that, but I also know she is in the States. I had this dream, you see. And then there was the writing on the wall.'

Although Ms Martin kept on smiling, she was beginning to look a little puzzled.

'The details are not important,' said Kumari hurriedly. 'You have to believe me, I know she's here somewhere. And the best way to track her down is to start with Simon Razzle.'

'Such awful people,' said Ms Martin, barely suppressing a shudder. 'Kumari, you must take care.'

'I will' said Kumari. 'Raider offered to help find Razzle, but I don't trust him.'

'You're wise,' said Ms Martin. 'He has big plans for himself. The presidential nominations are up for grabs this year.' She was about to say more when Theo caught her by the wrist and whisked her off to dance.

Kumari was working her way back towards the kitchen when she noticed someone slip in the front door.

'Ch-Chico,' she stuttered. There was a girl on his arm. A stunning girl with coal-black hair and a face that was made for TV. She was clinging tight to Chico, gazing up at him with adoring eyes.

'Kumari.' He was standing in front of her and so was she, the celluloid angel. 'Kumari, you remember Angie.' Oh great, they'd even named her for a celestial being.

'Hi, Angie,' Kumari spluttered, convinced she had never seen this girl before in her life.

'Hi Kumari. It's great to see you again.'

Really? I wish I could say the same for you

Rooted to the spot, Kumari had an overwhelming desire to run. The hubbub around her faded to nothing. She felt like she'd been dropped down a very deep mine-shaft. Even the light appeared to grow dimmer as she gazed into Angie's eyes. So this was why Chico hadn't called. All the stuff he'd said on the roof was absolute garbage.

'Excuse me,' muttered Kumari. 'I . . . uh . . . I need the bathroom right now.'

Wonderful, Kumari. Just brilliant. Always come up with an embarrassing excuse.

'Sure,' smiled Angie. 'See you later.'

'Yeah, later.'

And with that, they were weaving through the crowd, Chico's arm placed solicitously at her back, his eyes ever watchful and protective.

Choking back a sob, Kumari dived for the kitchen. The route to the bathroom was blocked. At least in here, among the food wrappers and debris, she could hide like a frightened mouse. Except there was no hiding when it came to eagle-eyed Ma.

'Kumari, whatchoo doin' in here, girl?' she demanded.

'It's Chico. He came with this girl.' There was no point in even trying to lie. Ma might not be quite her old self yet, but she was still sharp.

'So? You just get back out there and show him what he's been missing. And besides, have you asked him who she is? That girl could be his sister for all you know.'

'She is, actually,' came Chico's voice from the doorway.

Ohmigod. Angie. Chico's little sister. Last time she'd seen her, Angie had been wearing pigtails and braces. There was absolutely no resemblance to the swan she had become. Although, now Kumari thought about it, she should have recognised her by her resemblance to Chico. She had the same dark locks and olive skin, the same caramel eyes. Blinded by jealousy as she was, Kumari had been well and truly caught out. *Great. Fantastic.* Just like that time he'd brought Maria to the school dance and she'd turned out to be his cousin's girlfriend.

'Your sister. Wonderful,' mumbled Kumari.

Ma looked from one to the other and left them to it.

'She asked if she could come. She's been dying to see you again. We've had a lousy few months with Grandma being ill. I thought this might cheer her up.' Chico's expression was a mixture of disbelief and disappointment. He was looking at her as if for the first time. As if she was someone he did not know.

Double, double great. She hadn't even asked about his family. She had been so caught up in herself, she hadn't thought he might have his own problems.

'The worst thing, though,' said Chico, 'is that you still don't seem to trust me. Why is that, Kumari? What exactly have I done?'

It was a good question. And one for which she had no answer.

'I dunno,' mumbled Kumari. 'You haven't done anything, Chico.'

Self-hatred started to suck at her, along with the beginnings of fear. Why oh why could she not manage cool? Cool was good when it came to emotions. It meant you never got hurt. It provided you with a shell.

'Anyway,' she added. 'It's none of my business who you bring to the party. I mean, it's not like we're dating or anything.'

'If that's the way you feel . . .'

'It is.' Kumari raised her chin defiantly.

'I don't get it.' Chico frowned.

'You don't get what?'

'You. Me. The other night. I thought we agreed we had something special.'

'We did?' She couldn't meet his eyes.

'I thought so.'

Kumari shrugged.

'Have it your way,' said Chico. 'I'm sorry. Sorry I troubled you and sorry I got it so wrong.'

All at once, the speedball of fear that had driven Kumari stopped rolling. Real pain marked his handsome face. *No*, she wanted to shout out, *turn the clock back. Forget I said all that. I'm sorry. I'm an idiot. I got scared.* Instead, she watched him disappear into the party, gazing at the way his hair curled into the nape of his neck. Once she had loved to nuzzle into those shoulders. Now it seemed she had killed any chance of ever doing that again.

Why oh why did I say those things? she asked herself. *Is it because I'm terrified he'll leave too? Mamma was snatched from me – so he might be as well. But that's not true. It's illogical. I know that.* There was nothing logical, however, about emotion. What she had mistaken for cool was, in fact, fear. And now, by giving in to it, she had made it all come true. She had driven Chico away before he had the chance to leave her.

My bedroom at Ma's

Day four in New York

I cannot believe I did that. I mean, what was I thinking?! I love Chico and I went and behaved liked that. Sometimes I just don't understand myself. First I go and get all worked up just like I did over Maria. And then, even when it turns out it's only his little sister, I go and push him away like that. Ma says not to worry – all I have to do is explain. But how do you explain to someone you had a psycho moment for which you have no motive or excuse?

Now I feel guilty I kept Ma up talking, even though she said it was absolutely fine. It is so obviously not fine to keep her from her bed when she is still not her normal self. Sure, she seems like the old Ma when she talks, but I can see the tiredness in her eyes. She's trying hard to put on a good show, but I can tell she's a long way from being happy. I'll give her another blast of Power 5 tomorrow – that should help a bit.

Then there's having to deal with Jack Raider – that guy is so obvious. A grin that only stretches to the top of his cheeks. I don't know how he does it. Well, actually, I do know. It's called keeping your eye on the main chance. Well, I've picked up a few tips from Mr Raider. Let's see who plays the game better. The thing is, we still need his help, or at least the help of his people. There is no way we can find Razzle and the Ayah on our own. As the RHM said, we have no resources, other than my goddess Powers.

Of course, he emphasised the Powers bit a lot but I pretended to ignore him. He is really getting heavy about Power 5 – I'm sure he knows that I've used it. It is pretty obvious, I guess – Ma is doing amazingly. But she might have done that all on her own, so how can the RHM really tell? Anyway, he's right that we need Raider's help. If anyone can find Razzle it has to be the mayor. I'll just have to keep Raider sweet even though he makes me feel sick.

CHAPTER 9

Rita Moreno Middle School looked much the same from the outside apart from the shiny new sign at the gate:

Rita Moreno Middle School
Proudly Sponsored by Raider Enterprises

Dwarfing the lettering, Raider's logo dominated the sign and everything else in sight. It consisted of a rearing lion which had a laurel wreath clamped between its jaws while above it a bird flapped.

'You like it?' asked Raider. 'I got the idea after the HUNK fundraiser.'

The RHM glared at it stony-faced, clearly unimpressed.

So that was supposed to be Mamma's lion. But what of the bird?

'That's a dove,' said Raider, as Kumari stared at it. Badmash let out a dismissive squawk. He had little time for other birds, probably because he considered himself human.

'It signifies peace,' added Raider unnecessarily. 'Which is a central part of my message. Or rather, HUNK's message. It's so important the kids get it.'

And what would you know about kids? thought Kumari, although she smiled and said nothing.

As they approached the main entrance door, Raider announced: 'I have a little surprise for you.'

Oh really, thought Kumari. The only surprise was he'd waited so long. Whatever was up was clearly of immense importance to Raider. He even straightened his tie before pushing the door open. Kumari noticed another of his logos on the handle.

And then they were standing in the echoing entrance hall, the security guards springing to attention. Each wore a sweat-shirt emblazoned with that wretched logo. Had Raider never heard of overkill? The entrance hall was a hive of activity as people carrying clipboards scurried to and fro. One man was laying cables, another adjusting cameras.

'What on earth . . . ?' said the RHM. Kumari watched his mouth fall into instant disapproval mode.

'My new project,' said Raider, flinging his arms wide. 'It's called "School for Happiness".'

Kumari stared at him, dumbstruck.

'It's a reality TV show,' he added.

So this was it, his grand plan. She had known something was cooking. Never in her wildest imagination, however, would she have thought of something like this. A reality show at Rita Moreno? Some hokey Happiness theme? Before Raider even opened his mouth, Kumari knew what was coming next.

'And you, my dear, are to be the star of it.'

'Oh no,' said Kumari.

'Absolutely not,' snapped the RHM. 'I will not countenance such a thing.'

For a second, Raider was taken aback – but only for a second. He had not climbed to the top of the political pile without developing a rhino's hide for a skin, along with the adaptive cunning of an urban fox.

'Of course, RHM, of course. I should have shared my plans with you. But I wanted to surprise Kumari. I thought she would enjoy being with her friends once more. The benefits to them will be incalculable as well as to every one of our viewers. We have a chance here to bring Happiness to the masses, to spread more of the message Kumari brought us.'

Brilliantly done, thought Kumari. Even the RHM faltered in his tracks. No slouch in the wiliness stakes himself, he had more than met his match. Raider had effectively laid on a platform for the other part of their mission. Papa had charged her to bring Happiness to the World Beyond. Now here was a wonderful chance to spread the word.

'Papa did say . . .' she murmured to the RHM.

'I know, child, I know.' The RHM met Raider's benign gaze with a hard stare. 'I need to speak to Kumari for moment.'

'Go right ahead,' said Raider. 'I'll just talk with my producer here.'

A thin man wearing a baseball cap smiled as Raider approached, exposing perfectly straight teeth. Behind him, several people hung about sipping coffee from cartons. It was low-key chaos; the hallmark of a TV set.

'I am not happy about this,' pronounced the RHM.

'I know,' said Kumari. 'But it could help in so many ways. I know it's risky but Raider is the best-connected person we know. If his contacts can't lead us to the Ayah then no one can, simple as that.'

'I fail to understand how,' said the RHM. 'Putting you on television may destroy our chances. We need to proceed with stealth.'

'If I may interrupt,' said Raider, reappearing just in time to hear the RHM. 'The show will be taped so that it goes out after Kumari leaves. By the time it's on air, she won't even be in the country any more.'

The RHM stared into space as his mind processed this information.

'It could, perhaps, work.'

Kumari clapped her hands together. 'I knew you'd come round, RHM!'

'I haven't "come round" as you put it, Kumari. I am merely considering it as an option.'

Considering was enough, as far as Kumari was concerned. She waited, holding her breath, until finally the RHM turned to Raider.

'I will permit Kumari's participation under controlled circumstances. First of all you must recognise we are only here for a short time.'

'No problem. We can tape everything we need in three weeks,' said Raider.

'Secondly and most importantly, you must guarantee Kumari's safety at all times.'

'Why, of course,' said Raider, guilelessly. 'I look on Kumari as the daughter I never had. There will be absolutely no risk to her well-being.'

Oh puke, thought Kumari. *The daughter I never had.*

As soon as the RHM had given the nod, Raider went into full-spin. Make-up girls were summoned to powder his nose and chin. Another set to work on Kumari while a hairdresser brushed out her long, raven hair. The layers Ma had cut into it during her stay in the Hidden Kingdom had grown out but it still looked a darn sight better than it once had.

The RHM shook his head firmly as the make-up girl produced a lipstick.

'That's enough,' he said. 'His holy majesty would not approve. Come to that, he would not find your outfit acceptable, Kumari. What have you done with your imperial robes? If you are to represent the Kingdom you cannot do it dressed like that. We must send someone to fetch them at once.'

'No way,' wailed Kumari. 'I won't do it. I'm not appearing on TV dressed in a silk sack.'

'I'm sure we can sort something out,' said Raider hastily, clearly anxious not to alienate the RHM once more.

'I'm not wearing them,' Kumari insisted. 'All my friends will think I look like a dork.'

Out of the corner of her eye, she could see kids hovering in the corridor beyond. How soon before the bell rang and then they were all out? She was dying to see her friends but not like that, not dressed up in an ankle-length thing. It might be the height of imperial fashion, but even in the Kingdom she felt out of place next to her friends at Palace School. How much worse would it be here among the sneakers and sweatshirts that comprised the Rita Moreno uniform? OK, so they weren't exactly on trend either, but at least everyone looked more or less the same.

'Look RHM,' Kumari piped up. 'We could just make sure my clothes don't appear in shot. If the camera focuses on my head and shoulders, no one will really see what I am wearing.

The RHM thought hard for a moment then glanced at Raider, obviously impatient. Ever the diplomat, he would not want to upset their host. At last, he nodded his head gravely.

'Very well, Kumari, you may proceed dressed as you are, provided the camera focuses on your head and shoulders.'

'At last,' muttered Raider under his breath. 'OK, folks, let's rock and roll.'

'Positions please,' said a young woman with an open, pleasant face. She walked over to Kumari and smiled with genuine warmth. 'Hi Kumari, I'm the director of the show and my name's Lucy Gillman. Could you just stand right here for a moment and then we'll show you your mark.'

'Um . . . sure . . .' said Kumari. What was a mark exactly? There were two crosses laid down on the floor with tape. Raider was being positioned on one, which meant the other must be for her. She was led to a spot near to where Raider stood, already practising his smile for the camera.

'Quiet please. Action . . . and cut! Can we get rid of the bird please?'

They were all staring at Badmash, who had decided to inspect the camera. Or rather, he had decided to inspect the cameraman's pockets, which were bulging with sweet treats.

'That's Badmash and you can't "get rid" of him,' said Kumari. 'You'll hurt his feelings.'

'OK,' said Lucy. 'Badmash, come over here.'

She was holding out a cookie purloined from the catering

table. Sensing a new best friend, Badmash hopped happily towards her.

With the cameras once more rolling, Raider took a deep breath.

'Hello there and welcome to *School for Happiness*,' he said. 'This is a project that is dear to my heart . . .'

On and on he rambled, extolling the virtues of his precious programme. How the kids who participated would find their lives transformed, how the folks at home could benefit too. Finally, Kumari felt someone prod her in the back.

'And cut,' said Lucy.

Kumari was bundled into position beside Raider and the whole farrago recommenced.

'I am proud,' he said, 'to introduce a young lady who has taught me a great deal. This here is Kumari and she will be telling us how to bring more Happiness into our lives, courtesy of the special place that she calls home.'

Kumari could feel her face freezing in a stupid smile. What on earth was she supposed to say? She heard Lucy call 'Cut!' again. They tried another time and another.

'All you have to say is, "Thank you, Jack. It's great to be here",' said Lucy encouragingly. Raider's impatience was building a head of steam but he somehow managed to keep a lid on it.

Try as she might, Kumari stumbled over the words. It was so hard so say something she did not mean. Sure, she had appeared on *Oprah* that one time but this was a whole different experience. For one thing, Jack Raider was no Oprah Winfrey, skilled in making her guests feel relaxed. The more Kumari tried, the worse it got. They were going for one more take.

Diiiiiiiiiiiiiiiiiing. The second bell. Which meant that any moment the kids would be spilling out of class. There was only one thing worse than humiliation and that was public humiliation. All of a sudden, Kumari was word perfect.

'OK, just one more time for luck,' said Lucy. 'Take it from the top, Jack.'

Out of the corner of her eye, Kumari could see kids surging down the corridor towards them. Too late. She was trapped. She caught a glimpse of a familiar face: Eddie, the sneering bully who had once shut her in a locker. To Kumari's gratification, he had put on extra layers of lard to complement his zits. Clearly Eddie had been eating one too many buckets of fried chicken to stoke his campaigns of terror.

Casually, she scanned the rest of the growing throng and smiled as she caught sight of Hannah. No sign of Chico, but plenty of other faces she knew. Great. Maximum embarrassment factor. Shutting her eyes, Kumari waited for her cue, listening as Raider droned on about *School for Happiness*, deepening his voice as he spoke of his HUNK campaign and how it meant so much to him. With sincerity oozing from every pore, he touched on his mayoral achievements before smoothly segueing into a promise to every voter that he hoped and prayed to do so much more.

It was a masterful oration, the best performance yet. And then the jeers started. As Raider smiled into the camera, the kids could be heard chanting: 'Raider out!' in the background.

'Cuuuuuuut!' screamed Raider himself this time before rounding on the culprits. 'What in the world do you think you are doing?'

'Raider out, out, out!' they yelled.

Infuriated, Raider waded in, cuffing an ear here, an arm there. His own security detail had to pull him off. The crew looked on, horrified. Open-mouthed, Kumari stared before giving in to an attack of giggles. In the *mêlée*, Raider's toupee had slipped to one side. It hung over an ear, all askew. She had not even known he was bald. One more thing about him that was fake. For that was what the kids were chanting now: 'Fake Raider, Fake Raider.'

'Silence!' a voice called from the direction of the door.

Turning, Kumari saw Ms LaMotta, the formidable head of Rita Moreno.

'What is going on here?' she demanded. 'Mr Raider, you assured me there would be minimal disruption. When I agreed to let this camera crew into my school, I did not expect to have to contain a riot.'

'Ahh, Ms LaMotta,' beamed Raider, surreptitiously shoving his toupee back into place. Kumari heard a snigger from one of the kids.

'I said silence!' snapped Ms LaMotta.

Her eyes swept the entire entrance hall and then settled on Kumari.

'Kumari, my dear. We heard you were coming. Welcome back to Rita Moreno – although I had no idea you were to be involved in the show.'

'Kumari,' said Raider, 'is to be the centrepiece of *School for Happiness*. Her winning entry to the state essay contest did, after all, bring me into the Moreno fold. It also taught us all a great deal about true Happiness, as I am sure we will agree. Which is what I was just about to say on camera when I was so rudely interrupted.'

'Well, there will be no more interruptions,' said Ms LaMotta, her eyes sweeping the throng of kids. 'Please, Mr Raider, go right ahead.'

This time, when the cameras rolled, the kids remained silent. They knew better to cross Ms LaMotta, who stood by the security desk, arms folded. Even the two guards looked terrified as she flicked them a dismissive glance. Ms LaMotta had turned Rita Moreno around. She was not about to let standards slip once more. When Kumari had first come to Rita Moreno, there were still remnants of the old regime. A lack of discipline had led to abysmal results and an air of ill-contained anarchy. Now it was a place the kids and teachers could be proud of and she had played a part in its renaissance.

Dimly, Kumari became aware that Raider was reaching the climax of his introductory speech: 'I am proud,' he said yet again, 'to introduce a young lady who has taught me a great deal. This here is Kumari and she will be telling us how to bring more Happiness into our lives, courtesy of the special place that she calls home.'

Cue a big smile and her line.

'Thank you, Jack. It's great to be here.'

At last, the director yelled a final 'Cut!'

Kumari felt her shoulders sag in relief. It was then that she saw Chico, standing half hidden by a pillar. Next to him, Hannah raised a thumb and grinned, then melted tactfully away as Kumari approached.

'Hey.'

'Hey there.'

'How you doing?' He was looking at her warily.

'I'm good, Chico, but there's something we need to talk about. Have you got a minute?'

She waited, hardly daring to breathe. She could see him hesitate and then he said, 'I, uh . . . not now. Gotta go.'

Unbelievable. He was turning her down. She opened her mouth to speak, but he had already turned away. Maybe it was not so unbelievable. She had behaved pretty badly. Numbly, Kumari watched as he walked away from her and out of the door. Every single step that he took felt like a nail being hammered into her heart.

KUMARI'S JOURNAL
(TOP SECRET. FOR MY EYES ONLY.
EVERYONE ELSE KEEP OUT!)
THIS MEANS YOU!

Still at Ma's

Day five in New York

I deserved it, I guess. I mean, why should Chico speak to me? That's not once but twice now I've treated him like a cheat. He was so great to me that night on the roof and he never once mentioned his family had been having a hard time and I didn't even bother to ask, so what kind of friend am I anyway? Never mind girlfriend, I failed him at the most basic, buddy level. And I would do anything to make it better, but it seems like right now I can't. All I can do is keep trying. Will he even want me to keep trying? I don't know. This is yet another mess. But in some ways it's good – I have something else to think about besides finding Razzle. Like trying to get Chico back.

So maybe School for Happiness is not such a bad idea, even though it does sound really cheesey. Theo thinks it will be an interesting experiment but then he thinks that about most things. And Raider has asked him to scientifically measure the results although I'm not sure how he's going to manage that. I mean, how exactly do you measure Happiness, especially if you are a scientist? Theo says they have come up with a way but it's kind of complicated, so I said why bother. After all, Happiness is not exactly complicated is it? You're either happy or you're not. Theo said there was a little more to it than that and, besides, the audience likes to think something is scientific.

At least he'll get to see Ms Martin twenty-four/seven while he's working on the show. Some people might not think that's a good thing, but they get on great the whole time. Ms Martin is so busy with the school and Theo with his work that it seems to me they hardly get to see one another. When they do they're all googly-eyed – honestly, they're like a pair of teenagers. Some people say it's so uncool, but I think it's kind of cute. And at least they like one another and aren't scared to show it. I wish I could do that with Chico, but it's obvious he's not interested.

So I'd better get on with working out what I'm going to teach at School for Happiness. It's all very well throwing me in there and saying I'm the expert, but the trouble is, I've never had to think about it. Back in the Kingdom, Happiness is all around. It's in the air that we breathe, for heaven's sake. Every single person has been brought up to believe Happiness is all. That's why maintaining Maximum National Happiness is Papa's most sacred duty.

One day it will be my duty too so maybe I should look on this as good practice. After all, Happiness is about living certain attitudes. That's what I need to teach the other kids. There may not be a Haze of Happiness here but we can try and create our own version. I mean, every tiny action that brings Happiness will spread out to others, so that will act almost like a haze. Will you listen to me? I sound like some kind of guru! Maybe I really am getting the Gift of Wisdom. On second thoughts, maybe not. That's far too close to being a full goddess. I'd better sign off now – I have a date with Hannah. Time to sort out one more mess . . .

CHAPTER 10

Hannah was waiting outside the corner store when Kumari came running up. She was still not used to living once more by the clock. In the Kingdom, they measured time differently, by the passage of the sun and moon.

'Hey, Hannah, sorry I'm late.'

'No problem. I brought you a present.' And with that, Hannah slid an oversized bag from her shoulder and gave it to Kumari.

'The Badmash Bag! Ohmigosh. I can't believe you still have it.'

'You betcha,' grinned Hannah. 'Couldn't get rid of your hidey hole, could we, Badmash?'

Her words, however, were lost on Badmash, who had already dived straight in. Squeaks of excitement matched his frantic wriggles. The bottom of the bag was lined with doughnuts.

'You shouldn't have,' said Kumari. 'He can barely fly as it is.'

Judging by the gobbling sounds, there would soon be even more ballast on Badmash's already well-padded belly.

'So, where are we going?' asked Kumari.

Hannah's face grew serious. 'To this scuzzy store on Fordham Road. Charley's new friends like to hang there.'

Fordham Road. Sonny's old haunt. Poor Ma would always suffer his loss despite the fact he had been a total rat. She was his mother, after all. Their bond was unbreakable. Just as hers had been with Mamma. Still was, come to that. Kumari shook her arm so her amulet slipped to her wrist. That way, she could feel it. Most of the time she was so used to wearing it she was unaware of its presence, but now and then she liked to be reminded. It strengthened her determination to find the Ayah.

They took the bus most of the way, heading west of Webster Avenue. This part of Fordham Road was jam-packed with shops that sold anything and everything, their garish signs covering up what had once been beautiful buildings.

'This is it,' said Hannah, dragging Kumari into the store.

The place somehow managed to be both cavernous and dingy. It was set out on several levels with concession stands adding to the maze-like effect. They were piled high with an array of cheap-looking items. Everything was here, mostly designer rip-offs with labels that kept them just this side of legal. They headed down to the basement sales floor, the Badmash bag weighing heavy on Kumari's shoulder. Sated, Badmash had gone to sleep. Not even the sounds blasting from giant speakers would wake him after a doughnut feast.

'There they are,' said Hannah, dodging behind a stand. Kumari looked where she was pointing. At first she did not recognise Charley, giggling at the centre of a gang of five. Then she realised the redhead with the cigarette was, in fact, her friend.

'Oh my god, her hair,' she gasped.

'I know,' said Hannah grimly.

'And smoking . . . I thought that was prohibited.'

'Like they'd worry about that in here.'

In that instant, Kumari saw Charley slip something inside her purse. She turned, incredulous, to Hannah.

'She's . . . ?'

'Shoplifting, oh sure. They do it for kicks. She dyes her hair so often they never recognise her. She told me that, you know. Like she's proud of it or something. Honestly, Kumari, I just don't know what's happening to her.'

Hannah's eyes filled with tears as she shook her head in despair.

'She cut class again today. Pretty soon, they'll throw her out. The teachers try, but no one can get through to her.'

'Hey, it'll be OK, you'll see,' said Kumari. 'That's still the old Charley in there, somewhere. All we have to do is find her and bring her back. Why don't we go over and say hello?'

And with that, she strolled up to the gang, smiled and said, 'Hi.'

There was a pause and then they turned as one to stare at her.

'You talkin' to us?' sneered a guy whose hood could not conceal a virulent crop of acne.

For a moment, Kumari was reminded of the time she faced

down Eddie and his crew in an alleyway. Then, as now, she had been outnumbered, but at least this time she was not trapped. There would be no need to summon Power No 7, the Power to Move Freely Through the Earth, Mountains and Solid Walls.

'I am,' said Kumari coolly. First rule of combat: show no fear.

'And who the hell are you?'

Second rule: stay calm under pressure.

'Kumari! Oh my god!' Charley let out a squeal.

'You *know* her?'

'You bet I do. So just butt out, loser.'

And with that, Charley flung her arms around Kumari, forgetting all about her new persona for a moment.

'It's so good to see you,' she whispered. 'But how did you find me here?'

'Hannah brought me,' said Kumari. 'She's worried about you.'

It was the worst thing she could have said. Instantly, the shutters went up.

'Oh yeah? I don't know why,' sneered Charley. She looked to her new friends for support. 'You guys worried about me at all?'

They fell about laughing like a bunch of hyenas.

'Only thing worries me about you, babe, is that cute little tush of yours.' A tall, spindly guy made a passable attempt at leering.

The only other girl in the gang had stayed silent until now.

'Hey, you're that weirdo,' she said to Kumari. 'You used to be at Moreno.'

Kumari stared at the girl. She did not recognise her at all.

'You don't remember me, do you?' said the girl. 'I used to be with Chico's cousin, Joe.'

And then it all came flooding back.

'Maria?' Kumari gasped. Could this pasty, strung-out creature really be Joe's gorgeous girlfriend? Correction, ex-girlfriend. She had been so vibrant and pretty. Too pretty, in fact. Kumari could still remember the violent surge of jealousy when she had seen her with Chico at the Halloween Ball.

'Yeah, Maria,' said the girl. 'I kinda moved on from Moreno and Joe.' She winked at the others and yet again they sniggered. 'Say, aren't you supposed to be some kinda witch?' added Maria.

'Leave her alone,' muttered Charley.

'Yeah, that's right. You do some kinda hoodoo voodoo stuff.' Maria's eyes were glittering with a bully's certainty.

'I said leave her alone,' snarled Charley. 'You deaf or something?'

'Butt out, kid,' said Maria, shoving her aside. 'You always were a whiner.'

Now they were practically nose to nose, Maria taller than Kumari, trying to intimidate her. *Stand back*, thought Kumari. *Make her come to you.*

As Maria lunged, Kumari's foot shot out and caught her by the ankle. A carefully aimed elbow to the chest and Maria was down. Shocked, she did not move for a moment and then she started spitting with fury.

'Why, you little —'

'Run!' squeaked Hannah from somewhere behind, but Kumari was not going anywhere. The tallest boy made a grab for her and she dealt with him easily. Within moments he, too, was on the floor and the others were looking nervous. That was the great thing about Karali, or any martial art, come to that – you could handle people twice your size without hurting them too much.

'I'm outta here,' muttered the guy in the hood. 'The girl is crazy.'

Maria, however, was not finished. With a howl of rage, she lunged once more.

'Bring it on!' she screamed. 'Whattsa matter? Can't do your voodoo?'

This time, Kumari just had enough room to spin out of the way before catching her under the knee. Yet again, Maria went down and the look of surprise on her face was priceless. From across the shop floor, they could hear shouts. The store clerks had spotted them. Now, it really was time to run. Seizing Hannah by the arm, Kumari headed for the stairs.

'Come on,' she yelled to Charley who hesitated before she, too, sprinted for the exit. Behind them, they could hear Maria shrieking as the store clerks descended upon the gang.

'Hey, wait for me.' Charley came panting after them. Kumari grinned at her friend over her shoulder. She had hoped that little display might convince her. They could still hear Maria screaming incomprehensible oaths as they emerged into the sunlight.

'This way,' said Hannah and they took off at a fast walk along Fordham Road. 'In here,' called Kumari as they reached a McDonald's. She could see a security guard standing near the door. Charley simply followed them, mute. Kumari chose a booth from where they could see out, but not be seen too easily. Once they were settled with their milkshakes, Hannah let out a huge sigh of relief.

'Oh my god,' she said. 'I thought we were dead there. That girl, she is scary. What's with her, anyway?'

They both looked at Charley, still staring silently at the table.

'I dunno,' she finally muttered. 'Just leave it, OK?'

Kumari looked at Hannah. 'OK,' she said easily.

They sat in silence for a few minutes, sipping their milk-shakes.

'My mom and dad,' said Charley, all of a sudden. 'They're splitting up.'

She looked as if she were about to cry and, instinctively, Kumari reached for her hand.

'Why didn't you tell me?' said Hannah.

'How could I? You were so busy with Daniel.'

'That is just not true,' said Hannah. 'And anyway you never said anything about your parents until now. What do you think I am, a mind reader?'

'Yeah, well, whatever,' said Charley. Her lower lip was wobbling.

'Guys, please,' said Kumari. 'It sounds like you need to talk, that's all.'

'Oh, right, and then everything will be better, just like that?' The sneer was back in Charley's voice.

'No, but it might help,' said Kumari, deliberately keeping her own voice soft. These two clearly had their problems outside of Charley's own situation, but the biggest of them all was staring in through the window. Maria and Mr Zitty Hood were looking in their direction, only they couldn't quite see them thanks to Kumari's strategic choice of table.

'So,' she said, instinctively ducking lower into the booth. 'Why don't you start first, Hannah?'

'Uh, sure,' said Hannah, ever reasonable. 'Look, Charley, I'm sorry you feel the way you do.'

Good start, thought Kumari, *but keep going and faster.* She was praying Maria and Mr Zitty Hood would not walk in and spoil this opportunity. She glanced as casually as she could at the window. Fantastic. They had gone.

'And I'm not, like, with Daniel every second. I spend plenty of time with you. Or at least, I spent plenty of time with you until you started cutting school.'

'I couldn't face it,' said Charley sadly. 'Hey, Hannah, I'm sorry.'

That's it, thought Kumari. *Wonderful. They're talking.* Even better than that, they were smiling at one another. It was a great start back to normality. Then Charley glanced up and her face hardened. Kumari did not even need to look round to see what was coming – or rather, who.

'It's the Kung Fu Kid,' she heard Maria say. Great, they must have walked in when she wasn't looking.

'Actually, it's Karali,' said Kumari, turning to look into Maria's mean little eyes.

'Whatever,' said Maria, obviously itching for a fight. Not even she, however, would take on the security guard hovering near the door. 'You coming, Charley?' she added. It was more a command than a question.

'Yeah, sure,' mumbled Charley, pushing away the rest of her milkshake. Mr Zitty Hood attempted a menacing grin that exposed snarled, yellowing teeth.

'You don't have to go with them,' said Kumari.

Maria cocked her head to one side and smiled almost nicely. 'Sure she does,' she said sweetly. 'She's not stupid, are you, Charley?'

'Just leave it, Kumari,' said Charley. 'I'm going with them, OK?'

They've got some kind of hold over her, thought Kumari. *She looks almost scared of them.*

'Charley, please,' she tried again. 'Don't let them scare you. Whatever it is, we can sort it out. You don't have to do what she says.'

'Oh, I think she does. Don't you, Charley?' Maria's eyes shone with triumph. *She's enjoying this,* thought Kumari. *What is it Charley's so afraid of?*

'Charley, please don't go,' said Hannah. 'We'd just started talking.'

'Oh yeah? What'd you tell them?' demanded Maria. 'I told you to keep your mouth shut.'

'I didn't tell them anything,' whined Charley. 'Let's just go. Later.' She turned without a backward glance and headed for the door.

'See you later, girls,' said Maria sarcastically.

'In your dreams,' smiled Kumari.

There was no way she would show them the fear she felt in her heart for Charley.

The RHM watched the group emerge from McDonald's. The red-haired girl was walking with her head down while the other, dark-haired one appeared to be berating her. A third person, probably male although it was hard to judge, slouched along a few steps behind. Really, the clothing these young people adopted in the World Beyond made it so hard to identify them.

A short while later Kumari, too, emerged with her friend and walked in the opposite direction from the one the others had taken. Her friend was evidently upset and Kumari was doing her best to comfort her. While this was laudable, the RHM found it hard to contain his disappointment. Kumari had had every opportunity today to use her Powers, but she had chosen instead to employ Karali.

Back in that revolting emporium, he had found it easy to hide behind a rack of clothing and observe her conduct. At first he had hoped she might fall back on her divine attributes, but it was not to be. Even better would have been to acquire a new Power, so she was one step closer to acquiring Power No 1. Naturally, he did not expect Kumari to become a full goddess overnight, but her rate of progress was painfully slow. Gentle encouragement had failed. Perhaps it was time for a change of tactics. It would not hurt to have an added incentive , for example. If only Raider's agents would come up with something on Razzle, but they, too, were working at a snail's pace. It was then that an idea struck the RHM, one so beautifully simple he almost clapped himself on the back.

Excitedly, he scurried towards the subway station, already working out how to put his plan into action.

From his vantage point across the street, the man sporting wrap-around shades watched the foreign guy scuttle off. He sighed and folded his newspaper. This case was getting more complicated by the minute. It was obvious the girl did not know he had been following her. And how come he was sneaking around after her when this same guy seemed to be her guardian? Sure, it was the client's dollar paid the bills, but he had a bad feeling about this one.

Why were they all so interested in what Kumari did? The kid seemed fairly normal to him. OK, so she was beautiful and somehow different, but there were a thousand girls in New York City like that. The place was a magnet for pretty girls who could be kind of kooky. What was it about Kumari they found so fascinating? Two grown men were watching her every move. One paid him, one didn't. Which kind of dictated what he had to do next. Wearily, he picked up his cell phone and punched in a number. Sometimes he hated what he did.

KUMARI'S JOURNAL
(TOP SECRET. FOR MY EYES ONLY.
EVERYONE ELSE KEEP OUT!)
THIS MEANS YOU!

My bedroom at Ma's

Day 7 in New York
I have twelve hours and around twenty minutes to come up with something. We start shooting tomorrow at nine a.m. and I still don't have a clue what I'm going to teach them. I mean, Happiness is Happiness. You can't really teach it. You can tell someone how they might achieve it, but then it's up to them.

And I pretty much told them how to do it in my essay the last time I was here. Thank goodness Ma kept a copy. There has to be something here I can use.

It won a prize, after all – that means they must have liked what was in it. Or at least they understood what I was trying to say. And I only said it really quickly. What I mean is, I sort of gave them the main points, just like Ms Martin used to get us to do in class. I mean, I went on about how health, true wealth, love and expressing yourself are all you need to be truly happy – but how on earth am I going to teach them that?! Especially when half the class thinks Happiness equals a thick shake and a burger.

The thing is, the people here in the World Beyond will never escape Time no matter what they do. They might as well eat a ton of junk food – they're going to die anyway. Hmm – seeing that written down does not look too good. Now I think about it, I may have taken on too much with this. So what else is new?! What is it Ma says? That I've bitten off more than I can chew. Yeah, well, that's what Eddie does and all . . . Oh, ha, ha, Kumari.

OK, how about this next bit of the essay – the part where I say we listen to and trust ourselves. Oh my god, I can't believe I wrote this stuff. I mean, it didn't exactly work with Chico, did it? And that might just be the problem. I mean, how can I possibly teach anyone anything about Happiness? I'm not even happy myself right now – in fact, my life sucks. I have yet to avenge Mamma. I have no clue where the Ayah is. I can't even manage to track Razzle down. Where's the Gift of Wisdom when you need it?

That's supposed to be one of the five great gifts of a goddess.

Well, it's not working. If it was, I would know what to do –
and I don't – not about anything. Chico won't even speak to
me and one of my best friends has gone and become some
kind of gangster chick. My other best friend here is in pieces
because of it and I don't know how to make it better. At least
Ma is on the mend – hey, that's something I have done right.
I know it's not all me, but I think Power 5 has helped a lot.
And that's another worry – I don't want the RHM to find out
for sure about it. I have him breathing down my neck want-
ing me to be a full goddess.

Frankly, everything's gone nuts. Or maybe it's me that's
gone nuts. Well, I can't help it. My life is nuts. And so are most
of my friends. Even my pet bird is nuts, although he's nuts in
a nice way. Badmash is the one who should be teaching
Happiness. So long as he has a doughnut he's content.

Hey – maybe that's it. That could be Lesson One –
Happiness comes from appreciating what you've got. But how
do I teach that to a bunch of kids from the World Beyond? Oh
look, I've got eleven hours and fifteen minutes in which to
come up with something. Eleven hours and fourteen minutes.
Boy, do I hate this thing called Time. Eleven hours and thirteen
minutes. Come on, Kumari . . .

CHAPTER 11

They were all staring at her expectantly, a ring of faces that blurred into one. Her friends and a handpicked bunch of her old classmates. Her former teacher, Ms Martin. Even the principal, Ms LaMotta, had turned up to participate in *School for Happiness*. To one side, Jack Raider hovered, arms crossed as he surveyed what he considered to be his domain. Next to him, the RHM maintained an expression that was entirely inscrutable. All of these people plus, of course, an entire film crew, would soon be waiting for her to open her mouth and come out with something profound. Trouble was, she had nothing to say, nothing to teach them about Happiness. One sleepless night later, she was no further along.

'OK, Kumari, I'd just like to go over it with you,' said Lucy, the director. 'So, you'll introduce yourself to camera and then you'll take us through Lesson One.'

'Ah, yes,' said Kumari. 'Lesson One. No problem.' Desperately, she prayed for a sudden blast of goddess wisdom. Of course, none came.

'Wonderful,' smiled Lucy. 'Now, can we just run through the main points? I know this is meant to be fly-on-the-wall, but I do need some idea of where you're going with it.'

'Uh, sure,' said Kumari, trying to ignore the bead of sweat that was forming at the base of her skull. It grew larger and larger until it trickled in a ticklish rivulet down her spine. She beamed at Lucy, trying to look more confident than she felt. *Come on, Kumari. Say something. Improvise.* She opened her mouth to speak and somehow the words fell out: 'Lesson One is all about the Importance of Nothing.'

Lucy stared at her for a moment. 'I see.'

'Or at least, it's about getting rid of Things.'

'Go on,' Lucy smiled encouragingly.

Kumari was winging it now and something coherent was coming out. Maybe the goddess Wisdom thing was working after all. Yeah, right, in her dreams.

'I have to start with Nothing,' went on Kumari, 'before I can build up to Something.' She was well and truly warming to her theme, so much so the sweat was springing up else-where. She could feel it prickling at her brow and pooling in places she had never thought could perspire. *Oh great,* thought Kumari. *I'm all shiny before we even start.* Never mind worrying about Happiness – she now had to deal with looking like a walking oil-slick.

Kumari licked her lips. Her mouth felt as if she had sucked on a thousand lemons. Lucy was still looking at her in that puzzled way. The kids were beginning to whisper amongst themselves. At least Chico was not here. Not that she had scoped out the room or anything. But a whole bunch of other kids she knew were and all eyes were upon her. Any moment now they would smell her fear and then Kumari was done for. She could see Eddie out of the corner of her eye, wearing his habitual sneer. *Oh my god, how did he get picked?*

'Nothing,' said Kumari desperately, 'is the essence of Happiness. Without Nothing we are . . . nothing. I need to teach the kids to be . . .'

Oh my god – he had just walked in. She caught Ms LaMotta's look of displeasure. How come he was always late these days? That was so unlike Chico. He was talking to Ms LaMotta now, apologising. Chico was good at smoothing things over. Except with her, of course. It seemed he didn't want to do that. Well, if that was the way things were to be, she would simply pretend he wasn't there. Subconsciously, her fingers reached for her amulet. It always made her feel better.

Kumari looked at Lucy, at her open, friendly face. All of a sudden, she knew what she was going to say. It was going to be all right.

'You see,' she said. 'It's all about letting things just kind of flow. Like water, you know? You just have to let it happen.'

Lucy looked at her for a moment. 'And that's what you're telling me you want to do.'

'Well, yes,' said Kumari. 'If you trust me, that is.'

Lucy's eyes searched out her own. Then she gave a little nod, as if satisfied.

'OK, Kumari,' she said. 'We'll just go with the flow, shall we?'

Lucy glanced over to where Raider stood, tapping his foot impatiently. 'Close the set,' she said.

It took Raider a moment to realise and then his face darkened with fury.

'Are you asking me to leave?' he demanded.

'I think it's best for the show.' Lucy's voice was polite but firm. It was clear she was not intimidated.

Good for you, thought Kumari. Raider could be a bully.

After much huffing and puffing, Raider edged towards the door, followed by his security man.

'And you too, sir,' said Lucy to the RHM. Kumari had to suppress a giggle. No one talked to the RHM like that back in the Hidden Kingdom. His authority was more or less absolute, second only to the King's.

'But I must stay with Kumari,' protested the RHM. 'I am acting upon the King's orders. I assured his holy majesty I would protect her at all times.'

Slightly hypocritical, thought Kumari, seeing as he was perfectly happy to let her stay at Ma's. OK, maybe not perfectly happy, but it was obvious he only wanted to stay to make sure she said the right thing.

'Kumari will be just fine,' said Lucy. 'We have an entire crew here to protect her.'

She was holding the door open now, the steel evident behind her smile.

'Come on, RHM,' said Raider, mindful of how much any delay would cost him. Ms LaMotta, too, was gently but firmly shown the door.

And then it was just the class and Ms Martin, exactly like the old days. Except that in the old days there had not been a camera crew shadowing their every move. Kumari glanced at Lucy once more and felt another prickle of panic. Again, her fingers reached for her amulet. The confidence surged back through her. It seemed Mamma was watching over her in the only way she could, through the slender silver bracelet she had once given her daughter to protect her from harm.

Kumari smiled at Lucy. 'I'm going to start by getting them to realise Nothing is more important than Anything.'

Lucy looked at Kumari for a long moment. 'OK, you're the boss. Rolling. Speed. ACTION!'

Kumari took a deep breath. This was worse than the essay competition. She glimpsed Hannah's sweet face, but carefully avoided looking at Chico.

'I'm going to tell you about my Mamma,' she began, ignoring the snort of derision from Eddie. 'You see, my Mamma was murdered.' Now she had their attention. 'And ever since then I have been trying to find Happiness myself. That's why I think I might be the best person to help you all find it, too. Not because I am perfectly happy, but because I am not.'

She was scarcely aware now of the cameras rolling in the background or of Lucy's approving gaze or Ms Martin's supportive smile. As she spoke, she could almost see her Mamma and feel her strong arms about her.

'The only times that I am truly happy are those when I forget what has happened, when I lose myself for a moment in whatever I am doing. It is during those times that I let go of the anger and pain, that I know what it is to be free and happy once more. You see, we don't need things to make us happy. In fact, the more things we have, the more we worry.

Back home in my kingdom I could have many things, but we don't see them as necessary.'

She glanced up and saw the camera and almost froze for a second. Quickly, she averted her eyes and looked instead at her classmates. No longer a blurred mass, she could make out individual faces. Written on those faces were a variety of expressions, many of them echoing how she felt.

'I have learned,' went on Kumari, 'to let life flow around me. It's not the easiest thing to do, but when it happens it works. But stuff gets in the way – people, thoughts, objects. Just like stones in a stream, they force water to flow another way. Sometimes they even dam it up – and that's when you're in real trouble. Let water or life stagnate and it soon begins to stink.'

She heard a giggle from the back. *Don't worry about it.* A little humour was a good thing if it got her point across.

'What I would like you to do,' she said, 'is make a list of everything and anything you think is important in your life. And then I want you to go through it with a partner and cross out anything that might be a stone in your stream.'

They were still staring at her, wide-eyed, waiting for she knew not what.

'So come on,' said Kumari. 'Let's get writing. Make lists!'

And so they did, debating heatedly amongst themselves as they wrote.

'Why do you think you need a catapult?' someone demanded of Eddie.

'Because I do,' he snapped.

'What's with the hair straighteners?' Hannah asked of the glossy girl sat next to her. The girl looked at her in horror.

119

'I can't live without those!' she cried.

All of it, Lucy captured on camera, working the room unobtrusively. All human emotion was there to be viewed as each and everyone had their most precious needs challenged.

'And cut!' called Lucy but the debated still raged on.

'What the heck is "reconciliation"?' Kumari heard somebody demand. She glanced over her shoulder and realised it was the boy sitting next to Chico. For a fraction of a second, her gaze locked with his and then Chico looked down at the list before him.

'I guess it's not that important,' he muttered and drew a line through the word. As his pencil tore through the paper, Kumari felt a similar rip through her guts. *He hates me,* she thought. Well, if that was the way he felt she would leave him to it. *Let it flow, Kumari.*

KUMARI'S JOURNAL
(TOP SECRET. FOR MY EYES ONLY.
EVERYONE ELSE KEEP OUT!)
THIS MEANS YOU!

My bedroom at Ma's

Day eight in New York

I need to make my own list. I need to clear out the stones from my own stream. But there's so much to write about and I don't even know where to start. OK, let's start with the big one – the Ayah. How can I cross her off until I've avenged Mamma? The same goes for Razzle and, in a different way, the RHM. Raider's people still haven't come up with any real leads and I can tell the RHM thinks that if only I was in total control of my Powers, we wouldn't need to rely on their help.

But all this pressure to get my Powers is just getting in the way of what's important. And what's important is finding the Ayah so I can avenge Mamma. Keeping Raider sweet is supposed to be a part of that, but is it really too high a price to pay? I mean, this reality show thing sucks and I've only been doing it one day. All right, so it doesn't totally suck – one kid actually came up to me and said how much he liked it. And Lucy's pretty cool, but the whole thing is really just another way of bigging up Raider . . .

So that's the biggest stone in my stream right now: tracking down the Ayah so I can free Mamma from limbo. Then there's the way Ma still hurts so much over Sonny. OK, so it's her pain, but I feel it for her. And what about the Charley situation and the way it makes Hannah so unhappy? Not to mention Chico and my getting it so wrong. Of course I had to mention Chico. How could I not? It's in my mind all the time. OK, so it's in my heart. And boy, can I feel it.

You know, sometimes you can't just get rid of situations you don't like – you have to work them through and that's hard. There is no such thing as instant Happiness. I should know – I've been working on it my whole life. And I'm not doing too well so far. OK, Kumari – must try harder!

CHAPTER 12

Kumari stared at the pile of photographs on the table before them. On the top lay a blurred picture of Razzle. It was obviously taken from some distance away and at first glance did not look like him at all. But then Kumari remembered her vision in his old Park Avenue clinic – this was the new, improved Razzle. The patrician nose, painfully perfected, extended from under designer sunglasses. The bleached locks clashed badly with an acid-yellow T-shirt on which some kind of slogan was written. If anyone was ever not made to wear a T-shirt it was Simon Razzle. He belonged in a couture suit and handmade shoes, preferably crafted from Italian leather.

'These were sent anonymously,' said one of Raider's people. 'There was a note stating they were taken in LA, but that's all the information we have for now. We are, of course, investigating and trying to find Mr Razzle's exact location.'

LA was a big place. Still, it was a start.

The other agent extracted another photograph from the pile.

'In a lot of these photographs Razzle's with different women, but there's one who pops up all the time. Do you recognise her?'

Kumari braced herself. Taking a deep breath, she looked and then let out a sigh. It wasn't the Ayah after all. There was, however, something familiar about the face that was turned in conversation towards Razzle. The two had been photographed at some kind of restaurant table and it was clear they were deep in discussion.

'We have another picture of her if that will help.'

Kumari glanced at the man and then took the photograph he was holding out. This time, she let out a gasp. She knew where she had seen the woman before: in Razzle's clinic, where he had kept her incarcerated.

'That's her,' she stammered. 'The woman who wanted my face. Razzle was going to cut it off and sell it to her.'

One of Raider's people looked faintly nauseous.

'That is just sick.'

'It is indeed,' said the RHM. 'A good measure of Razzle's ruthlessness. This makes it all the more important that we hunt him down without delay.'

Not to mention we need to find the Ayah.

'Well, now, here's the thing,' said Raider. 'We're in a *quid pro quo* situation.'

'A what?' asked Kumari.

'You scratch my back, I scratch yours.'

'I see,' said the RHM. 'And what exactly are you proposing?

123

I thought Kumari had done everything you required of her, fronting your show.'

Raider waved a hand at his people. 'You can leave now. We're done here.'

Without another word, the two of them gathered their things and departed. Now they were alone in Raider's office. Raider exposed his veneered teeth in a facsimile of a smile. It reminded Kumari of a shark going in for the kill.

'The thing is,' said Raider, 'the show will not simply sell itself. We need Kumari to spread the word, to give people a sneak preview.'

'And what precisely do you mean by that?' The RHM's tone was clipped.

'I mean *The Tonight Show*. They want Kumari on to talk about *School for Happiness*.'

Smug was not the word for it. Raider was positively licking his grinning lips. The RHM, however, was not easily impressed.

'The late-night talk show?'

'The very same filmed in LA. You'll have a great trip. Take in some sights. I would come too, but there's a little something I need to take care of here.'

LA, where Razzle was hiding out like a sewer rat.

'But that's great!' said Kumari.

'Absolutely not. Under no circumstances.' The RHM's tone was final.

Raider's grin faded instantly.

'Are you telling me "no"?'

'I am telling you to tell them "no".' The RHM's gaze did not waver.

Raider stuttered, incredulous. 'B-but it's *The Tonight*

124

Show. With Jay Leno. It's the biggest talk show in America. You want me to turn down the biggest talk show in America? I do not believe I'm hearing this. We need this. I need this. You want me to find this Razzle guy, you'll do it.'

For what felt like the longest second ever, the RHM stared him down. Then, with impressive dignity, he rose.

'Come, Kumari. We're leaving.'

'You can't leave.'

'Oh yes we can. This discussion is over. I will not expose Kumari to any danger. Your idea is utter lunacy.'

Kumari looked from one to the other, not sure where this was heading. All she knew was that it felt bad. She needed to find the Ayah more than anything. If Raider would not help them, then who would? All he was asking her to do was one lousy show. It was worth it to find Razzle, to get him to lead her to the Ayah, whatever the risks. She was about to open her mouth and say as much, but the RHM was already hustling her out of the door. Glancing over her shoulder, she saw Raider's face, his mouth hanging in slack-jawed astonishment.

'The trouble is, we need him.' Kumari watched the RHM pace to and fro across Ma's bedroom. The only place they could go was Ma's apartment. Somehow, Kumari did not feel they were too welcome right now at Gracie Mansion. It was a small room, which meant he had to turn every five paces, but he never once broke stride, his expression impenetrable.

'*He* needs *you*, Kumari,' he said. 'He needs you more than you need him.'

'Maybe,' said Kumari. 'But without his help we'll never find Razzle. And if we don't find Razzle then we certainly have no hope of finding the Ayah. His people just said those pictures were taken in LA.'

'Kumari, my mission is to protect you. I promised his holy majesty. I said from the beginning this television show was madness and I feel I have been proved abundantly correct. Far from aiding our efforts, it has merely placed you in more danger. And by going to Los Angeles you could be walking right into the lion's den.'

'Please, RHM.'

'No, Kumari. And that is my final word.'

Kumari knew better than to press the point. When the RHM was in this mood, there was no persuading him. In which case, she would have to try something else. Something the RHM would not like.

Casually, Kumari glanced at the alarm clock beside Ma's bed. A neon pink copy of the Taj Mahal, its chimes were straight out of Bollywood. The digital dial indicated it was nearly six o'clock. Time for Ma's evening dose of Power 5 and the perfect opportunity for a little chat.

'Is something wrong, Kumari?'

Excellent. He had caught her sneaky peek, just as she had intended.

'Uh, no,' she said, eyes wide. 'It's just that *The Simpsons* is about to start.'

'*The Simpsons*?'

'It's a TV show.'

'About what?'

'Um . . . just an average family.'

'I see.'

The RHM studied her for a moment.

'Sometimes I find it difficult to understand you, Kumari.'

Likewise, thought Kumari. The RHM was just about the hardest person to read in the world. Well, apart from her Papa now and then, and Chico. Actually, Chico came a close second.

'I'm sorry RHM, but I am tired. It's been a long day and I just want to kind of relax.'

It was true, she was exhausted. There seemed to be such a lot to deal with on a daily basis. Nevertheless, she thought she should throw in a yawn, if only to underline her words.

The RHM softened a fraction. 'Of course you are, child. But we must talk again. And I must return to Gracie Mansion. I have much to discuss with Mr Raider.'

'Absolutely. Most definitely. You deal with him, RHM.'

She was edging towards the door now, nearly home and dry. The one thing the RHM must not discover was her use of Power No 5. Once he knew that, he would also know she was that much closer to full goddess status. Which would not be a good thing. At least, not for Kumari. The RHM was an excellent teacher; she could not fault him on that. He only wanted her to become a full goddess. And she only wanted to be herself.

'Just one more thing, Kumari.'

'Ah, yes, RHM?'

'Ma appears to have made a remarkable recovery in the short time you have been here.'

Kumari felt her mouth go dry, but forced herself to smile at him. 'Yes, I suppose she has. I think she's glad to see me.'

'She must be very glad indeed to have made such progress.'

'She is. She told me so herself. And now I had better get back to her.'

Her hand was on the door handle now, turning it as she kept smiling. He knows, she thought. Or at least he suspects. I have to be more careful. Just two more Powers to acquire and that's it. I'm finished.

Several thousand miles away, Simon Razzle stared at the package in his hand. It had been couriered overnight from New York, courtesy of the agent working there on his behalf. The man was good, he would give him that. He had been straight on to Kumari as soon as those Sherpas had tipped them off that she was on her way back to New York. He had taken care of the Sonny problem. He had also provided updates on the Ma Hernandez situation. So far, the woman had no idea who had disposed of her useless son. Or if she did, she had not gone to the authorities. Not that they would find Razzle in any case. Any fool could try and slip back into the United States and be caught literally red-handed by the new fingerprinting regime. It took a master surgeon to avoid that one. Automatically, Razzle flexed his fingers. They still felt somewhat raw from the surgery. As for his eyes, thanks to laser correction he had passed the iris recognition test with ease. Simon Razzle was, to all intents and purposes, a new man.

He removed the DVD from its package and inserted it into the machine. As he did so, he caught sight of himself reflected in the TV screen. A fine job, if he said so himself. Naturally, DIY cosmetic surgery was not without its hazards, but he could not have entrusted the job to anybody else. Apart from the ethical issues, he was, quite simply, the best. He turned his face to profile, admiring the straight lines of his new nose. In some ways he wished he had done it long before, but then patients seemed to prefer a lack of perfection in their practitioner.

They might not be on to him but you could never be too careful. Only a very few people knew he was even here – old clients, mostly. Sometimes they discreetly sent along a potential client to meet with him at his unofficial office, the Polo Lounge. It was the perfect place to trawl for trade, a hive of Hollywood's movers and shakers. Then there was one very special client, a woman who was still waiting impatiently for her new face. And not just any face at that. The woman wanted Kumari's. Sometimes Razzle wished he had never let her see the girl, then he would not be plagued by her constant nagging. Once a movie star, always a movie star, even when the looks started fading.

'We could easily find you another face,' Razzle had cajoled. 'After all, it's really only the skin we need. The bone structure underneath will still be yours. I cannot turn you into another person.'

'I know that,' the movie legend had snarled. 'But it's her skin I want, Simon. It has the most remarkable quality. Why, the girl almost shimmers.'

Ah yes, shimmer. The kind of translucence the camera loved. Never mind that everyone knew she was past her best, the movie star wanted her youth back. And if it meant carving the face off someone younger then so be it. A movie star is used to getting what she wants. A little murder here and there was a mere trifle.

Dead or alive, Kumari was invaluable to him, as long as death had occurred within a few hours so her body was still fresh. All he needed to do was extract her blood and some organs, and the secret of eternal youth would be within his grasp. Somewhere in that exquisite form of hers lay the key to billions. Cosmetic companies worldwide would kill for such knowledge. And so, of course, would Simon Razzle.

Almost as soon as he had made it back to the United States along with the Ayah, they had started to plan their next kidnap attempt. Knowing that Kumari's year and a day in the World Beyond was already up, they had thought they would have to go back to the Hidden Kingdom for the girl-goddess. Her reappearance in the World Beyond was an unexpected gift. This time, nothing must go wrong. This time, everything was at stake. Not least his own neck, as his new financial backers had made abundantly clear.

Razzle pressed the 'play' button on the DVD player. A moment's pause and then he sighed. He was gazing at his beloved Manhattan. All of a sudden, Razzle felt homesick for those New York streets. Here in LA, life was simply not the same. He was an exile, stranded far from his natural habitat. They wore Hawaiian shirts here, for goodness' sake. He had even sunk to sporting lurid T-shirts himself to aid his disguise. And for that he blamed Kumari, fairly and squarely. If she had complied, he would not be here now in this plastic hell-hole of a place.

And then he saw her, walking along, cool as you like, that wretched bird perched on her shoulder as she entered Rita Moreno Middle School. It was the final confirmation he needed; absolute proof of all the reports. The girl was most definitely in New York City.

Kumari had come to him.

CHAPTER 13

'You want us to go to Los Angeles? Girl, you gone lost your mind.' Ma was staring at her in disbelief. 'And how do you think we're going to get there? Thumb a lift? Kumari, I only just got the salon back to full speed. I ain't got no money for no plane ticket.'

'Don't worry about that,' said Kumari. 'I've been invited on *The Tonight Show*. The TV people will pay. I'll say you're my guardian.'

'*The TONIGHT SHOW*? Holy macaroni! *The Tonight Show* with Jay Leno? No way. You are kidding me. So when are we leaving?'

That was more like it: Ma practically rebounding off the walls. Kumari thought she might have overdone it with Power 5, so excited was she.

'Well, that's the thing. I need to call Jack Raider.'

'Jack Raider? That scumbag. He's just using you, Kumari.'

'I know. And I also know I'm using him just as much as he's using me. It's Raider who wants me to do the show to publicise *School for Happiness*.'

'Say what? Now you're telling me you're doing this for Jack Raider? Uh, uh. Count me out. He can do his own dirty work.'

'It's not dirty work – it's publicity. OK, so maybe there's not much difference. But just hear me out, Ma. I really am doing this for me. Simon Razzle, he's in LA. He's my one hope of finding the Ayah. Right now, I've got no other leads. I need to get to her through Razzle.'

'And you think he's just going to tell you where she is?' Ma snorted in disbelief.

'No but he might lead me to her. Chances are she'll be close by.'

'It could work,' said Ma. 'But then that's what they said about time travel.'

'Ma, I really need you on my side otherwise I won't be able to do it.'

Kumari held her breath. It was really important Ma said yes. Not just because she wanted her along; she did, very much. But it would be so good for Ma. She needed her mojo back, in more ways than one. Helping Kumari hunt down Razzle would give her a great, big karmic boost. Especially if, as Kumari suspected, Razzle had something to do with Sonny's death.

In the end, it was easy, even if Raider did sound smug.

'I knew you'd see sense, Kumari,' he said.

'You know the deal, Mr Raider. I want to see those photographs again.' She needed to examine them one more time to see if she could pick up any clues.

'No problem, Kumari. I'll have copies sent right over.'

'And not a word to the RHM.'

'You can count on my discretion, Kumari.'

Of course I can, she thought. *You'd do anything to get me on that show. You need me, Jack Raider. And I'm going to make sure I use that to my advantage.*

The minute she put down the phone it rang again. Thinking it was Raider, Kumari picked it up.

'Yes?'

'Don't sound so friendly.'

'Chico!'

'How ya doin'?'

He sounded . . . hesitant. Even nervous. Kumari felt her heart start to pound. Chico had called her. Maybe he wanted to make things up.

'I'm good. And you?'

'Yeah, I'm OK.' A silence. Kumari clutched the phone pressed to her ear and listened to the faint hum on the line, waiting, hoping and praying that he would carry on. Unable to bear it any longer, she was about to crack when he cleared his throat.

'So . . .' his voice wavered. 'You want to meet up, take a walk or something?'

'A walk with you?'

'Uh, yeah. Is that such a bad idea?'

'No, no. Not at all. I just . . . I would love to.'

'Great. So meet you at the secret garden?'

The secret garden, where he had once saved her from Razzle's henchmen. It was their special place.

'OK, see you there in twenty minutes?'

'That's great. Can't wait.'

Can't wait? He'd said "can't wait". Kumari punched the air.

The moment she put the phone down for the second time, she was racing for her meagre wardrobe.

'Oh my god,' she wailed. 'I've got nothing to wear!'

'Hush, child, what you fussing for?'

'Ma, you have to help me. That was Chico on the phone. He's asked me to meet him.'

'He has?' Ma's face lit up with one enormous smile. 'We have to find you something real pretty to wear.'

'Pretty is good, but not *too* pretty like I'm trying.'

'You *are* trying,' said Ma. 'We'll just make it look like you ain't.'

'I'm meeting him in twenty minutes. He said he couldn't wait to see me.'

'He said that? Well, honey, we need to get you looking good fast.' Ma was dragging Kumari towards the twins' room, hollering at the top of her voice.

'CeeCee, LeeLee, you in there? Kumari here needs some clothes.'

A bespectacled face looked round the door.

'Keep it down, can't you, Ma? We've got an exam tomorrow,' said LeeLee.

'And Kumari has a date now with Chico. This will take two minutes.'

Another face appeared above the first, wearing an identical pair of glasses.

'You got a date with Chico? Well, why didn't you say?'

Fifteen minutes later, Kumari was looking good. A few swift stitches in CeeCee's new dress made sure it clung in all the right places and LeeLee's favourite belt set it off to perfection. Even Badmash looked impressed, cooing as he hopped round her to get a better view. Then again, maybe that was due to the doughnut bribe LeeLee was holding in her hand. Much as Kumari loved Badmash, this was no time for a chaperone. Especially not a jealous, guzzleguts chaperone with a whole lot of attitude.

'Wish me luck,' yelled Kumari as she skipped out of the door moments later.

'Good luck!' they all cried, although Badmash was busily silent.

All the way to the secret garden, Kumari wondered what lay ahead. He had rung her, hadn't he? *Can't wait.* Those were his words. Can't wait for what? To break her heart big time? To tell her face to face what he thought of her psycho behaviour? By the time she reached the scrubby waste patch that formed the secret garden, Kumari's nerves were jangling so loud she thought he surely must hear.

If he did, he gave no sign, but maybe that was because he looked equally nervous. As soon as he saw her he sprang up from the broken old bench on which he had been sitting.

'You look great,' he said simply, his eyes travelling over her outfit.

'Thanks,' she said, suddenly shy. Only Chico could make her feel like this.

'So . . . you want to sit down?'

'I thought we were going to take a walk.'

135

'A walk. Oh, uh, sure. If that's what you want.'

'I don't mind if you want to sit here. That's fine with me, really.'

'No, no. We'll take a walk. Um . . . where would you like to go?'

She looked at him, all anxious to please, and her heart dissolved. 'Chico, I don't want to walk anywhere. I want to stay here with you.'

The smile that flashed across his face told her everything she needed to know. Well, not quite everything.

'So . . . why did you ask me here?' said Kumari.

Oof. Not exactly subtle. It had just slipped out before she could stop herself. She had meant to say something far less up front, had rehearsed all sorts of other options. But there it was, it was out and he was looking at her with his serious face on.

'Because I think we need to talk.'

'You're right. We do.'

She could feel her scalp prickling. *Oh please,* she begged silently, *please let us sort this out.*

'I've been thinking a lot about that night. You know, the party. And the thing is, Kumari, I think you were right.'

'You do?' she gazed at him, astonished.

'It's kind of flattering in a way, that you care enough to get so jealous.'

'It is?' Oh dear. It was also incredibly uncool. She was supposed to be mature about these things. *Yeah, right, Kumari.*

'I guess I should have told you I was bringing Angie. Then the whole thing would not have happened.'

'Hey, wait, back up a minute,' said Kumari. 'You were

entitled to bring who you wanted. I mean, it's not up to me who you invite and it's not like I have first call on you.'

'Thing is, you do,' said Chico.

'I do?'

'And you know it.'

'I . . .' All they had was the here and now. Might as well make the most of it. 'I'm not afraid of anything,' said Kumari, slipping her hand into his. 'At least, not when I'm with you.'

'Likewise,' said Chico.

They stared into one another's eyes, for once deadly serious. *I'll just pretend,* thought Kumari. *I'll make believe it could happen.* Never mind the full goddess thing, she had to live for the moment. They both had to live for the moment, however long it would last.

And then Chico shook his head. 'I almost forgot,' he said with a smile. 'My grandpa wants to meet you. The whole family do.'

Aaargh. Ohmigosh. 'That sounds great,' said Kumari.

'Liar,' teased Chico. 'Don't worry, they won't eat you. In fact, Grandpa says he'll cook dinner – and that's an honour, let me tell you. Grandpa's quesadillas are legendary. The neighbours line up round the block for them. He was thinking Thursday night around seven.'

Thursday night. She'd be back from LA by then. Today was Monday, and she and Ma were due to fly out Wednesday morning. Kumari would record *The Tonight Show* early that evening and they would fly back the next day. It gave precious little time to find Razzle, but it was better than nothing and the RHM would start asking questions if she was gone any longer.

As it was, CeeCee and LeeLee would have to stall him if he called. The cover story was that she and Ma were ill, both confined to their beds. It was a story she would stick to with everyone else, even with Chico. Kumari had learned what it was to keep secrets. Sometimes it was the safest thing to do.

'Thursday it is,' she smiled.

CHAPTER 14

'Kumari, there's something you need to see.' Theo's voice sounded urgent on the phone. So much so that Kumari forgot how tired she was after a long day's filming and the fact that she was trying to pack for their flight early the next morning.

'Uh, sure, why don't you come over now?'

Kumari wondered what on earth it could be. Theo was trying to collate some results from the show. So far it did not look good. Maybe he was coming to tell her that the whole thing was a waste of time. Well, she hardly needed Theo to tell her that. *School for Happiness* was becoming a nightmare. There was no way you could teach Happiness in that time, especially for a reality show. Reality show: what a stupid name. Like there was anything real about it.

It was not a pile of results, however, that Theo thrust in

front of her an hour later. It was a pile of newspaper clippings printed from an archive, along with one yellowing original.

'Someone put these in among my notes,' said Theo. 'It must have happened when I left them lying around on set. I was going through them this evening when these clippings fell out. This one is dated sixteenth of June 1976 and it's taken from *The San Francisco Observer*.'

Kumari stared at the newspaper clipping in her hand. The headline read: *Cult Conman Jailed*.

Beneath that was a grainy photograph of a man dressed in flowing robes, his long hair hanging lank. A bushy moustache adorned his upper lip and he wore some kind of garland around his neck.

'Look closer,' said Theo. 'Try to imagine him without the moustache.'

There was something familiar about his eyes; they were the snake-eyes of a politician.

'It's Jack Raider!' Kumari gasped.

'The very same,' grinned Theo.

'Let me see that,' said Ma, snatching the clipping away. 'Land's sakes but it's him! And what's this he called himself? Brother Joyful? You're kidding me! That man is about as joyful as stomach flu. No wonder they called him a conman.'

'And you said someone just left these for you to find?' said Kumari. 'I wonder who that was. Obviously someone who hates Raider. Look, there's one here says: *Conman Escapes from Jail*. And another one: *Conman on the Run*. But there's nothing that says they ever caught him.'

'I know,' said Theo. 'Which means . . .'

'Brother Joyful is still a fugitive. Or should that be: Jack Raider?'

'No way!' Ma's eyes were wide with excitement. 'There is a god after all! Of course I knew that, what with you being a goddess and all, but you know what I mean.'

'I know what you mean,' said Kumari. 'And I know what this means. If this gets out then Jack Raider is finished.'

'That's right. He'll be exposed to everyone as a sham.'

Theo's dark curls bobbed as he nodded. He really was a cute super-geek, thought Kumari. She could quite see what Ms Martin saw in him.

'Helen's on her way over,' he said, as if reading her thoughts. 'I left her at the cuttings library. We think we've found everything there is, but she just wanted to double-check. You know how Helen is. A stickler for thoroughness.'

His eyes went all dreamy as he spoke. *He's got it bad,* thought Kumari. *Or should that be good,* she corrected herself. After all, love was a good thing, wasn't it? Sometimes she was not so sure. It seemed love also made life way too complicated. At least she and Chico had made things up. Now she had to figure out the future.

Riiiiiing. Saved by the bell. Kumari could save figuring out for later. Right now, here was Ms Martin brandishing an envelope.

'There's more on Raider!' she cried.

They all gathered round as she shook out two more clippings, both dated March 1979. One proclaimed Brother Joyful to be dead; the other reported his supposed funeral. Only they did not refer to him by his assumed moniker, except as an alias. The man in the coffin was apparently one

John Monroe, aka Brother Joyful.

'But he's not dead,' said Kumari. 'He's alive, as we all know.'

'So who was that in the coffin?' asked Theo.

They looked at one another.

'Don't tell me he murdered someone,' said Ma. 'I knew that man was a no-good from the start.'

'How do we know there was anyone in the coffin at all?' said Ms Martin. 'We only have the newspaper's word on that.'

'And presumably the family's,' said Theo. 'Although there don't seem to be too many blood relatives.'

There was, in fact, only one elderly woman identified in the photograph of the funeral as Monroe's mother and a young boy who looked to be about eight years old named as his brother, Mike. The rest were all his former disciples, apparently loyal to the last. *'He brought happiness to so many,'* one was reported as saying. *'It was something that was dear to his heart.'*

'Hurrrrrrm,' rumbled Ma in disgust. 'He was even using the same schtick way back then.'

'This complicates things a whole lot,' said Theo. 'For one, we don't know who sent the original clipping. This could be about to blow up in all our faces.'

'And then again, maybe not,' said Kumari. 'Whoever sent it now did it for a reason. If they'd wanted to expose Raider they could have done it long ago. Which means they must have some other purpose.'

'The main thing, Kumari,' said Ms Martin. 'Is to make sure he doesn't drag you down with him. I think Raider should be exposed, but I also think it must be done at the right time.'

'Meaning . . . ?' asked Kumari.

'Meaning you should wait and watch for the right moment. This information is dynamite, Kumari. You need to choose when to light the fuse.'

She's right, thought Kumari. Good old Ms Martin. All right, so she was not so old. She was still fantastically, brilliantly clever.

'So what do we do now?' she asked.

'We wait,' said Ms Martin. 'That is, if everyone is agreed?'

They all nodded solemnly.

'And we must keep this between ourselves. No telling anyone, not even Chico.'

'Not even Chico,' echoed Kumari. Great. Another secret to keep from him. First her trip to LA and now this. Was life always going to be full of secrets?

Downtown in City Hall, Jack Raider put down the telephone. A most interesting discussion. The caller had a proposition to put to him and it concerned Kumari. There were not only vast sums to be made but also a leg-up towards the White House. More intriguingly, he was insisting they meet in a public place alone, which suggested his proposition was not entirely kosher. Raider pressed a button on his desk and waited impatiently. Within minutes, one of his security team appeared.

'We're going out,' he announced. 'Get someone to bring an unmarked car around. On second thoughts, make that two and organise some back-up.'

'Yes, Mr Mayor,' said his bodyguard. 'May I ask where we are going?'

'The south side of the Brooklyn Bridge,' growled Raider. 'And make it snappy.'

His contact had stipulated seven o'clock. That gave them ten minutes to get there. It would be tight, given the Manhattan traffic, but they should just about be able to do it.

In fact, they made it in seven minutes thanks to some impressive driving on his chauffeur's part. They had left a trail of unhappy motorists in their wake, but that was of no concern to Jack Raider. What did bother him was the absence of anyone to meet him at the bridge, despite his having got there at the allotted time.

It was a glorious summer's evening and there was a steady stream of walkers, joggers and cyclists moving past him towards the bridge itself. Raider tweaked the peak of his baseball cap and adjusted his sunglasses. As a disguise, it was effective enough to shield him from any nosy passers-by. The cars were parked some two hundred metres away across the street, separated from him by the concrete wall of the walkway. He glanced back at the slender spider's web of the cables dipping and soaring towards Manhattan, the gothic arches from which they were suspended, framing the city lighting up behind. He looked ahead of him to the bustling streets of Brooklyn, where traffic never ceased to blare and honk. He was about to give up when his cell phone rang.

'Get rid of your people,' said a voice.

'But I have no one with me,' protested Raider. 'I came alone, just like you said.' Alone apart from the cars parked at a discreet distance and the two bodyguards posing as tourists.

'Come on, Jack. You know the score. Get rid of them now or no meet.'

With great reluctance, Raider called his lead security man. 'He wants you to back off,' he said.

'Mr Mayor, sir, with all due respect I am not happy to do that. You are already dangerously exposed out here. How do you know you are not dealing with some terrorist?'

'I don't,' snapped Raider. 'But I have no choice. Now back off like I said.'

'Is that an order, sir?'

'It's an order.'

'Very well, Mr Mayor, we'll stand down.'

Jack Raider waited ten minutes more, cracking his fingers in frustration. He hated to be vulnerable like this. Whoever it was, they wanted to make him sweat. Finally, his phone rang once more.

'Well done, Jack. That was very intelligent.'

'It's "Mr Raider" to you. Now where the hell are you?'

'Look behind you, Jack. Just make sure you turn round very slowly. I wouldn't want anyone to get trigger-happy here. Let's keep things nice and smooth.'

Slowly, cautiously, Raider turned around. There was something in the man's voice that meant business. He regretted having ordered his team to stand down. In fact, he regretted ever coming here. But the voice on the phone had said big bucks were at stake. They were talking millions. If there was one thing Jack had never been able to resist it was easy cash. It was what had got him into trouble all his life.

Correction. Had once got him into trouble and he made sure he killed that one off. Or, at least, he had made sure he killed the man he had once been. John Monroe no longer existed. It had been easy enough to substitute bags of sand of the appropriate weight. His mother had insisted upon a closed coffin. But then she would do, wouldn't she? She thought he'd been mangled in a horrific accident.

'I'm here,' said the voice. 'Right beside you, Jack, on your left.'

Raider shifted his gaze and saw a man standing by the wall, a cell phone pressed to his ear.

Clever, thought Raider. *He's got the concrete wall between him and the traffic.* If anything came at him from that side, he was pretty much covered. In fact, the whole choice of venue had been clever: close to City Hall but not too close. Several ready avenues of escape and no chance to park a car right beside him. The constant movement of people walking by meant there was also natural gun cover. No one would dare shoot into such a crowd, not even the mayor's security team.

Not that he was expecting shooting. The man looked surprisingly benign and entirely ordinary. He was dressed in the scuffed suit of someone who did not need to exert control, his shirt open at the collar. There was something about him that was vaguely familiar, but Raider could not place his finger on it. He met thousands of people in his job. Probably seen the guy somewhere before.

'Mr Raider.' The man moved closer. 'I have a message for you from my client.'

Ah, so that was it. This was the hired hand. Raider might have known.

'Who is your client, Mr . . . ?'

'My name is not important.'

Raider suppressed a flash of irritation. The guy could at least have made something up. It was what he would have done in his position. Had done several times, in fact.

'My client,' continued the man, 'is a Mr Simon Razzle. You may have come across him before.'

'I sure have,' said Raider.

This was becoming very interesting indeed. Was Razzle aware that he was being hunted? Perhaps this gofer had come trying to broker a deal. Suddenly, Raider was all ears.

'Mr Razzle,' said the man, 'would like to suggest a collaboration. He understands you are working with a young lady called Kumari. He has some information you may find invaluable.'

'Information? What kind of information?'

'The sort that would make you very rich indeed. All Mr Razzle requires is access to the young lady concerned. For that you will be handsomely rewarded.'

'I get it,' snarled Raider. 'You're suggesting I let him harm my star. Well, you tell Mr Razzle where he can stick his suggestion. I ain't playing ball.'

'If you would hear me out,' said the man. 'All Mr Razzle is suggesting is a little accident. The sort that would instantly turn your star into a tragic heroine. Just imagine the ratings.'

'A tragic heroine? Have you lost your mind? The show is about Happiness. If something happened to Kumari that would blow the whole message, the one my entire campaign is built upon.' Raider turned on his heel. He had heard enough for one day. This lunatic was wasting his time. He was probably some schmuck trying his luck.

'Remember Monroe,' said the man.

Raider blanched, but held his nerve. He turned once more and looked the guy in the eye.

'Monroe?'

'Marilyn Monroe. Screen goddess.'

Raider could feel a twitch set in at the corner of his eye. Just how much did this guy know? Enough, it seemed, to send his blood pressure shooting up. Maybe it was better to hear him out.

'Imagine,' said the man, 'you have another Monroe. A tragic, beautiful heroine. Death made Monroe into a megastar. More than that, it made her an icon.'

'Go on,' said Raider, glancing across the road. His men were still out there, somewhere.

'Were Kumari to die, then you would solve two problems at a stroke. You would not need to prove her methods worked.'

'But they do,' said Raider. 'The results are promising.' Actually, they were the exact opposite, but he was not about to divulge that.

'That's not what I hear. What are you going to do, Jack, if at the end of the show Kumari does not succeed? You will have failed to deliver to your people.'

The same thought had occurred to Raider, only each time it did he ignored it. He had learned long ago that people would buy into an illusion if they really wanted to do so. Happiness was just such an illusion. Frame it right and they could not fail. There was still, though, a nagging seed of doubt in his mind and the man's words had only caused it to germinate.

'So what's the second problem I would solve, supposing

something did happen to Kumari?' He was intrigued to know where this was going. This guy seemed pretty confident.

'Money, Jack. You need money for your presidential campaign and right now your company coffers are pretty empty. Imagine what will happen if the show fails. It won't just be your image that's hurt. We also know that you have brokered a book deal based on the show; a deal that will be cancelled if Kumari does not succeed. My client is prepared to pay extremely well for your cooperation. We're talking a seven-figure sum, Jack.'

Jack Raider blinked, which was something he hardly ever did. He was, after all, a seasoned poker player. And life was the greatest poker game of the lot. Blinking was a sign of weakness.

'It's "Mr Raider",' he growled. 'And I'd like to know where you get your information. My company is doing very nicely, thank you. As will the book when it is published. Now why don't you get your sorry ass out of here before I call the cops?'

'Come, come, Jack. We both know you won't do that.'

Without another word, Raider turned and stalked off. The man knew way, way too much.

CHAPTER 15

Ma gazed, bleary-eyed, out of the plane window. 'I cannot believe I am on a flight at six a.m.,' she muttered. 'Where's the steward with the coffee? I need my fix, fast.'

Beside her, Kumari stared one more time at the photographs Raider had sent over. There had to be something in them she had not yet seen, a clue to Razzle's whereabouts. Every time she tried to concentrate, however, other pictures invaded her mind. Pictures of Jack Raider with a moustache – or should that be Brother Joyful? It certainly added a new dimension to her problems. One she'd have to investigate when she got back.

Right now, she had six hours before they landed in LA. Six hours in which to work out where that other low-life was hiding so he could lead her to the Ayah. There were lots of different women pictured with Razzle, always at the same table. But one kept popping up again and again. She had to force herself to focus on the ageing movie star. Right through the safety demonstration, she continued to scrutinise the photographs. Not even Ma popping open her packet of peanuts could distract her from her task.

'Four lousy nuts,' said Ma. 'And they expect a grown woman to survive on this? Please someone tell me this is not my breakfast. Where is that darn steward?'

'Breakfast. That's what they're having,' muttered Kumari, looking at the picture in her hand. Two coffee cups and an untouched croissant were set on the table at which Razzle and the ageing movie star sat. Great. Well, that really helped. There must a million places in Los Angeles that served breakfast. Although this place did look rather chi-chi. There were gorgeous flowers on the table and more just visible in the background. Flowers in the background? And they were cascading down a wall. That meant the table must be outside. Well, duh, it was Los Angeles. With all that Californian sunshine, it was not exactly unusual.

But maybe there was something else, some detail she was missing. The sort of detail you could not see through ordinary eyes. The type that required the use of goddess Powers. A blink of the eye and it was there: Power 2. The Power of Extraordinary Sight had become second nature. It was like that with all the Powers, or so the RHM had said. The more you practised, the easier they became. Until one day you were a full goddess.

As quickly as it entered her head, Kumari thrust the thought aside. She would never be a full goddess until she wielded the Sacred Sword. And she had zero intention of doing so. Right now, she was only practising those Powers she already had and, boy, was Power 2 proving useful. Half closing her eyes, she gazed at the table in the photograph. A crisp edge caught her eye: the corner of something lying just in shot. Focusing on it, Kumari realised she was staring at the menu. An image swam into view. It was a picture of a man on a horse.

Beneath the picture, a list of breakfast items. Kumari scanned through them. All of a sudden, she let out a little shriek.

'Polo Lounge Famous French Toast!'

'Say what?' said Ma. 'French toast, now that does sound good. But I don't see none coming our way. Kumari, what are you talking about?'

'It says Polo Lounge on the menu,' said Kumari.

'It does? I don't see it. In fact, I don't see no menu either. Lord, but I am starving!'

'No, not on the plane,' said Kumari. 'It's here, in the picture. There's a menu on the table in front of Razzle and it says: *Polo Lounge Famous French Toast, $17.50.*'

'$17.50 for French toast? You have got to be kidding me. Hang on one second, I don't see no menu there either. Girl, you're making this up.' Ma snatched the photo and stared at it.

'I am not,' said Kumari, snatching it back. 'It's there, in the picture. Only you can't see it Ma because you don't have Extraordinary Sight.'

'I may not have Extraordinary Sight but I do have Extraordinary Good Sense. Who in the world would pay $17.50 for French toast?'

'People in Beverly Hills, that's who. The Polo Lounge is famous. It's where all the movie stars hang out. I saw it on the Entertainment Channel.'

'Well, someone oughta tell those folk they can get French toast just as good for three dollars. That's what I pay at the diner. Of course, I ain't no movie star. Now can you please tell me what all of this has to do with us? Especially when I am starving and all you can talk about is food.'

'It's the first place we're going to look,' said Kumari. 'As soon as we land in LA.'

'What – you think Razzle's just going to be sitting there waiting for you?'

'No, but I do know he goes there a lot and it seems to be at about the same time. Look at these photos. They were taken on different days. Different women, same table. Look at the shadows: very similar. That means the sun was in the same position each time, throwing shortish shadows. If the shadows are short, it has to be late morning or early afternoon. And the stuff on the table, it's usually a coffee cup or a glass of juice. I reckon he goes there for breakfast most days. Razzle does love swanky places.'

'You are one clever girl,' said Ma, peering at the pictures. 'And at least there I might get some breakfast. What's a woman gotta do to get service around here? Steward! Hey STEWARD!'

They landed at LAX at 9.20 a.m. and by 10.20 a.m. they were in the studio limousine.

'The Beverly Hills Hotel, please,' said Kumari.

'My instructions are to take you to Burbank,' said the driver.

'Yes, well I have a meeting first,' said Kumari.

'I thought you said we were going to the Polo Lounge?'

squeaked Ma. A plastic bowl of stale cornflakes had done nothing to ease her hunger. As if to underline the fact, her stomach let out an ominous growl.

'Relax, Ma,' said Kumari. 'The Polo Lounge is in the Beverly Hills Hotel.'

'Thank the Lord,' muttered Ma. 'I might even have to have some of that fancy French toast.'

As the car drew up outside the famous pink hotel, Kumari felt a twinge of anxiety. Was this just one big wild goose chase or would Razzle actually be there? And if he was, what would she do? Walk right up to him and demand to know where the Ayah was? *Of course not,* she told herself fiercely. *Think RHM. Proceed with stealth.*

'Wait here,' she told the driver as she helped a half-faint Ma from the car. The only thing that was going to get them through this was attitude. She pulled out a pair of CeeCee's fake Chanel shades. They swept past reception without a hitch, but the real test would come at the restaurant. Sure enough, it was guarded by a frosty *maitre d'*, his lips as starched as his collar.

'Can I help you?' he enquired in tones that suggested otherwise.

'A table for two,' said Kumari, sounding much braver than she felt.

'Do you have a reservation?'

'Yes I do. In the name of Razzle.' It was a long-shot and it seemed to fall short. The *maitre d'* raised an immaculate eyebrow. 'I'm afraid I have nothing in that name,' he announced, having perused his reservation book.

'Oh really?' said Kumari. 'That's too bad. We're supposed

to be meeting Mr Spielberg.'

'Mr Spielberg is already at his usual table. I thought you said you required a table for two?'

'Of course he is,' said Kumari. 'What I mean is, we're meeting him later on. After breakfast.'

Ma's stomach growled on cue.

'For goodness' sakes, man,' she suddenly hollered. 'I need to eat. Right. Now. And if I don't, I won't be held responsible – so, buddy, just lead me to my table, double-quick. Don't you know who I am? The nerve of some people!'

The *maitre d'* took a step back as Ma skewered him with her wildest look.

'I, uh, I'll see what we can do,' he said. 'Just wait right there Ms . . . uh . . .'

'Goldberg.'

'Ms Goldberg. Of course. I'm so sorry. It's been a while.'

A couple of minutes later, they were seated, looking out at the tables on the patio. Each one was covered in a heavy, green-and-white checked cloth with glorious flowers set in the middle. Quickly, Kumari scanned all of them. Most were occupied by A-list celebrities, their tans perfect, their limbs impossibly lean. Kumari had never seen so many designer labels in one place, all worn with casual ease. Oh my god, there was Harrison Ford. But no sign of Simon Razzle. *This is no time to be staring at movie stars,* Kumari told herself. Still, she could not help but sneak in another peek. Ma was already clutching the menu, running a rabid eye down the list.

'Dutch Apple Pancake,' she sighed. 'Belgian Waffles. Eggs Benedict.'

'Oh my god,' Kumari's voice shook. Her heart was beating so fast she could hardly breathe. 'He's here. He's coming towards us.'

She had no idea what to do. Hastily, she held her menu up so it hid her face. The *maitre d'* must have told him they had used his name. What on earth was she going to say? 'Hi Simon, good to see you?' There was nowhere to run, nowhere to hide. They were sitting ducks. But as they drew level with Kumari's table, the two men kept on walking.

She could hear the *maitre d'* talking to him as they passed: 'Your guest is already here, Mr Kingdom.'

Mr Kingdom? The cheek of it! Of *course*, Razzle would use a false name, but did he have to refer to her homeland? When she glanced up again, he had disappeared from view. A movement outside caught her eye. Simon Razzle was being seated at a table where a woman in a white hat sat. Kumari felt the blood ice over in her veins. It was the woman from the photograph. The ageing movie star: the one who would pay anything to have her face. And she was sitting not ten metres away, perched on her wrought-iron chair.

All thoughts of food deserted Kumari. The woman and Razzle sat, heads close together, deep in discussion. The woman appeared agitated, Razzle unctuous. Kumari felt a surge of hatred towards him. *He's a means to an end*, she told herself. *He's my route to the Ayah. Don't get emotional, Kumari. Just watch and try to work out what to do.*

All of a sudden, the woman got up and slapped something on the table before storming out. Razzle was on his feet in an instant, running after her.

'Quick, Ma,' said Kumari. 'We're leaving.'

'We're what? No way. Oh no. I can see my waffles coming towards me.'

'Never mind your waffles,' said Kumari, grabbing her by the hand. 'Razzle's on the move and so are we.'

They sped past the waiter carrying a steaming plate of waffles. Ma let out a low moan. They raced on, skirting the *maitre d'*. This time, both eyebrows shot up. And then they were skidding to a halt just inside the covered entrance way, Kumari desperately looking round for Razzle.

'There he is!' she hissed, ducking behind a pillar. He was getting into a grey sports car that the valet had brought round. There was no sign of the ageing movie star save the disappearing tail lights of a Rolls Royce.

'Follow that car!' she told the driver as they dived into their waiting studio limo.

'Honey, this is not the movies,' he sighed. 'Hollywood, it does that to people.'

Nevertheless, he gunned the engine and there was a satisfying squeal of tyres as they whipped out of the driveway and on to Sunset Boulevard. Kumari could see the grey sports car ahead, weaving in and out of the traffic. After about a mile, he slowed down and settled into one lane. Razzle must have given up trying to catch the Rolls Royce, which meant he might head for home. And if he headed for home, wherever that was, they could follow and find out what he was up to. Once she knew where he lived, she could start to stake him out.

Kumari knew in her gut that where Razzle was, the Ayah would not be far away. Call it goddess wisdom or a plain old hunch, she was absolutely sure he would lead them to her. Gently, she reached out and stroked her amulet. 'I'm trying, Mamma,' she whispered.

There was no answering flash of insight, no heavenly tremor. Mamma was well and truly cut off. Kumari had to avenge her fast or risk losing her to limbo forever.

'He's turning off!' she cried as the silver sports car took a left. They followed it along winding streets before it pulled into a driveway. A pair of electric gates swung open at its approach and then the sports car disappeared from view.

'Wait here,' cried Kumari for a second time as she swung her legs out of the car.

'We should get you to the studio, Miss,' said the driver.

'I'll be two minutes. I promise.'

'You ain't going nowhere on your own,' said Ma, heaving herself out to join Kumari. Together, they walked up to the gates, careful to keep out of the way of the camera perched above them.

'You know,' said Kumari. 'They're not all that high. I could climb them.'

'Oh yeah?' said Ma. 'And get shot down by some security guard?'

There seemed no other way on to the property. A high wall ran all around the perimeter, backed by tall Californian pines. From the top of it, lethal-looking spikes protruded. That's when Kumari had her idea. She looked up at the wall. The spikes reminded her of the rocks she had once stared down at from the palace parapet just before she used Power No 6, the Power to Levitate or Fly Through the Sky.

'OM BEMA TARE SENDARA

HRI SARVA LOKA KURU SOHA . . .'
Kumari began to chant under her breath.
'OM TARE TUTTARE TURE
DZALA BHAYA SHINDHAM KURU SOHA . . .'
She could feel herself rising, hear Ma's suppressed shriek of surprise. And then she was soaring over the spiked wall in the gap between two cameras, clearing the tops of the trees. She landed amongst some bushes at the edge of an endless marble-edged swimming pool. Its azure water looked inviting, but she had other things on her mind. For one thing, she could hear voices coming through the open French windows that opened on to the pool area from the house. For another, one of those voices was Razzle's and it was raised in rage.

'What do you mean the electricity went down?' he was shouting. 'The generator should have kicked in. You're lucky her machines kept on working. If the Ayah had awoken now, it would have been a disaster.'

Kumari felt her throat go dry. He had said 'the Ayah'. So she *was* here. Here and asleep for some reason. Or maybe uncon-scious. Razzle had dropped his voice now. It was harder to hear him. She crept closer, staying close to the low wall that ran by the pool. And then she heard them: the sound of footsteps approaching.

Any second, someone would appear and she would be discovered. Not for the first time, Kumari wished she had acquired Power 4, the Power to Become Invisible, but it was one of the trickiest of Powers and this was no time to start. Casting about for somewhere to hide, Kumari spotted an open door from which a hosepipe snaked. Jumping behind the door, she pulled the hosepipe in after her and found herself in a cupboard full of cleaning materials. Moments later, she heard someone walk up, pull the door to and turn the key in the lock.

Great. Fantastic. Now what was she supposed to do? She might be safe for the moment, but sooner or later someone would come along and find her in the cupboard. Not to mention the fact she was supposed to be getting to the studio in time to do the show. For the first and only time in her life, Kumari wished she wore a watch. The show was due to record at four-thirty. She had strict instructions to be there an hour and a half before. When they had left the Polo Lounge it had been after midday and the driver had been getting twitchy when she asked him to wait. She could not, dare not miss the show or Raider would never trust her again.

Although, frankly that did not matter so much, seeing as she had managed to find Razzle. And not only Razzle, but the ultimate prize: the Ayah herself. Although what they would do when they discovered her made Kumari's heart beat all the faster. The blood pounded so loudly in her ears she was convinced someone would hear it thudding. She had to get out of there, sooner rather than later. A Power had got her into this mess. She'd use another to get her out of it.

But which one to choose? Power 7 seemed the most suitable: the Power to Move Freely Through the Earth, Mountains and Solid Walls. The only problem was, she had no idea what lay on the other side. She might burst through the door and straight into whoever had locked her in. Or worse, straight into Simon Razzle. But she simply had to take the risk; there was no other way around it. Stay in the cupboard and wait to be discovered or burst out and possibly reveal herself anyway.

The decision was made for her when she heard voices once more. This time, they sounded light-hearted. One of them was even laughing. As they drew closer she could hear them speak. 'Water looks good,' said one male voice.

'Sure does,' said another.

'Mr Razzle, he's gone to take a nap and then he'll be working. Trust me, we won't see him for hours.' A short pause and then a splash. 'Come on in, man, it feels good.'

Another splash and more laughter. It sounded like two of the guards were playing hooky. Which meant that she was forced to stay in her cupboard listening to them splash around, wishing and hoping they would go away so she could get out of this stinking hole. The guards clearly had other ideas: they splashed around for what felt like forever. Slumped against a dank wall, Kumari rested her head on her knees. Now she could hear some women giggling. Great. They'd invited their girlfriends over.

She'd have loved to have been splashing in a pool instead of stuck in some damp cupboard. To keep herself from descending into total despair, she tried to imagine she was out there with Chico. *Chico. Tomorrow night.* She had to get out of here before then. His grandpa had invited her for dinner. It was one huge deal, a total honour. *Calm down, Kumari. Of course you'll get out before then. They can't stay around the pool all day.* Actually, it was probably getting towards evening. *Oh my god, the show.* There's nothing you can do about it. *Raider will kill me.* Who cares about Raider? He's a lowdown conman, for goodness' sake.

Finally, one of the guards called to the other: 'We'd better get dressed, man. It's nearly eight.'

Nearly eight? Oh my god. She had been in there for hours. Ma would be worried sick. She had well and truly missed the show. Leno's people would be furious. And not only Leno's people – she could not even begin to think what Raider would have to say. *Too bad,* thought Kumari. It was much more important to find the Ayah. But now she had, how was she supposed to get to her? This place was crawling with guards.

At last, silence fell. Holding her breath, Kumari began to chant in her head, summoning up the Power that would get her out of there: Power No 7. She was tired now and wrung out. It was hot and stuffy in the cupboard. Power 7 did not come so easily, but finally she could feel it rising. Concentrating all her energies, she managed to burst her way through the door, breaking it from its hinges. Fresh air filled her lungs as her eyes raked the pool area.

The place was deserted, thank goodness, although lights shone from inside the house. She had just taken a couple of cautious steps towards the bushes when she heard a shout.

'Over there! I saw something.'

Oh god, no, they had seen her. What to do, where to run? She caught a glimpse of two men. They had guns. She had to get out of there, *now*. There was no time to think or to worry. Kumari was already chanting once more, summoning up Power 3, the Power to Run with Incredible Swiftness. It had stood her in good stead the time she trapped the Ayah in the labyrinth and it worked for her now. One moment she was hovering like a trapped deer in headlights, the next she was running for her life. Racing over the lush lawns, bounding towards the dense line of trees, crashing through them as if they weren't even there, using Power 6 to get over. It all flowed like a dream, like it was second nature to Kumari. From behind the wall she heard more shouts but she was safe on the other side. Along the road, she could see Ma sitting on their suitcases, waving at her frantically. The studio limo was nowhere to be seen.

'What happened?' cried Ma, staggering up to her. 'I've been so worried. That darn fool driver kept taking calls from the studio. They were yelling down the phone. Then he said he had to go. I told him we couldn't just leave you here and he said that was my problem. My problem! I tried to grab his keys and then he threw me and all our stuff out the car.' Ma was rubbing her hip, obviously in some pain.

'The creep!' said Kumari. 'Did you try and call a cab?'

'I couldn't,' said Ma. 'My phone is out of credit.'

Fantastic. The one cell phone they had between them and it was useless. They were stuck.

'In that case,' said Kumari. 'We had better start walking. Fast.'

They had to get out of there before Razzle's men came looking. It was going to be a long trek back to town.

KUMARI'S JOURNAL
(TOP SECRET. FOR MY EYES ONLY.
EVERYONE ELSE KEEP OUT!)
THIS MEANS YOU!

My bedroom at Ma's

Day sixteen in New York

I can't believe I was so close and then everything went so horribly wrong. It took us hours and hours to find a callbox and then I had to try to explain it all to Raider. He's mad as hell, of course. By that time it was nearly midnight and we had no idea where our hotel was supposed to be, so I suggested we just head out to the airport on the bus and wait for our morning flight and then we found it had been cancelled.

It took us all day to get on another flight and we landed back in New York really late – too late for dinner at Chico's and too late for us, I suspect. I did call him from the airport and explain but of course I'd promised Ms Martin I wouldn't tell him the truth and he wasn't buying the illness story when it was so obvious I was not at home. I mean, what can you do when there are constant airport noises in the background? 'The flight for Bogota is now leaving from gate thirty-two . . .' did not exactly make my story sound convincing.

So that's it, I guess. I've blown it once and for all. I found Razzle and the Ayah and couldn't get near either of them. I thought about trying to go back, but now he knows that I am around. Great stuff, Kumari. No revenge and no boyfriend. Might as well make it a hat trick and blow the show.

CHAPTER 16

Another day, another attempt at teaching Happiness. Today's task: learn to trust yourself. Kumari turned over in her bed with a yawn, her limbs heavy as lead. She was still exhausted from the LA trip. *Yeah, right,* she thought. *Like that's going to go down well.* Especially with Chico in the class, more mistrustful of her than ever. They were headed out to Long Island to learn to surf. It was Lucy's idea. She had grown up on Long Island, about an hour away from Manhattan. When Kumari had told her what she needed to teach, surfing seemed the obvious choice.

For a bunch of kids from the Bronx it would be a whole new experience, learning to ride the waves with nothing but a board and their own tenacity to rely upon. At least, thought Kumari as she dozed, this would be a whole new experience for her too. There was no such thing as a big roller in the Kingdom. All right, so there was a swell now and again on the lake, but nothing like the sort of wave you surfed.

'Kumari, are you in there?' It was Ma banging on her door. 'Kumari, it's nine o'clock.'

Oh my god, she must have fallen back to sleep.

Refusing Ma's offer of French toast, she bolted out of the door, still pulling on her clothes. Luckily, one of the Long Island buses was still waiting when she finally made it to the meeting point.

'Where have you been?' said Hannah. 'The other bus has already gone. I said I'd wait until you got here.'

'Thanks,' puffed Kumari, still breathless from jogging up the road. Badmash, too, was panting, having trailed her all the way.

'You seen that?' asked Hannah, jerking her head towards the waiting group.

At first Kumari did not understand what she was talking about. Thirty seconds later she clocked Charley – and not just Charley but a couple of her cronies, sitting sniggering amongst themselves.

'What are they doing here?' she whispered.

'Search me,' said Hannah. 'They showed up just as the other bus was leaving. All the teachers were on that one. Ms LaMotta, she just kind of grabbed the RHM and shoved him on. I think she secretly fancies him.'

Well, that was a relief, thought Kumari, trying to ignore the bizarre image of Ms LaMotta with the RHM. If there was one thing the RHM could not abide it was tardiness, as he reminded her so often. The absence of the teachers, though, did present them with a problem. What on earth was she supposed to do with Charley and her crew? She could either ignore them or say hello. Kumari chose the latter.

'Hey Charley,' she smiled at her, conscious of the evils she was getting from the girl beside her. Really, Maria was one nasty little number and she had come plastered in make-up and hair product. Well, that would soon wash off in the sea. Pity the rest of her could not follow. Kumari wished with all her heart she would just disappear. Goddess Powers, however, did not run to vaporising people. In which case she would have to do the second-best thing and ignore her totally.

'Uh, hi,' mumbled Charley and then dipped her head, a smirk upon her face.

'Glad you could make it.'

'You are?' Just for a second, it was the old Charley. And then her eager smile dissolved into that hard, tight set of her mouth Kumari had come to know.

'Yeah, well, thought we would check this out, seeing as we're, like, invited.'

'You were all invited?' asked Kumari, wondering what on earth Ms LaMotta could have been thinking. Charley and Maria were definitely on the Moreno roll, but she wasn't too sure about Lanky Boy sat beside them. It took her a moment, but then she recognised him. He was the tall, skinny one she'd floored at the store.

'That's right,' snapped Maria. 'All of us – we just never showed before. Too much to do, you know what I mean? Too many other places to be.'

What a shame she wasn't in one of those other places right now, thought Kumari. They had to show up today of all days. The surf trip was supposed to be special and now they were here, threatening to spoil it. To be honest, she was not even happy to see Charley. This was not the time nor the place. Maybe it's for the best, she told herself. Charley might even benefit from *School for Happiness*. Kumari said as much to Hannah as they clambered on board the bus.

'Yeah, right,' snorted Hannah.

All the way to Long Island, Kumari stared out of the window into space. Badmash worked his way down the bus, cadging treats, but she didn't even notice. By the time he got back to their seat, belly bulging, they were getting ready to disembark. He let out a loud belch which would ordinarily have earned him a telling off. This time, however, Kumari did not even hear. She was too busy thinking about everything: the Ayah, Chico, Charley. Especially Charley. What had caused things to go so wrong?

OK, so Charley's parents had split up, but many people's parents split up. Almost half the kids in school came from broken homes. Even her own Papa and Mamma were no longer together although that was for different reasons. Come to think of it, she had every reason to go off the rails herself. Murder was not exactly good for the mind or spirit. Admittedly she could be naughty sometimes but nothing like the self-destructive spiral Charley had chosen.

When Kumari was disobedient it was generally in a good cause. Or so she liked to tell herself. And at least no one else got hurt. But Charley was lashing out at everyone she had once cared about. It was as if their happiness hurt her all the more and so she would do anything to destroy it. All of which left a large, leaden lump sticking in Kumari's stomach. What was Charley really up to?

And then they were arriving at surf school and Kumari had no more time to worry. It was into the classroom for basic instruction and safety drill and then clothes off and wetsuits on. Kumari could not help but notice how cute Chico looked in his. It showed off his muscles to perfection. As they practised on their boards on dry land, their happy shrieks began to dispel Kumari's fears. Lucy's cameras worked unobtrusively as they practised lying prone and putting their arms in the 'chicken wing' position, laughing all the while. Then they were standing up, sliding a foot forward, riding imaginary waves.

'Everyone ready to try it for real?' asked their instructor.

'You bet!' cried Hannah.

Kumari grinned at her friend's eager face. This was Hannah, whose nose was never normally out of a book. Yet she was here, on a surf board, looking for all the world like she owned it. Maybe things would be different out there on the water, but right now she'd become a surf chick.

The instructors divided them up into smaller groups, eight to an instructor. Chico was put in a group with Hannah's guy, Daniel. Ms Martin and Theo were split up as the instructors mixed and matched. Kumari saw their looks of disappointment. *Awww, cute,* she thought. All of a sudden, she noticed that Maria was headed their way.

'Oh great,' she muttered to Hannah, mercifully still in her group. 'Here comes trouble big time. Just look at her face.'

Maria's snide smile bore a knowing edge that suggested she was up to no good. She whispered to Charley and Lanky Boy before heading their way. Something was definitely up.

Before they began, Kumari gave them her little speech, reminding everyone of why they were really here.

'It's about learning to trust yourself,' she said. 'It's an essential part of Happiness. It doesn't matter if you fall off or, er, "wipeout". It's only important that you do your best. If you do that, you will have mastered this task. If you master this task, you'll have mastered yourself.'

She felt a pang of nervousness and thanked the heavens the RHM had elected to stay in the bus away from all that nasty sand. It had not been strictly true about the wipeout thing. She, of all people, could not afford to fall. She reached a hand up to the pendant now encased in a waterproof bag, the material permeable to smoke so that she could still breathe in the holy fires of Happiness. Carefully, she tucked it inside her wetsuit and prayed it would stay dry. The fires could not be extinguished by water, but there was still a risk they might be damaged if the pendant was submerged for too long. Kumari would have to do her best to keep her head above water. Otherwise, she was dicing with death, and a horrible and swift one at that.

She felt someone's eyes upon her and looked up to see Theo.

'Are you sure about this, Kumari?' he asked.

'Perfectly sure,' she answered.

'Just remember, if you go under, come back up fast.'

'I will do. Don't worry.'

She smiled at Theo with a confidence she did not entirely feel. Some risks were worth taking. She had thought long and hard about whether she should surf at all, but in the end the old desires had won out. Above all, she wanted to join in

170

with her friends, especially when she was now teacher rather than student. It was weird enough being on the other side of the whiteboard divide without also seeming to be a wuss.

'Let's do it!' yelled the chief instructor, and they were swarming towards the sea, lugging their surf boards with them. Some looked excited, some plain terrified. One or two even managed to look unimpressed. Once in the water, though, they were forced to concentrate. Above all, they must respect the sea and the possible dangers out there.

One by one, Kumari's group lay belly-flat on their boards and paddled out. For the first couple of times they would come in like this until their instructor was satisfied they could progress.

Hovering above Kumari's head, a concerned Badmash circled anxiously. He had never seen her doing such an out-landish thing and it worried him greatly. Once or twice he attempted to land and perch on the end of her surf board. Each time Kumari yelled: 'No, Badmash!'

It was bad enough trying to paddle without a bird tipping the balance. They were turning now, waiting for their wave, a small group bobbing in the water. Kumari could feel the water swelling beneath her, heralding the roller they needed. At the exact moment it reached its zenith, she heard their instructor shout and began to paddle for all she was worth. She was riding it, surging in, laughing in exhilaration.

They all reached the beach at more or less the same time. Kumari noticed Maria's dishevelment. 'Not so good for the hair, is it?' she teased and saw the flash of fury that crossed Maria's face. Streaks of mascara adorned her cheeks and her lip-gloss was nowhere. Hannah saw her too and began to giggle. Maria really was a sight.

A mocking wolf-whistle sounded from the group next to them.

'Hey babe, looking good,' someone called out.

Maria scowled and turned her back. At that moment, Kumari saw Chico. He was there, in the next group, already heading back into the water. She noticed he did not give Maria a second glance but then he did not give her one either.

They practised body-boarding a few more times before their instructor gathered them together.

'OK, listen up,' he said. 'This time we do it for real.'

A frisson of excitement thrilled through the group. Kumari and Hannah looked at one another. This was what it was all about. They were going to master the waves. A flash of sunlight glinted off the camera pointed at them, but Kumari had ceased to notice its presence. It was all about surfing now. She absolutely had to catch that wave, stand up and ride it high.

They paddled out and waited. Kumari flicked a glance at Hannah. She was bobbing in the water some three metres away. There was no sign of Maria. Once again, Kumari felt the swell. Here it came – a big one. She recited the technique in her head: *Foot down. Other one through. Stand up slowly. Put your arms out and . . .* splash!

She was down, covering her head with her arms just as she had been taught. Kicking hard, she propelled herself to the surface and broke free. A wipeout on her first attempt. It was only to be expected. She checked her pendant and it was fine. Hauling her board towards her on its leash, Kumari scrambled aboard and paddled in. She could see Hannah in a similar state and, ahead of them on the beach, Maria. *She didn't even try,* thought Kumari. *She simply sat there, sulking.* An instructor was talking to her now, trying to persuade her into the water.

As they waited, Kumari watched the next group along catch their wave. All but one wobbled and fell within seconds of standing up. Then she noticed the exception. There was Chico, poised on his board, riding the surf. 'It's Chico,' she murmured under her breath. 'He's done it! Go Chico!' She was jumping up and down now in the shallows, punching the air with her free arm. As Chico reached the shore, he glanced her way and she felt their eyes lock on. Then he was high-fiving the rest of his group, completely ignoring her. Crushed, Kumari dropped her arm and heard a soft, lethal snigger. Looking round, she saw Maria's face alight with glee.

'Aw, too bad,' sneered Maria. 'Guess you weren't enough for him. It takes a real woman to keep a guy like Chico. Watch and learn, Kumari.'

And with that, she struck a pose and sauntered over to the next group. Kumari saw her fling her arms around Chico and haul his head round for a kiss. She could feel the rage swelling inside her. Just like the waves, it surged and broke and, for an instant, she would cheerfully have flattened her. Then Kumari caught sight of her amulet glinting on her wrist and the anger drained away.

Let Maria taunt her if she wished. Kumari would not rise to it. If she did, Maria would have won. She would have become Kumari's master. Besides, Chico was pushing her away. She could see Maria pout as she flounced back. Something else surged through Kumari. This time it was triumph. And this

173

time she could not resist. The temptation was too great.

'Too bad,' she snickered as Maria drew close. 'Guess you weren't real enough for him.'

As soon as she said it, Kumari regretted the words. The look Maria shot her was lethal. She had no time to worry about it, however. They were heading further out this time, hoping to catch a better break. Kumari's arms had started to ache, but she was still determined to make it.

This time she would stay on her board. She would show Chico she could do it. That glint in his eye had acted like a gauntlet thrown down and there was nothing Kumari loved more than a challenge. Out on the water, they were all equal. Sure, she could use a Power to cheat, but she didn't want to. She was doing this as one of them, without any special advantage. Once more, her amulet caught the sunlight, gleaming as she held on to her board. *Forget Chico*, thought Kumari. *I'm doing this for me. Me, and no one else.*

The swell was stronger this time. She could feel the water suction pulling her out. And then the wave, swelling towards her, threatening to break. *Come on, Kumari, paddle hard.* She caught it at the perfect point. *Up now. Leg through. Arms out.* Yessss! She was riding her wave. Above her head, Badmash flew, letting out squawks of excitement. Even he had caught the surfing bug. The sheer thrill was infectious. Whooping and hollering, Kumari headed in, knees bent, constantly adjusting. She could feel the wind and salt on her skin. It was a delicious combination.

'Good work!' called the instructor.

'You go girl!' shouted Hannah.

Kumari glanced at Chico's group. He was watching her,

smiling. There was no time to linger, however. They were paddling out for a final wave. Kumari could see other kids up on their boards, some riding it, some falling off. All of them, however, were laughing and smiling. She even thought she saw Charley shrieking with delight. But Maria's scowl was permanent. This was one lesson she was determined not to learn. Lanky Boy was nowhere to be seen. He'd probably sloped off to pick his nose or do something equally productive.

'Make it a good one!' Kumari called to Hannah. In return, she got a thumbs up. Then it was concentration to the max as she waited for her wave. When it came, Kumari realised with a thrill that it was an absolute monster. Its pull almost tore the board from her grasp and then it rolled towards them, a raging, swirling beast barely contained within its own swell.

She glanced sideways and saw she had floated several feet from her group. *Don't be scared,* Kumari told herself. *It's only a wave, just the same as all the others.* She heard shrieking from elsewhere in the water and, above that, the calm voice of their instructor. He was calling instructions out, trying to keep them focused. Then there was no time to be afraid. The wave was under them, rising high.

She could either master it or let it master her. *Pull yourself forward, step up,* thought Kumari.

This time, if anything, it was even smoother. One foot in place, the other sliding through, standing up in perfect balance. Despite the thunder of the wave and the rush of air, she felt a profound sense of peace. For a few moments, she was like a bird, flying over the water. All of a sudden, she heard a squawk. It was her real bird, hovering above her. Kumari did

175

her best to ignore him – this was her final wave, after all.

'Aaark, aarrk!' Badmash cried again.

Kumari did not dare twist her neck up to look at him. If she did so, she might lose her balance and come crashing down off her board.

'Aaaaaark!'

'Shhh, Badmash!' she yelled. So much for peace and being at one with nature. And then she saw it, poking out of the water. An upended board, sticking up a couple of feet out of the water and she was headed straight for it. There was no time to try to swerve even if she could have done so. The boards collided with an awful smash. Kumari already had her arms around her head as she desperately flung herself sideways.

Round and round the water whirled, sucking and pulling her this way and that. She must have swallowed water without meaning to. Her lungs felt as if they were on fire. Desperately, she grappled for her pendant, trying to clasp one fist around it. She felt herself bash against something. A rock, maybe, or a board. Then something else thudded against her skull. The entire force of the wave seemed to bear down on her, pushing her down, down towards the bottom. *I'm losing it,* thought Kumari. *I can't breathe. I can't see.*

Just when she thought she could take no more, the sea relinquished its merciless grip. Like a cork she bobbed to the surface, emerging gasping and spluttering. She could hear people calling her name, but her ears were full of water and they seemed so far away. Then strong arms were grabbing her and holding her tight, hauling her towards the shore. Somehow she was sitting on the sand, still half-blinded and coughing. From somewhere she heard a feeble squawk and then a feathery bundle was nestling up to her.

'Badmash,' she spluttered. 'Badmash. You tried to save me.'

'Don't try to talk,' she heard someone say. 'Take a few more deep breaths.'

A few more coughs and finally she could breathe easily. She raised her head and brushed the salt from her eyes.

'Chico.'

'You heard the man. Don't try to talk.'

He was sitting on the sand beside her, one arm around her shoulders, helping her sit upright. On the other side was her instructor and, surrounding them, a ring of faces. She saw Hannah, her face contorted with anxiety, and next to her Daniel. Lucy Gillman was there along with the crew. Fantastic. Another filming washout. Others were running up to join them as word spread. Among them, she noticed Charley. Way behind her, sprinting up the sands, she thought she could see Theo.

'I said I'd give you good TV,' Kumari joked, before succumbing to another fit of coughing. Her throat felt red raw, as did her eyes. Her head pounded painfully.

'There is such a thing as trying too hard,' said Lucy. She was smiling, but her eyes were concerned.

'What the hell happened?' demanded Kumari's instructor.

'There was this board sticking up out of the water,' said Kumari. Her tongue felt thick and her head muzzy. Weird, it hadn't been so shallow there. Which meant someone must have been holding that board in place. The others had been some distance from her, but surely someone else must have seen it?

'A board sticking up? How come?' demanded the instructor.

Chico glanced up at the small crowd surrounding them. All of a sudden, he noticed Lanky Boy.

'You were out there,' said Chico in a curiously flat voice.

'Hey, I was the one raised the alarm.' Lanky Boy waved his arms in an exaggerated shrug.

Too much, thought Kumari. The guy thought it uncool to so much as blink. This display was out of character. But her head was spinning so fast it was hard to think. What was it she was supposed to remember?

'And you,' said Chico to Maria. 'You were watching from the beach. I saw you, staring at Kumari. Waiting for your little plan to work.'

'No way,' snorted Maria. She tossed her head and glared defiantly down, daring Chico to contradict her.

'It's your style, Maria,' he said in tones of disgust. 'It's exactly the kind of thing you would do. You're so jealous of Kumari it burns you. I've seen you giving her the evil eye. So you got your boyfriend here to do your dirty work.'

'Oh please,' sneered Maria. 'He is not my boyfriend. At least give me credit for having some taste. You should know that, Chico.'

The insinuation was all too clear. Chico looked her up and down.

'Don't flatter yourself,' he said. 'I would rather stick needles in my eyeballs than look at you.' Someone in the crowd sniggered.

The colour flared in Maria's cheeks. She turned on Kumari, eyes blazing.

'You deserved it!' she shrieked, the spittle flying from her mouth. 'I only wish you'd died out there.'

In the sudden, shocked silence that fell, Kumari heard Charley cry out.

'How could you?' she wailed, rounding on Maria. 'You evil cow. We're finished.'

Flinging herself down into the sand by Kumari, she grabbed her hand and held it tight.

'I am so, so sorry,' mumbled Charley, on the verge of tears. 'I can't believe she did that to you.'

'It's OK,' said Kumari. 'At least you've seen what she's truly like.'

'You bet I have,' said Charley, her damp hair clinging to her face. Under that dye job, she was still Charley. She always had been, really.

'I think we all have,' said Chico.

'Oh yeah? Maybe it's time you learned what your little friend here is really like? Whaddya say, Charley?' Maria's face was alight with malice, her eyes feverish, her mouth twisted.

'No, don't Maria, please . . .' Charley's face was awash with guilt.

What is it? wondered Kumari. *What is it she's been hiding?* Maria's hard gaze fell on Hannah. 'I guess you didn't know about your boyfriend cheating.'

'My what?' Hannah's eyes flicked to Daniel.

'And with your best friend too. Oh dear.' Maria shook her head in mock sympathy.

Hannah was looking at Charley now, her eyes burning into her. 'Is this true?' she demanded, her voice very quiet and very low.

'No. Yes. I mean, it was only one kiss. I forced it on him. It's not his fault.'

'I don't think so,' crowed Maria. 'From where I was standing it looked mutual.'

'Daniel?' Hannah stared at him, daring him to lie.

'It was when we broke up for that week. I missed you. I'm sorry.'

'You missed me so you kissed my friend?'

'It wasn't like that. She kissed me.'

'It's true,' whispered Charley. 'Daniel came to talk to me about you. Maria told him he should. She knew I was feeling really low. Daniel said he wanted to get back with you and, I don't know, I felt so jealous. He obviously cared about you so much and I had no one, not even my mom and dad. It was all my fault, Hannah. Blame me, not Daniel.'

Hannah's eyes swivelled to Maria. 'And this is the hold you've had over her? You evil, scheming cow. You probably set the whole thing up.'

Maria let out a forced laugh. 'Same old do-gooding Hannah. Always going for the sob story. Maybe it's time you got yourself a better boyfriend.'

'Maybe it's time you got lost.'

Kumari had never seen Hannah this angry and she admired her for it. The girl was standing up for what she believed in; standing up for her friends.

'I am so, so sorry, Hannah,' whispered Charley.

'Forget it. Let's move on.'

Hannah turned and walked away along the beach. It was obvious she needed a little time.

Kumari looked at Charley's stricken face. At least some good had come out of it. The truth might hurt, but it was always good, and at least Charley was free now of Maria. Now if only she and Chico could sort things out. Impulsively, she turned to him. 'We need to talk,' she murmured. His arm was still about her shoulders. She could feel the heat of his skin burnishing hers. She was staring at Chico's face but it was dipping around crazily. All of a sudden, she remembered. Her pendant. Her fingers fluttered to her neck. Her head was whirling. She could hardly breathe. It was just like being back in the water.

'Kumari?' she heard Chico say. 'Kumari, are you OK?'

'P-pendant . . .' she managed to gasp out before the darkness engulfed her.

KUMARI'S JOURNAL
(TOP SECRET. FOR MY EYES ONLY.
EVERYONE ELSE KEEP OUT!)
THIS MEANS YOU!

My bedroom at Ma's

Day thirteen in New York

That was way, way too embarrassing and also really scary. Theo tells me it was touch and go. Thank goodness he was on the beach. No wonder I was feeling so weird – the salt reacted with the fire mixture. Theo says he adjusted the balance by throwing on fresh water, which sounds mad but it worked. At least we know for sure the pendant will stand up to water – just not lots of sea water.

Anyway, I can't believe I had to go and pass out on Chico all over again. Chico says I must be allergic to him. OK, so I only did that once before and long ago, when he rescued me from Razzle's clinic. But I hate that damsel in distress thing. It is just so not me. The thing is, it worked. In fact, it acted as what Theo would call a catalyst. Chico came this evening just to check I was OK. Guess we're friends again. Ma, being Ma, gave him a bit of a hard time, but only in a joking way. When he asked me if I wanted to go for a walk, she rolled her eyes in that way of hers and suggested Badmash stay with her. I felt a bit bad about that – it's kind of like when the grown-ups exclude the kids – but Badmash seemed perfectly happy to stay and lick peanut butter from a plate.

Yup – another walk. And guess where we ended up? That's right, the secret garden again. Our super-significant place. I said once more how sorry I was for not showing up for dinner and he just looked at me in the way he does – like I am a lunatic. Then I took a deep breath and asked if I could make it up by going to meet his family. He liked that idea so much I couldn't speak for a full ten minutes thanks to the fact he was kissing me. And, of course, I was kissing him back. It felt so, so good.

CHAPTER 17

As they approached the apartment building, Kumari began to drag her feet.

'Come on, they won't bite,' said Chico.

'Yeah, I know. But Badmash might.' She glanced at the vulture perched on her shoulder and he favoured her with his beady stare. 'I didn't mean it,' she said. 'I know you'll be on best behaviour. Or else.'

She couldn't leave Badmash behind again, especially not when there was food involved. Actually, it was the food thing that was worrying her most. Badmash was so very greedy. But he was a part of her, a big part, and if they wanted to meet her they needed to meet him too. Badmash was her first friend, for so long her best friend. For one thing, he had no expectations of her – beyond doughnuts.

Chico, on the other hand, was now steering her towards

the door behind which his family lay in wait. And it really felt like that, like she was walking into a lion's den. *What will they think of me? Will they like me? I musn't let Chico down.* So many thoughts whirling in her head, even when the door swung open.

'Chico. And you must be Kumari. Hey, everyone, Chico's home. Well, what do we have here? A vulture? It's Badmash, isn't it?'

Grandpa was obviously well primed because he was holding a doughnut in his hand. Uttering cries of ecstasy, Badmash hopped from her shoulder and snaffled it in one peck.

'Badmash! Don't be rude,' scolded Kumari, mortified.

'Don't worry about it. He's a vulture. That's what vultures do, don't they?'

Kumari smiled at Grandpa and found herself staring into the liveliest eyes she had ever seen. As dark as Chico's, they were set in a face that seemed young despite its scores of lines. What was left of Grandpa's hair was silver and his weathered skin a tanned olive. Kumari could see Chico's features reflected in his face. It was like staring at Chico in fifty years' time. A tiny ripple of dread ran through Kumari. Of course, she knew Chico had to age. It was just that staring at Grandpa was proof positive that, unlike her, he would not live forever.

'Grandpa – Kumari. Kumari – this is my grandpa.' Chico spoke with such affectionate pride that Kumari almost curtsied.

'Well, come on in, Kumari. It is wonderful to have you here. We have heard so much about you. All good, I might add.'

'You have?' squeaked Kumari, following Chico's grandpa through into the living room. There, two more people were waiting, their faces wreathed in smiles. They were sat together on a couch, its material worn but immaculately clean.

'Hi Kumari,' chirped Angie. 'It's so great to see you.'

'Ah, likewise,' said Kumari. Had Chico told Angie about her jealous outburst? If he had, Angie gave no sign. She seemed genuinely pleased to see her. Beside Angie sat an old lady swathed in a blanket despite the heat of the day. She, too, smiled at Kumari, although it was obviously with some effort.

'This is my grandma,' said Chico. 'She's not been too well lately.'

Grandma held out a frail hand and Kumari took it in her own. It felt papery and so very thin, as if Grandma was a tiny bird.

'I'm so glad you came,' said Grandma. Kumari felt tears prick, hot at her eyes. Without warning, a premonition had flashed through her mind. Call it goddess wisdom or intuition, she knew without a doubt that Grandma was going to die soon. Speechless, Kumari simply kept a hold of her hand, forcing herself to keep smiling.

'I hope you're hungry,' said Grandpa. 'I have made a stack of quesadillas.' Kumari looked up and saw him watching her. *He knows,* she thought. He knows his wife is not going to be here long, but he's doing his best to hold it together. Chico had told her how very special his grandparents were. Now she understood why. They had taken Chico and his sister in when Chico's mum got sick. They had brought the kids up as their own – no easy task when you were old.

It's so unfair, Kumari wanted to shout. I hate this thing called Time. I hate what it does to you people in the World Beyond. You grow old so fast and then you die. Instead, she kept smiling, for her hosts and for Chico. All the way through dinner, which was delicious, even if Badmash did his best to clean everyone else's plates. As the evening wore on, that smile became easier to sustain. She found herself laughing at Grandpa's jokes and giggling with Angie over photos. Grandma had insisted they got the albums out after dinner. Chico was one cute baby.

'Awww, no,' moaned Chico as Grandma pointed out his best moments.

'And here he is as an altar boy,' she said. Kumari leaned in for a closer look. Weird, Chico looked a bit like Tenzin in his tunic. And what was with the white ruffles around his neck and the red skirt poking from underneath?

'What's an altar boy?' she asked.

'It's someone who helps the priest out in our church,' Grandpa explained. 'I guess you're not Catholic.'

'Ah, no,' said Kumari. One more difference between them. Strange – she had never even thought about it before. In the Kingdom, there was only one religion. Actually, more than a religion, it was a way of life and she was a big part of it. One day, she would be at its helm, worshipped rather than worshipper. The thought always creeped her out, but then it came with the territory. If you were born a goddess, what could you expect? At least she'd had a normal life for a while. And she would continue to lead one for as long as she could, for as long as she could stave off the full goddess thing.

Kumari shut Chico's album with a sigh. There were no photos of her as a baby. They had no cameras in the Kingdom, no pictorial records, save portraits. It was why

Mamma's portrait meant so much to her. It was literally all she had left. All of a sudden, she wanted a picture of them all together, right here in Chico's living room. It would be a memory that would mean a lot, not just to her but to Chico's family.

'You know what,' said Grandpa at that precise moment. 'Why don't I fetch my camera and take a picture of you all? You look so good sat there together.'

'I swear he's a mind reader,' muttered Kumari to Chico. 'I was just thinking the same.'

'Grandpa's like that,' said Chico. 'He's real quick to pick up on people. He likes you a lot, I can tell.'

'You think so?' beamed Kumari.

'I know so – now here he comes. Hey everyone, photo opportunity.' And with that, Chico put one arm around Kumari and the other round Grandma.

'Say "chillis",' instructed Grandpa.

Several flashes later they were done, but not before Grandpa had insisted on taking a few shots of Kumari and Chico together.

'Don't they look cute together?' whispered Angie to Grandma, just loud enough for Kumari to hear. Grandma merely nodded and smiled.

She looks tired, thought Kumari. This would be a good time to leave, even though she found it hard to tear herself away.

'Thank you so much,' she said to Grandma, bending to kiss her goodbye.

'Thank you,' murmured Grandma, 'for making my Chico so happy.'

Once more, Kumari felt a lump choke up her throat.

'I'll get prints of those pictures for you,' said Grandpa as he hugged her tight. 'You come again soon now, you hear?'

'I will,' said Kumari. 'And thank you again.'

She had to practically drag Badmash out of the door. In his beak he carried a doggy bag, courtesy of Grandpa. There was no way he was letting anyone else touch his booty, as his flashing eyes made quite clear.

'So you had a good time?' said Chico as they walked downstairs together.

'I had a great time,' answered Kumari.

'They're good people,' said Chico.

'The best. And so are you.' She squeezed his hand tighter. It helped her fend off the tears that threatened. They were a wonderful family. She would so love to be a part of them. But it could never be; they could never be.

At least they had these moments. She remembered the way Grandpa had looked at Grandma, relishing every second he had with her. He knew they would be parted soon and yet he accepted the inevitable. *Why can't I be like that?* thought Kumari. *Why do I fight against everything? I didn't want to lose Mamma and I don't want to lose Chico. I don't even want to be a full goddess.*

But maybe some things could not be fought against. Perhaps they even happened for a reason. The trouble was, she could not think of a single reason why losing someone you loved could ever be a good thing.

'I won't do it,' muttered Kumari.

'What did you say?'

'Uh, nothing.'

She would spare him the pain of the inevitable. Let Chico find out in the fullness of Time. Meanwhile, she would handle the goddess thing herself. She had no other choice.

CHAPTER 18

The man looked at the scrawny girl in front of him. She had clearly once been very pretty. But her hard little features spoke of tough times on the mean streets and an attitude spawned to match. He had been watching her for some time now, as soon as he'd realised her connection to Kumari that day on Fordham Road. The girl was trouble with a capital T, but she could be very useful to him.

Now that the client was putting on the squeeze, he needed to come up with answers. The client wanted to know exactly what was happening to Kumari every minute of the day. The man needed to find more resources. He could not be everywhere at once and sometimes it was impossible to follow without being spotted. The day the kids had gone out to Long Island, he had been caught wrong-footed. How was he to know they would not be in the classroom that day?

Generally, folk followed a routine.

He had been in the game long enough to know not to go asking questions of the wrong people. Teachers were notoriously tight-lipped and had far too much lie-detecting experience. An attempt to infiltrate the crew had almost blown his cover. Some woman director had given him the once-over and then demanded to know what he was doing. His tale about being a sub on the catering wagon had not washed with her. The woman was astute, he would give her that. The wisest thing had been to skedaddle.

Over the years, he had learned that Lady Luck played a big part in success – and she had turned up in the form of Maria. He had bumped into the girl by chance when he was hanging round near Moreno. She was obviously waiting round for someone too and bought his story of being a reporter working on a follow-up to the Manhattan Mystery Girl story.

Maria had been only too eager to talk, once he had waved some of those dollar bills at her. It helped that she hated Kumari's guts. In his experience, emotion worked even better than hard cash and particularly if that emotion was as naked as Maria's resentment of Kumari. He wondered what had gone down between them. Unsurprisingly, he did not have to wonder long. Maria spilled her guts messily. It all came out – the guy, the surfing 'accident'. Some mumbo jumbo about Kumari having strange powers. He filed that one away for later and pressed home about the beach incident. Maria swore it had nothing to do with her and blamed Kumari for her punishment. Turned out Maria had been suspended, although why that would bother her he found hard to work out. It was obvious the kid skipped school most of the time. How would a suspension make any difference? He guessed it had more to do with Maria losing out, or at least that was how she saw it. And the girl was set on revenge which was all the better for him.

'Was there anything else you remember?' he pressed. 'Anything she said you thought seemed odd?'

'Yeah, actually, right before she passed out. She said something about her pendant.'

'Her pendant?' Now this could be interesting.

'Uh huh. She wears a couple of things around her neck. One of them Chico gave her.' Maria practically spat out his name. Obviously, there was no love lost there either. Rejection had turned her feelings for him upside down. It was easier to hate him as well.

'And the other?'

'I dunno. It's just a pendant. Kind of big and clunky and smells sorta strange. Like she has perfume in it or something. You know those perfume necklaces you can get?'

He didn't, but he nodded encouragingly. This could be something or nothing, but Kumari had mentioned her pendant – and right before she passed out. People who were losing consciousness often talked total garbage. Then again, they often talked perfect sense and usually about something that mattered. If it was on her mind right before she fainted, chances were it was important. He needed to get his hands on it and fast.

'OK, Maria, you come up with anything else you call me.'

'It'll cost you – and you owe me for today.'

'Fifty bucks should cover it.'

'Make it a hundred and we're talking.'

'You drive a hard bargain,' he said mildly. It was, in fact, less than he expected to pay and, besides, it was not his money. He was interested, though, to see how far she would push him. It seemed Maria was not as tough as she thought.

He counted out the notes, watching her greedy eyes flicker over them. She snatched them from him and recounted twice before she was satisfied.

'I'll call you,' she said, 'on your cell, when I have something to give you.'

'Make it soon, Maria,' he said. 'And don't try anything stupid.'

For a fraction of a second their eyes met, and then she dropped her thickly mascaraed lashes. Maria had blinked first. It was all the information he needed. When the chips were down, Maria folded. The kid was easy pickings.

CHAPTER 19

Simon Razzle snatched his cell phone from the table and barked into it impatiently. 'Where the hell have you been? I've been waiting to hear from you.'

'I'm following up something right now. It could turn out to be very interesting.'

'So? Why not tell me what it is?'

'It concerns a pendant worn by Kumari. Apparently she was talking about it right before she passed out on the beach. My contact says she was very agitated. She thinks it has some significance.'

'She? Who is she?'

'You know I can't reveal my sources.'

'For what I'm paying you, you can reveal anything right down to your inside leg measurement.'

'My source attends Rita Moreno Middle School. Or at least, she's on the roll. Attendance seems to be optional as far as she is concerned, but she does know Kumari and her friends. More than that, there's some history between them. Something about a boyfriend. Some kid called Chico who seems hot and heavy with Kumari. That's all I can tell you.'

Razzle sucked in his breath. He remembered Chico well. Cocky kid had come barging into his clinic like he had a perfect right and had carried Kumari back out with him. It was a score he would settle in good time. Right now, he needed to concentrate on Kumari. This pendant could turn out to be very interesting indeed. He would have to ask the Ayah about it.

Throwing his cell phone aside, Razzle clicked his fingers at his omnipresent guard.

'Unlock the surgery door,' he commanded. 'I need to visit my patient.'

These guards were really beginning to get on his nerves, especially since the incident the other evening. Apparently they had spotted an intruder and had given chase, but had somehow managed to lose the person. Worse, there was no CCTV footage thanks to the earlier electricity outage. Some darn fool had forgotten to reset the cameras. All they could do was bleat on about the intruder being small. As if Razzle cared about the size; all he cared about was his security. His and that of the Ayah, who had to stay alive – at least until they could execute their plan.

The guard rose gracefully to his feet, a look of disdain on his chiselled face. Taking his time, he sauntered through the vast, open hall before stopping in front of a door. Extracting a bunch of keys, he inserted one in the lock. The door swung inwards silently to reveal a stark white room with a bed in the centre. A low hum filled the air along with a curious, medicinal smell. On the bed, a figure was scarcely visible under a mass of snaking tubes and electronic sensors. Razzle hesitated a moment, surveying his work, before he moved closer to the bed.

Suspended animation: the cutting edge of surgical science. And he, Simon Razzle, had achieved it with ease. But then, why would he not? He had always been underrated as a surgeon and as scientist. A drawback of the cosmetic industry, he supposed, along with the age-old professional envy. Scientists were far worse than movie queens and far more ruthless. Just wait until he unleashed his discoveries upon the world. People would kill for eternal youth. As he knew from personal experience, flesh was just one more commodity to be sold. Make that young, beautiful flesh and the potential rewards were incalculable. Add in a soupçon of divinity and you had a licence to print money. Which was why he would never, ever give up until he had Kumari in his rubber-gloved clutches. He snapped on those gloves now in preparation for his checks. He had to ensure the Ayah's heart remained motionless, thanks to sophisticated cooling techniques. They were the same techniques pioneered for cardiac surgery and, as such, he maintained surgical conditions. Carefully, he checked each connection and valve, every switch and monitor.

All was just as it should be. The Ayah would survive indefinitely until the moment came to revive her. By stopping her heart he had effectively stopped the clock from ticking too. He had bought the Ayah extra time in the World Beyond.

Sometimes, when he looked at her like this, he had a heady rush of power. A valve disconnected here, a switch flicked there and he could consign her to oblivion. Unfortunately, though, he needed the wretched woman. She was the one who had come up with their latest grand plan. She was also the only one who could finish Kumari off once and for all. This time, they had a secret weapon.

A mirthless chuckle escaped Razzle's lips. Those idiots at the palace had been so busy worrying about their precious Secrets they had never even suspected something else might have been stolen. But it was during his and the Ayah's expedition to the inner sanctum that they had managed to switch the Sacred Sword for an exact replica, copied by a corrupt craftsman from the drawings the Ayah had painstakingly made. The woman thought long-term, he would give her that. She was definitely a forward planner. Those drawings had been kept hidden for years, waiting for the moment when she could use them.

And now that moment had come. The sword lay safely beneath the Ayah's bed. With it, she would kill off Kumari at last, enabling him to harvest what he needed from the girl's body. Frankly, he wished he could be the one to do it. His surgical skills would ensure precision. There would be nothing worse than the Ayah slicing up an organ that later turned out to be vital. The criteria, however, were clear: it had to be someone from that wretched Kingdom who wielded the sword. Otherwise, it would simply be a mundane act, devoid of sacred power.

Once she had carried out her dreadful task, the Ayah intended to return at once to the Kingdom. There she would enlist the help of the warlords to depose the king and replace him with herself as ruler. The whole plan required immaculate timing; the Ayah had already all but used up her time in the World Beyond. Her window for action was very tight. They needed to leave nothing to chance.

A man on the ground in New York had seemed prudent and now it was paying off. This information about Kumari's pendant could prove crucial to their plans. The more Razzle thought about it, the more he was convinced. Somehow that pendant must hold the key to Kumari's survival out here. It was an odd thing to be wearing when surfing, and to make such a fuss was a further clue. In which case, the pendant might save him a whole lot of trouble. Snatch it and the girl would perish – no need for the Sacred Sword – or the Ayah.

A slow smile spread across Simon Razzle's face. Cut out the Ayah and all the profit was his. And the beauty of it was that the woman would never know. He would simply switch her machines off. He glanced at the monitors once more. All was satisfactory for now. But if his plan succeeded, those readings would fly off the scale as things heated up for real. He almost wanted to laugh out loud, except that might have alerted the guard hovering by the door. The man was in cahoots with the Ayah, as were all the guards. Razzle would have to proceed very carefully indeed.

'We're done here,' he said. 'You can lock up.'

The man grunted and did as he was asked.

Razzle followed him back through the vast, echoing hall. Pretty soon it would be he who called the shots.

KUMARI'S JOURNAL
(TOP SECRET. FOR MY EYES ONLY.
EVERYONE ELSE KEEP OUT!)
THIS MEANS YOU!

My bedroom at Ma's

Day sixteen in New York

It's been over two weeks since I got back here. Time is flying by so fast. But then it always seems to in the World Beyond, or maybe that's just in New York. I know I can come back again, so long as I hold the full goddess thing at bay, but it still doesn't stop that empty feeling every time I think about leaving all my friends. Thank goodness for Theo and thank goodness for my pendant. Without it I would not be here now and I would not have been able to help Ma.

I would also not be back with Chico. What was he supposed to do, wait forever? Oh stop – that sent a shiver right down my spine. If I became a full goddess that's exactly what would happen. So much good has come out of this trip – School for Happiness, my friendships. But the really important stuff has still not happened – like avenging Mamma. What's worse is that I can't even tell the RHM that I've found Razzle and the Ayah and that we need to go after them. Somehow, I need to get Raider's people on their tail. I need to get back to LA.

It's not just a question of money – I'm sure Theo or Ms Martin would lend it. I need help to get in there, past those guards. The kind of help that comes armed. There's no use calling the police – if I do that, I'll never get the Ayah. And that is the whole point – to finish her off once and for all. Raider is the only one who can help here. The good thing is, I have leverage, but I need to choose the right moment to use it – when Raider is stressed to the max and will give me exactly what I want. The Brother Joyful stuff is not something Raider would want splashed across the papers. OK, so blackmail is really bad, but so is what Raider did back then. It's a means to an end, the only way I have of freeing Mamma. I promised I would do what it takes and the gods accepted my bargain.

CHAPTER 20

They got to the 38th Street entrance on the FDR Drive early, determined to bag themselves a great position. The fourth of July fireworks were not to be missed and it was all the better going as a gang. For once the cameras were not with them – this was strictly a fun outing. Of course, fun would up the Happiness quotient, but that was simply a by-product.

Badmash was nestled deep within the Badmash Bag, Ma's old earmuffs strapped tight to his head. If there was one thing he hated it was loud noise, but he had insisted upon coming.

'But you could stay here with Ma,' Kumari had pleaded. 'And watch it on TV with the sound turned down.'

Badmash had rolled his eyes in that way that suggested he would die if he did not come and so Kumari had had no option but to bring him. Feeling left out was far worse than a few loud bangs for Badmash, although he would spend the entire evening trembling. Ma was more than happy to stay home. She, too, hated fireworks. Or at least she did since Sonny's death. She said they smelled of smoke and gunpowder. CeeCee and LeeLee were also elsewhere, attending some kind of big chess tournament.

'Who holds a chess tournament on the fourth of July?' Kumari wondered aloud to Hannah and Charley.

'Chess players, that's who.'

Hannah pulled her nerd face. Charley and Kumari collapsed into giggles.

'What's so funny?' asked Chico.

'Uh nothing. Nothing you would understand.'

'Girls.' He rolled his eyes and carried on talking to Daniel. The Hannah and Daniel thing was now back on track after the Charley incident. Excluding that minor hiccup, they'd been an item for ten months. Was it really ten months since the Halloween Ball? It felt more like ten years at times. So much had happened. And yet they were all here together, Charley and Hannah, friends again. Kumari. Chico.

They hustled their way through the crowds, following Theo along the FDR Drive to 34th Street.

'It's the best,' he had promised. 'You get a fantastic view.'

And so it proved. Up river they could see the Queensborough Bridge which linked Manhattan to the low-rise sprawl visible across the water. Behind them, the endless skyscrapers of Manhattan jutted proudly, dwarfing all below. There was a firework barge to the left, one to the right and one directly ahead of them. There was no way they were going to miss a single rocket. Kumari patted the Badmash Bag reassuringly.

'Are you OK in there?' she cooed. Badmash studiously ignored her. He was far too busy listening to the iPod strapped on beneath his earmuffs – another stroke of Ma genius.

Kumari surveyed the river in front of them. It would be getting dark soon and then the fun would start. She could see the Macy's name picked out on large white letters everywhere. Of course, they sponsored the fireworks. Funny to think they also ran the Thanksgiving Parade through which she had escaped from her kidnappers on her first ever day in New York. It was almost as if things had come full circle. For some reason, the hairs on the back of her neck prickled.

Chico noticed her shiver and threw his arm around her.

'Let me warm you up,' he said.

'Thanks.' She smiled up into his eyes. The evening light lent them an unearthly glow. What would it be like, she wondered, if Chico, too, were a divine being? Then they could be together for eternity. No, it could never, would never happen. Chico was a human being through and through. Like all her friends here, he would grow old and die. Or perhaps, like poor Sonny, he would not even get that chance. Kumari could not bear to think about it.

They were all of them so vulnerable; even she had her Achilles heel. Kumari's fingers grasped for her pendant, her miniature fire of Happiness. She held on to it as if it were a talisman. Actually it was more – it was her lifeblood. Lose that and she would perish within minutes. The atmosphere it created for her replicated that of her homeland. In the World Beyond, she was a fish out of water.

Never mind the atmosphere emanating from her pendant – there was a party mood on the FDR Drive. All around them, people laughed and chattered, sharing drinks and food from their coolers. Some had brought chairs and rugs. Others stood around in happy groups. Ms Martin was passing water and juice around their gang. Eddie looked as if he would much rather have a beer. Thank goodness the RHM had also elected to stay away. This was really not his scene at all.

'Any minute,' whispered Chico in her ear. 'It's getting close to nine o'clock.'

At 9.06 p.m., the first silver stars burst across the sky to the strains of a fanfare and a collective 'Ooooooooh' from the thousands watching. Thundering over the Manhattan skyline, forty thousand shells were let off in a choreographed sequence. Kumari had never been so close to such an incredible display. She was both awestruck and entranced.

Chico murmured something in her ear, but it was impossible to hear him over the cacophony. Instead, she reached up and kissed him full on the lips. Red and gold fireworks exploded over their heads. The colours of the Kingdom. It was almost as if the heavens were blessing them, thought Kumari. Perhaps the gods could actually be appeased.

As they drew apart, she felt something tugging at her neck. Darn – she must have got her necklace caught on Chico's T-shirt. She patted his shirt, but there was nothing attached to the cloth. With the constant flashing of fireworks it was hard to see. Some of them were eyeball-blinding in intensity, leaving their imprint on her retina. She reached up to her neck and felt around. Another starburst above exploded dizzyingly. The colours were beginning to make her head whirl. There were so many of them, constantly coming.

'Oh my god,' Kumari gasped. Her pendant. It was no longer there.

'Chico,' she grabbed his arm and pulled it desperately. 'My pendant. It's gone.'

'What?' he mouthed at her.

This was crazy. No one could hear her.

'My pendant,' she screamed again. This time he understood. She was pointing frantically at her neck then at the ground, signalling it might have fallen off. Her wild gestures brought Badmash grumbling from his bag, his vulture fuzz sticking out in tufts, his earmuffs falling round his neck.

'What is it? What's wrong?' shouted Charley, as Chico scrambled on the floor. A terrible dread was stirring in Kumari's stomach. That tugging at her neck. Someone had deliberately taken it. She tried to breathe slowly but surely, fighting back the panic. How long would it take before she suffocated? Minutes. But how many?

Dimly, she was aware that Theo was thrusting towards them. Just to her right, she thought she saw another ripple of movement. Then something else caught her eye. Maybe thirty metres away the crowd was obviously agitated. Someone was trying to shove their way through. Could it be the person who had stolen her pendant? Summoning every ounce of courage she had, Kumari tried to focus. Come on, she thought. It may be the last chance I have. Power 2, the Power of Extraordinary Sight. The chant rose from nowhere, escaping her lips. Her Powers were becoming second nature.

It was working and so easily. She stared hard. She could see the person now. A figure swaddled in a dark hoodie. She homed in on the hands and there it was: her pendant, clutched in the left fist. It looked like a man's fingers. Her sight was fading now. There was only one chance.

'There, Badmash,' she yelled at the top of her lungs. 'There, Badmash. Go get him!'

For a heart-stopping second, Badmash hesitated then, crouching low, he took off. He was flying, swooping through the air, talons and beak at the ready. The effort of shouting almost finished Kumari. She could feel the shadows lengthening. Even the fireworks seemed to fade into the distance, the ear-shattering explosions receding. In their place she heard a quiet voice: 'It's time now, Kumari.' It was an unearthly voice, an inhuman voice. The voice of destiny.

Oh no it's not, she thought. *I'm not ready. I'm not done here. I haven't yet come what I came to do. You can't have me. Not yet.*

With every ounce of her being, she fought to stay conscious. She was scarcely aware of her friends clustered close, of Chico's arms holding her up. 'Stay with us, Kumari,' he was begging.

She wanted to. She really wanted to. The lights were going out now. She was falling.

'I love you,' she murmured. 'I love all of you.'

It was over. She was finished.

CHAPTER 21

They were slapping her face, shaking her like a rag-doll. 'Come on, Kumari. Wake up!'

'Leave me alone,' she mumbled, but the words did not seem to come out right. A bright, white light was burning her eyelids. Through them, the world seemed orange. Orange, a nice colour. She would just rest here a moment and enjoy it. Maybe even slip back into darkness.

'Kumari, breathe in. That's it, sweetheart. Take a deep breath. And another.'

It was almost too much effort, but she complied. That sounded like Theo's voice.

BANG!

'Oh my god!' She snapped her eyes open. The sky was exploding in front of her eyes. Was this what the heavens looked like? No, Theo would not be in the heavens. And nor would the rest of her buddies. Come to think of it, someone was holding her tight. With an irritated wriggle, Kumari broke free.

'What are you doing?' she snapped. 'I was just having a little rest.'

Chico's face shone out, illuminated by the constant flashes. His eyes appeared to be on fire. 'You're OK,' he said. At least that was what she assumed. It was hard to hear with all this noise going on. What on earth was happening? She turned and looked properly at the river. Of course, the fourth of July fireworks. And then she remembered her pendant. She fumbled at her neck.

It was there, back in place.

'Badmash,' mouthed Chico.

With one bound, Badmash was in her arms. A pair of beady eyes gazed at her with devotion.

'You saved me,' she whispered. 'I owe my life to you.'

Above them, the sky was ripped asunder by a final, spectacular volley. Then a sudden, deafening silence. The enormous crowd began to whistle and cheer. All along the FDR Drive people were applauding. From 23rd to 42nd Street they showed their appreciation in true, audible New York fashion.

'They're cheering for you, too,' said Kumari to Badmash. 'Or at least I am.'

At last, the applause died away. The crowds started to surge home. Kumari's group stayed where it was, united by the tragedy that had almost happened. Most were not aware of the exact details, but all knew Kumari had suffered some awful attack.

'He was incredible,' said Theo, stroking Badmash's head.

'He spotted the guy and dived on him. I only wish we could have gotten through the crowd quicker, but by the time we did the guy had disappeared.'

'So it was a man?' said Kumari.

'Definitely – although none of us saw his face. Eddie, Daniel and I gave chase, but we lost him. I'm sorry.'

'Don't be,' said Kumari. 'You did your best, all of you.' She looked at them with gratitude. Even Eddie had tried to help!

'But who would have wanted to steal your pendant?' asked Hannah. 'And how would they know it was important?'

'That,' said Kumari. 'Is something I have to find out.'

The man paused, panting, in the shadow of a doorway. He had walked fast from 38th Street. Not fast enough to attract attention; just fast enough to get away. One moment he had been clutching the pendant, the next that darn bird had swooped on him. It had happened so fast scarcely anyone had registered what was going on. Besides, they were all too busy gazing at the fireworks.

That was what he had been banking on – the fireworks were a perfect distraction. The plan had been to snatch the pendant and get away before the girl even realised what was happening. He wondered why the stupid thing had turned out to be so important anyway. That Razzle guy never gave him details. It was frustrating for a professional such as he. This job relied on adequate information. The more details he had the more he had to work on. It was a simple equation. And yet his clients seemed to think by holding back they were protecting themselves when, in fact, the reverse was true.

The man prided himself on his work. He was one of the best in the business. That was why Razzle had come to him in the first place. As one of the best, he would get to the bottom of things and what he saw so far worried him. More and more he was starting to question this job or at least certain aspects of it. The pieces were beginning to slot into place. He was no longer sure he was happy to carry on. Perhaps it was time to shift the focus away from Kumari and on to Raider. That, after all, was the other part of his mission, the more personal part, the chance for vengeance.

It had been a godsend when one connected with the other, although he had had Raider in his sights for some time now. Ever since the guy had become mayor, in fact, and raised himself above the radar. The Razzle job simply made things easier in many ways. For one, it meant he was actually paid now to follow Raider. All right, not directly, but as good as, in the form of Kumari. The guy was always hanging around the show, keeping an eye on what the girl did. Two birds with one stone. He loved it when that happened.

The man straightened up and carried on, this time sauntering casually towards the subway. He blended seamlessly with the crowd also heading that way. Blending in was his speciality. It was the lynchpin of his work and the reason he had succeeded this far. Sometimes it was good to be nondescript. It meant you could get away with a lot more. A small smile briefly lifted the corner of one lip before his mouth once more fell into a straight line. He had been waiting over thirty years for this chance. He was not about to blow it.

CHAPTER 22

'Land's sakes, girl, are you telling me someone tried to take your pendant?' Ma's face had gone as grey as it ever would, considering the deep copper colour of her skin.

'Yes, but Badmash got it back within minutes so everything's OK now . . .' Kumari's voice trailed off as she saw Ma's expression. It was the one that defied her to say another word. She glanced at Chico, hovering in the doorway, and at Theo and Ms Martin. All three looked as cowed as she felt. They obviously considered themselves to have failed Ma.

'And what if he hadn't? What if that low down, stinkin' thief got clean away? Then where would we be, Kumari? At your funeral, that's where, young lady.' Ma sat down heavily on the couch and buried her face in her hands. For an awful moment Kumari thought she might cry but then Ma raised her head.

'Kumari, it's not so long ago we buried Sonny. I don't plan on burying anyone else for a long time. I certainly don't plan on burying you. How would your poor Pops have felt? Imagine if I had to call him up and tell him you were not coming back to him after all? He already lost your Mamma, Kumari. I don't think he could bear to lose you too.'

Aside from the bit about calling Papa up, the rest more or less hit home. There were, after all, no telephones in the Kingdom, although a message might eventually have got through. If not, then Papa would have found out only when they brought her back to him. It was a sobering thought. Whoever had tried to snatch the pendant had obviously known its significance. She had been wearing it tucked into her top. It must have been quite a feat to even reach it. If they had known the pendant's significance then they had intended to kill her, no question.

A shudder ran through her, ice-cold. Someone had wanted her dead. Kumari could only think of a couple of people on the planet who would like to see her in that state. Somehow Razzle must be on to her and probably the Ayah too. Had they seen her at the house in LA? It was unlikely the CCTV had caught her pendant. But even if it had, how would they know what it was for? They couldn't and they wouldn't, which meant someone must have told them. And if someone had told them, it had to be someone close to Kumari.

Only a very few people knew about the pendant and all of them were her friends. There was Ma, of course, and the girls, as well as Chico, Charley and Hannah. The RHM, naturally, and Ms Martin and Theo. OK, one or two of the other kids may have worked something out that day at the beach. A sudden thought struck Kumari. Maria had been there. She and Lanky Boy had seen everything as they fought to revive her the first time. Had Maria put two and two together and passed the information on to someone else?

It was exactly the sort of thing she would do, out of spite if nothing else. The more Kumari thought about it, the more it seemed to make sense. No one else hated her in the way Maria did, apart from the Ayah. And someone must have extracted the information from her in order to hurt Kumari. All of this pointed to the fact that Maria was the potential missing link. Excitedly, Kumari leaped up from the couch.

'I have to go see the RHM at once!'

'You ain't going nowhere, honey,' said Ma. 'I am not letting you out of my sight from now on. Besides, the RHM is already on his way over. He sounded as upset as I am.'

Kumari flicked another glance at her friends. They still looked shell-shocked. In the ensuing lull, Ma delivered her *coup de grâce*.

'I am going to tell the RHM to get you back home on the first available plane. Ms Martin, I am sure you can help arrange that. After all, Kumari's life could be at stake.'

'I . . . er . . .' for once in her life, Ms Martin appeared speechless. But then Ma in full flow did that to people. It was almost heartening to see. Almost but not quite. Kumari still had a mission in the World Beyond to accomplish. Not even Ma could be allowed to stop her, not when she had got so close.

By the time the RHM arrived, Kumari was resolute. She had a foolproof plan in mind, one that would convince him she had to stay.

'RHM,' she smiled sweetly. 'It's good of you to come, but really there was no need. As you can see, I am absolutely fine and will be even better after a good night's sleep.'

'Fine, my buttocks!' snorted Ma. 'You're only breathing thanks to Badmash.'

Badmash inclined his head in a little bow. He did so like to take applause where it was due.

Kumari dropped a kiss on his fluffy forehead. 'I will always be grateful to Badmash, but this doesn't mean we have to give up. RHM, I have a plan. And I think you will approve.'

'I am listening,' said the RHM. His voice was as flat as his expression. For some reason, he did not appear too surprised at what had happened, but then he generally expected the worst.

'I will acquire Power 4,' said Kumari. 'The Power to be Invisible. That way, when I'm out and about, I'll be entirely safe.'

Easier said than done. She only wished she could have got it together in Los Angeles. But then, it had been too risky to attempt a Power that may or may not have worked when there were gun-toting guards on your tail.

The RHM's face took on a whole new glow. It was as if someone had flicked his inner light switch. 'Power 4,' he said, 'is difficult. But, you know, I think you are ready.'

Good old RHM, thought Kumari. Gave reticence a bad name. Still, this was about as enthusiastic as she had ever seen him. Stage one of her plan had worked.

'It will also come in useful,' said Kumari, 'when I start to follow Maria. I'm pretty sure she's responsible for this evening. She's got the knowledge, the motive and the opportunity.'

Kumari beamed at the assembled company. A good speech, if she said so herself. She'd got the last bit from *CSI*, but the RHM, for one, would not know that.

'Maria?' Chico's face darkened. 'Let me deal with her, Kumari. I know from my cousin Joe how her mind works. You don't want to get involved.'

'Oh but I do,' said Kumari. 'She's the one who led Charley astray. She also fancies you like crazy, which is why she hates me.'

That may have been a little too revelatory, but there was no time now for mincing her words. Maria had to be found – and fast, before Razzle cottoned on to the fact they were on to her.

'Very well, Kumari,' said the RHM. 'You have convinced me on this matter. We will continue our sojourn in New York so long as you acquire and practise Power 4.'

Bingo! thought Kumari. She had known he would go for it. Power 4 was another huge step towards becoming a full goddess. Almost the final step, in fact. The RHM did not know for sure she had mastered Power 5 and was practising it on Ma, but he certainly suspected that was the case. After Power 4 there was only one more Power to acquire; Power No 1, the Power to Be Invincible with the Sacred Sword. The Power that would change her life irrevocably.

'You're insane!' Ma spluttered. 'You want to sign your own death warrant? These people will stop at nothing Kumari, now they've crawled out of the woodwork.'

'I know,' said Kumari. 'But I can handle them, believe me.'

In her heart, though, she wondered if that were actually true.

Simon Razzle stared at the bank of equipment in front of him. The low hum throbbed ever louder. The lights on the console glowed in the semi-darkness. That medicinal smell filled his nostrils. It reminded him of being in a morgue; the Ayah was, after all, suspended between life and death. He glanced at her face, waxy white, and could almost imagine it in a coffin. His finger was poised above a switch. Press it and he would start the process of bringing the Ayah back. If only his plan to snatch the pendant had worked. He could still taste the bitter disappointment.

Now he was forced to follow Plan A after all. Was this really what he wanted? He could hear his guard shuffle in the doorway then clear this throat.

'Is there some problem?'

The man spoke English with a heavy accent, but his tone was unmistakable.

'No, no problem,' said Simon. 'I'm just making sure everything's OK.'

A small grunt of assent from the guard. Thank goodness he was no mind reader. If he were, there would no doubt be a knife at Simon's throat.

The secret of eternal youth. He had been searching for it all his professional life. And finally, when the Ayah had approached him, it had seemed as if all his prayers had been answered. Who would have guessed that Kumari would prove so troublesome? She was nothing more than a slip of a girl. Really, it would be a pleasure to silence her once and for all. She had become his nemesis. He would not be in this situation now if it were not for Kumari. She had forced him into living like this, hidden away in a gilded cage, his talents wasted.

A sibilant hiss escaped Razzle's lips as his finger hit the switch. It was the same noise a snake made just before it struck. The machines sprang to life with barely a whirr. The process would take around an hour. And then the Ayah would be back with them. Actually, that was the downside of his plan. He absolutely loathed the woman.

As much as he distrusted her, however, he needed her and she knew it. Just as she needed him. It was a *quid pro quo* situation. The plane was on standby; tonight they would depart for LaGuardia airport. From there, it was a short drive into Manhattan. He would be home at last. All these months spent in exile would be as a dream. He would be back where he belonged, on Park Avenue. Even better, Kumari would be his at last.

(TOP SECRET. FOR MY EYES ONLY.
EVERYONE ELSE KEEP OUT!)
THIS MEANS YOU!

My bedroom at Ma's

Day seventeen in New York

I don't even know if I can do it but I have to try. Power 4: the Power to Become Invisible. Of all the Powers it sounds the most fun and maybe that's why it's so difficult. I mean, Powers are not meant to be fun. They're deadly serious, at least according to the RHM. He says I acquire Powers so I can use them for the good of the kingdom and the people. Well, preserving their trainee goddess must be a good thing, although some might not necessarily agree.

I suppose giving them a full goddess would also be a good thing, but that's too bad as far as I'm concerned. I'm all for doing good and stuff but there is such a thing as self-preservation. Although if I was going to become a full goddess, which I'm not, I'd be a better full goddess if I'd lived a little first. A goddess who knows how to have a good time can pass that knowledge on to her people. OK, so some might say that was stretching things a little but I disagree. Knowing how to really enjoy yourself is important, after all. It's part of Happiness, so long as what you do does not make others unhappy.

Hmm – that's a tricky one. Does my staying a trainee goddess make others unhappy? Well, it would definitely make the RHM unhappy, but that's only because he wants to see results. He is my teacher, so I can understand that, but are results really the most important thing? Ms Martin always says the process is just as important and I agree with her. Learning how not to do something is just as important as learning how to do it. That's what that inventor guy Edison said and he was no slouch when it came to success. OK, so it took him a while, but what's so wrong with that? It's taking me a while to do a lot of things, like sort my feelings out.

And that's another thing – my mind and feelings have to be in the same place, right? If one is ahead of the other then that just won't work. I think it's what they call maturity. One of the Great Gifts of a Goddess is Wisdom and I'll happily hold my hand up and say I'm not there yet. How wise can you be at fourteen and a half anyway? You're supposed to be all mixed up at my age.

Or at least you're supposed to be all mixed up if you're totally human. I guess I only qualify for one per cent of that even though sometimes I am definitely, absolutely one hundred per cent mixed up and confused, especially where my feelings are concerned. Emotions are such a weird thing – sometimes I wish we didn't have so many. I seem to have thousands of them competing all at once and it's really, really hard to choose. Take Chico, for example – I love him, I know that. But I also love Papa and my kingdom and my friends there and my Mamma.

Loving all of those at the same time means life is pretty impossible. And then I also love New York and my friends here and Ma. It feels like I'm being tugged from all directions when all I want is to be happy too. But what would really *make me happy? That is such a difficult question. I don't know. I have no idea. And that is what makes everything ten times more difficult.*

CHAPTER 23

Invisibility was not as easy as it appeared – or rather as it did not appear. Kumari's first few attempts in the privacy of her bedroom resulted in hysterics from Badmash.

'Stop laughing!' she howled as he rolled on the bed in silent mirth. 'You try making flesh and bones disappear.'

So far she had managed a vague blurring around her edges and the momentary fuzziness of a couple of fingers.

'I thought the more Powers you got, the easier it became,' she grumbled.

Deep breath. Try again. Maybe a rub of her amulet for luck.

A half hour later she was on the verge of giving up. She'd been trying since the crack of dawn. She should have been ready for school ten minutes ago. Chico would soon be banging on the front door. He had offered to stand escort this morning instead of CeeCee and LeeLee. OK, one last attempt.

'OM HUM PHAT KALI KALI MAHAAKAALI MAAMSA.

SHONITAM KHAADAYA KHAADAYA DEVI MAA.

PASYATU MANUSETI . . .'

A loud rap on her bedroom door disturbed her just as she was getting into it. With a sigh, Kumari flung the door open and said crossly, 'Can't you just wait a minute?'

'Kumari? Are you there?' CeeCee peered into the room.

'Of course I'm here. I'm right in front of you. Stop kidding around, CeeCee.'

Both CeeCee and LeeLee had looked dubious when the invisibility thing was explained to them. All right so they might be cynical, but there was no need to be sarcastic too.

'I am not kidding around. Why don't you stop hiding? Come on, Kumari, this is no joke. Where are you – under the bed?'

CeeCee looked perfectly sincere and more than slightly worried. Slowly, it began to dawn on Kumari that her chant might actually have worked. She looked down at her arm. Or rather where she expected her arm to be. But there was nothing to see, not so much as an inch of flesh. She could still feel it, though, which was even weirder. She tried an experimental shake. Nothing. Even her amulet had disappeared. Fantastic – she could feel everything, move everything but she was entirely invisible. She reached out and tickled CeeCeeShe reached out and tickled CeeCee, who let out an ear-splitting shriek.

'What was that? Ohmigosh! Kumari? Was that you?'

'Yes it was,' said Kumari happily. 'I've done it! I've acquired Power 4!'

She leaped around her little room, throwing herself backwards on to the bed.

'Aaark!'

'Oops, sorry Badmash.' She noticed that he was shivering. 'Badmash, what is it? Come here, sweetie, what's wrong?'

As she reached out to scoop him up, Badmash flung himself to the other side of the pillow. Emitting frightened squeaks, he darted for the end of the bed and hurled himself into CeeCee's arms.

'Badmash, it's me!' cried Kumari. 'Can't you see it's your mamma?'

'No he can't,' said CeeCee. 'And nor can I, Kumari.'

Both of them were gazing in the direction of her voice, eyes wide open in fear and bewilderment. They had known she was trying to acquire Power 4, so what was all the fuss? LeeLee's face appeared over CeeCee's shoulder. She, too, was peering into the room.

'What's up? Where's Kumari? What's with all the screaming, you guys?'

'Kumari's there,' said CeeCee, pointing a trembling finger in her direction. 'Or at least I think she's there. She could have moved by now. She's invisible.'

'Have you gone and lost your senses, girl?' Ma, too, had joined the party. 'Kumari, enough's enough. Come on out before you scare them witless.'

'I can't come out,' said Kumari. 'I'm already here, right in front of you. Power 4, it worked! I'm really and truly invisible.'

'You can say that again,' said Ma. Her face was a picture. Kumari had never seen her mouth pinch up like that into a tiny, terrified 'o'.

'Can we touch you?' asked LeeLee.

'Go ahead, try,' said Kumari.

LeeLee extended a finger and poked around where she thought Kumari might be.

'Ouch!'

'Eek!'

They shrieked simultaneously.

'That is so bizarre,' said LeeLee. 'I can feel you, but I can't see you.'

'Good, isn't it?' said Kumari. 'I can play all kinds of tricks with this.'

Just at that moment, the doorbell signalled Chico's arrival. Now this was going to be interesting. Would he freak out or stay cool? In the event, he did neither. Having stared in her general direction for a few, dumbstruck moments, Chico burst out laughing. Only it was the sort of laughter that had a hysterical edge, tinged with sheer disbelief.

'No way,' he kept saying. 'No way is this happening.'

'Yes, it is,' snapped Kumari. What was wrong with them all? She had told them she was going to do this and she had done it, although now she could feel Power 4 fading. As her form began to re-emerge, she watched the expressions that flitted across Chico's face. They ranged from terror to awe to amazement to relief. But there was something else, something that made her breath catch and she could not blame him for it one bit. In Chico's eyes there was the fascinated horror of someone staring at an alien creature. For the first time ever in their relationship, he was looking at her as if she were not quite human.

Which, in a way, she was not, being a trainee goddess and

all. There was, however, that tiny part of her that was human and it was this part that hurt. A lot.

'Hey.' She smiled at him.

'Hey.' He could not quite meet her eye.

'Shall we get going?'

'Uh, sure.'

So this was how it was going to be. Him freaked out, but trying not to show it. It was what Kumari had always feared and yet had known was inevitable. She was different from Chico, from all her friends. And there was absolutely nothing she could do about it. If truth be told, she did not want to do anything about it. She had got past wanting to fit in. She was who she was, and that was fine by her. Kumari was not changing for anyone.

Maybe it was foolish to have expected Chico to be eternally accepting. Actually, Chico could not be eternally anything. That was the tragedy of their relationship: it could never be permanent. Of course, a lot of relationships were not permanent – and at their age hardly any – but somewhere in her soul Kumari knew that it could have been. If only. If only she were not destined to live forever, in one form or another. If only he were not mortal and she was divine. If only an entire culture did not separate them.

Mamma and Papa would be together forever one day when he finally joined her on the Holy Mountain, so long as Kumari could free Mamma from limbo so she could ascend. Gods and goddesses were not meant to be separated, but then they were not meant to be murdered either. What had happened to Mamma was unprecedented and all the more terrible for it. But Mamma had not been a goddess when she first met Papa. She had been elevated to that status by Papa, the god-king, who had the power to grant eternal life.

Kumari, too, had that power. It was another of the Great Gifts of a Goddess – the Gift of Eternal Life and the power to grant the same. In theory, at any rate, she could bestow it wherever she chose. Which meant, if she took that a stage further, she could turn Chico into a divine being, able to live forever just like her and to one day sit atop the Holy Mountain. But Mamma had chosen to become a goddess. It was impossible to bestow that gift without the person's consent. Chico would have to ask her to turn him into a god. Or she would have to ask him and he would have to say yes. Somehow she didn't see that happening. For one thing, she would never want him to have to make that choice.

Kumari sneaked a glance at Chico. He was hesitating by the door to the apartment building, his eyes still slightly averted.

'Guess you'd better do it then,' he said.

'Do what?'

'The invisible thing.'

'Oh that. Guess I better had.'

She looked at him, embarrassed.

'Do you mind not looking?' she asked.

'Oh. OK. Sure.' Politely, Chico turned his back. Was it relief that made his shoulders droop or the prospect of what was to come?

'OM HUM PHAT KALI KALI MAHAAKAALI . . .'

It was working almost immediately. Hey, this was pretty cool. Kumari stared at her arms admiringly. First her hands, then her forearms – everything faded then evaporated. She stared down at her legs and feet and saw the same thing –

which was nothing at all. Even her clothes and her amulet were entirely invisible. It was as if a cloak had been thrown over her or a bubble that shielded her from human eyes.

Bird eyes too, come to that. Badmash let out a squeak as Kumari's shoulder, on which he was perched, disappeared from view.

'Can I turn round now?'

'Wait a second.' Kumari plucked something from Chico's pocket.

'Hey . . .' He turned to see his wallet being waved at him and then a dollar bill dancing through the air. 'Give that back, you little —'

'Come and get it,' teased Kumari. 'Catch me if you can!'

She was off, racing through the door, running along the street ahead of him. Anyone watching would have seen nothing more than a wallet whizzing through the air at waist-height, hotly pursued by a young man with fire in his eyes.

'Gotcha!' He grabbed the wallet, simultaneously grasping for Kumari. She dodged out of the way and, giggling, danced ahead.

'Shhh – cool it, Kumari.'

Instantly, she slowed and sobered up. This was not a game, after all. But it was hard to remember that when being invisible offered so many opportunities for mischief. *This must be how ghosts feel,* thought Kumari, as she scooped a plastic bag from the pavement and made it do a little jig all by itself.

'Stop it, Kumari,' hissed Chico. 'Your feet – they're visible.'

She glanced down, saw her sandal-clad toes and instantly forced herself to concentrate. That was the trouble with

Powers – summoning them up was only the start. It was sustaining them that was the real trick, and not an easy one at that. Especially not when there was fun to be had and a freaked-out Chico to tease.

By the time they got to Moreno, he was white-faced with effort.

'I am going to kill you,' he muttered as she playfully tweaked his shorts up and down.

'Join the queue,' she murmured. 'Hey, look, there's Charley and Hannah!'

The two girls were standing just inside the entrance to the school, waiting for her to arrive. Kumari glanced around. There was no one following them. They were safe. Before Chico could say anything she was off, darting towards her friends. Charley was first to experience the Kumari effect as her schoolbag was whipped off her shoulder and flung into the air.

'What the . . .' Charley stared, open-mouthed and then Hannah let out a shriek. Her sunglasses were spinning around by themselves a few inches from her nose. Deciding her friends had suffered quite enough, Kumari called out: 'Don't worry, guys it's me.'

'Kumari?'

'In the flesh.' She grinned as she exhaled Power 4 away. Only it didn't disappear as fast as she thought it would, at least judging by Hannah's expression.

'Your arms,' Hannah gasped.

'What about them?'

'They're not there.'

'Oh, yes.' Nonchalantly Kumari gazed at the gap between shoulders and fingers. Letting out another deep breath, she released more Power. Gradually, her arms took shape again. Badmash bounced back in alarm, almost braining himself against the wall in the process.

'Oh my god,' said Charley. 'That was absolutely the most spooky thing I ever saw. How did you *do* that, Kumari? That was just gross.'

'It's Power 4,' said Kumari, slightly hurt. 'The Power to Become Invisible. I haven't quite got it right yet but it's to help keep me safe. After what happened with the pendant I had to come up with something. Otherwise Ma was going to pack me off home early. What else could I do?'

'Wow,' sighed Hannah. 'That must be so cool to be able to do that.'

'It is,' beamed Kumari. 'I wish you guys could have a go.'

'No thanks,' said Chico. 'You can count me out. It's too weird.'

Kumari gazed at him for a moment.

'If that's how you feel . . .' she said.

Without another word, they headed for the classroom and the penultimate Happiness session. Kumari's heart, though, sat heavy in her chest, a solid lump of growing dread. Her worst fears were coming true. Chico could never really, truly accept who and what she was. How could she have got it so wrong? She had always thought he was the one person who really understood. None of her other friends, not even Asha or Tenzin, could look at her in the way he did and know things without saying them. But now it seemed they were growing apart just when they needed to grow closer. In a few days she would be leaving the World Beyond and there was still so much left to resolve. The Ayah . . . her Powers . . . and now this with Chico. Who knew when they would next see one another? Would she have to leave it like this?

Two sets of eyes had, in fact, monitored Kumari's progress along the streets. Two sharp pairs attached to equally keen minds had observed her intermittent invisibility.

For the RHM, it was a triumphant vindication of everything he had worked towards. He was reasonably sure that Kumari had used Power 5 to restore Ma – he had seen the signs in Ma's astonishingly rapid recovery and in her sustained rejuvenation. Now, the girl's near-mastery of Power 4 meant they were only one step away from Power 1 and full goddess status.

Quietly, he slipped away, just as he had that night at the fireworks. It was better Kumari did not know he was always one step ahead of her.

Across the street, concealed in the entrance to the alleyway, the man watched the RHM walk away. Interesting that he never used the mayor's car now. He obviously did not want Jack Raider to know what he was doing. The man shook his head. He was still bending his mind around the trick the girl had pulled off. Must have been something to do with smoke and mirrors; David Blaine stuff.

The man did not believe in hocus pocus or any of that mumbo jumbo garbage, but he remembered what Maria had said – something about unusual powers. Well, unusual powers or not, Kumari was still living and breathing. Which was good news for him. As long as Kumari was alive she was a lure for Razzle and his partner in crime. Only this morning he had called from Los Angeles to say they were on their way.

The man rubbed his hands together and smiled grimly to

himself. Soon, now, this would be over. He could get on with his life. He glanced over at the school and saw the catering trucks parked on the playground. *School for Happiness* was doing well. Jack Raider was one lucky man. Well, luck could change in an instant, as the man knew only too well. His luck had changed when he was ten years old, and it was all thanks to Mr Raider. Or should that be Brother Joyful, or John Monroe, or one of the half dozen other names Raider had used over the years?

Whatever his name, Raider had destroyed his family. His own family, come to that – for John Monroe was the man's big brother. And a lowdown scumbag of a brother; always had been, always would be. His mom had told him how he used to scam pennies from the other kids at school and how he even stole from the church charity collection. John was his senior by sixteen years and he had hero-worshipped him despite everything. Then came the day his mom died of a broken heart, unable to bear the shame any longer.

The doctors called it a cardiac arrest, but he knew different. It was John who had killed his mom; John and the misery he had brought upon them. John had been his mom's first born, conceived when she was barely eighteen. She had loved him despite everything, but she was crushed by what he had done to others. And now here he was, alive and well, the Mayor of New York City. A man who had conned and thieved his whole life was sitting pretty in Gracie Mansion. Well, here was where the buck stopped. He was about to blow the whole sham sky-high. It had taken him months of patient detective work, but now he almost had the proof he needed. He could not wait to let the whole world know all about it, but he needed to be patient a little longer. He was a patient man. He could wait.

KUMARI'S JOURNAL
(TOP SECRET. FOR MY EYES ONLY.
EVERYONE ELSE KEEP OUT!)
THIS MEANS YOU!

My bedroom at Ma's

Day eighteen in New York

The show's finale is the day after tomorrow and there is absolutely no way I can pull this off. I have never felt so miserable in my life. Well, OK, maybe sometimes I have felt this miserable, but not when I'm expected to succeed in spreading Happiness. Everything seems to be going into reverse – Chico, the show, finding Razzle.

Chico is just so freaked out by the invisibility thing even though he keeps telling me he's not.

He also keeps staring at my pendant like it's going to disappear or something. Actually, I think it's me he expects to disappear at any moment, which is not so far from the truth. I have four days left in the World Beyond and I have achieved absolutely nothing. What are the gods going to do next if I don't find the Ayah and avenge Mamma?

And as for my second mission – well, that's also doomed to fail. How did I ever think I could teach Happiness in just a few weeks when it takes a lifetime in the Hidden Kingdom? Even then we have things to help us, like the haze of Happiness and our surroundings. Every little thing in the Kingdom aids Happiness, even the trees and flowers. What chance do I have of reproducing that in a concrete jungle in front of cameras? The whole thing was madness from the beginning, but I guess I went along with it so Raider's people could look for Razzle.

It's obvious Raider wants us to cheat the results, but no way. This is supposed to be a reality show, right?! He's on set all the time. The guy is practically foaming at the mouth he wants it so much, but when I look at him all I think of is Brother Joyful. I mean, what a hypocrite – the man is actually trying to run for office on a Happiness ticket. HUNK, his corporation, everything is all based on a lie. Raider does not believe in true Happiness – he believes in pure profit. All he sees are dollar signs if the show succeeds. And he'll do anything to make it happen.

Well, I have a surprise for Mr Raider. He wants reality, he's going to get it. I can't think of a better moment to reveal all than on camera. They may end up cutting it from the actual show but Lucy has promised to keep all the footage and I'll use that to get what I want from Raider. I haven't told her why, but she knows to expect something. Which is more than Raider knows – tee hee! Finally the creep is getting what he deserves.

CHAPTER 24

The process was nearly complete. Any moment now the Ayah would be reanimated, no longer suspended in a frozen half-life. Razzle glanced at the monitors; all the readings were nearly normal. He could detect a slight pinkening of her skin as the blood started to flow. Her heart, stilled for so long, had once more begun its relentless beat. It would be like waking up from a very deep sleep.

He winced as he studied her face. Her features, never attractive, were ravaged where the lion had done its worst. A livid scar ran from cheek to cheek and deep puncture marks scored her skin. One side of her face appeared to have been torn away. It was a part of their deal that Razzle would do his best to restore what looks she had once had. He did not relish the challenge; she was one demanding woman. The sooner he was free of her the better. If that meant rearranging her features then so be it; he would do his best. Although the results would hardly be a great advertisement for his not inconsiderable skills. Razzle sighed as he glanced at his hands. They were truly the instruments of a genius. Why waste such a gift on such a gorgon when there were so many more deserving and better-paying clients? For a split second he wondered if there was still time to stop the process. No – she was nearly conscious.

And then another idea occurred to him. What was to stop him taking the sword and trying it out for himself? After all, he only had the Ayah's word that it had to be someone from the Kingdom wielding it to deal Kumari a fatal blow. As he knew from bitter experience, her word was not to be relied upon. This was his last chance to cut her out of the equation, kill Kumari himself and rake in all the profits. He ducked his head to peer beneath the bed. It was still there, in its reinforced case. Neither of them was taking any chances when it came to the Sacred Sword – the thing was their salvation. He had just begun to reach for it when a malevolent voice stopped him in his tracks.

'Don't even think about it,' hissed the Ayah.

'Y-you're awake!' he stuttered.

'Awake and alive and freezing cold, you idiot.'

And as charming as ever, thought Razzle while he plastered a smile across his face. 'That's because I slightly underdid the process to buy you a little extra time. It's good to keep your body temperature a little low.' *Besides, you should be used to it, you lizard.*

'I see,' said the Ayah. 'We have a job to do. Let's get on with it. I assume you have a plan if you have woken me up, which means every second counts.'

'I do indeed,' smirked Razzle. 'And you are just going to love this one. We don't even have to travel too far. Kumari has come to us.'

'What do you mean, "come to us"?' The Ayah's eyes glittered.

'I mean she's here, in America. In New York City, to be precise.'

'Then what are we waiting for, you fool? We need to get on a plane fast. In case you had forgotten, I have limited time in which to carry out this act.'

Thirty-six hours, to be precise. That was what Razzle had calculated as giving them enough time to get the job done and the Ayah on a plane home. He had also picked out the best place: Coney Island, the setting for the grand finale of *School for Happiness*. Jack Raider had provided all the details and would be getting them in as crew. So much for his bravado at the Brooklyn Bridge – Razzle had known Raider would capitulate in the end. They had, after all, leaned on him just where it hurt.

Raider had promised to close the area the night before using his mayoral powers. That gave them plenty of time to set up a little accident for Kumari; the sort of little accident from which she would never recover. Then they would whisk her away in a private ambulance to a facility where Razzle could do his worst. By the time Kumari was returned to her loved ones, she would be in little bits.

Of course, they would cite the autopsy required of any unexplained death as the reason for her state. Kumari's death would be recorded as an accident – Raider would make sure of that. It was mighty handy having the mayor on your side.

It could be even handier if he became president. Naturally, that was all a long way off, but Raider was a strong candidate. If *School for Happiness* succeeded, he would be looking even stronger, which meant a sure-fire source of funds for Razzle for many years to come. The past had a way of resurfacing at the most inopportune moments. He was sure Raider would pay handsomely to ensure it remained buried away from press or public.

'Wipe that stupid smile off your face and get moving,' snapped the Ayah. She clicked her fingers at the bodyguard. 'Open this door at once.'

Trailing in her wake, Razzle kept his mouth firmly shut. He had not expected a gushing eulogy. A simple 'thank you' would have done. Thanks to him and his skills, this ghastly woman was alive and within reach of her greatest wish. It was really what he was all about: making dreams come true for others. Well, now it was time to make his own dreams come true, starting with Kumari.

The secret of eternal youth: the holy grail of the beauty industry. And he, Simon Razzle, was about to make it happen. Not only would he be drowning in dollars, he would also achieve the global fame and respect that he so deserved. His name would forever be associated with the greatest discovery of the century. He would be fêted, adored. Worshipped just as Kumari would have been. Actually, make that the greatest discovery *ever*, right up there with electricity and sliced bread. Forget cures for cancer, forget global peace. The Nobel Prize was practically his.

CHAPTER 25

It was the final day of filming and Kumari could not bring herself to touch her breakfast.

'Come on, child, eat up,' said Ma. 'You need the energy, girl.'

Energy schmernegy. She was running on empty. But it was a nervous kind of empty which would keep her going for a long while yet. Would they, could they pull this off while keeping Jack Raider at bay? He would cheat, lie, steal to make this show work for him and she was none too sure he had not done so already. Face facts, Kumari. *School for Happiness* was a fake.

Yesterday evening, she and Lucy had sat trying to work out what to do to try to save the show. Never mind Jack Raider, Kumari hated to fail.

'I've got it!' Kumari had yelled after much pondering.

'We've done too much on the inner and not the outer.'

'I'm sorry?' Lucy had looked puzzled.

'For true Happiness we need to look outside ourselves. Yes, Happiness comes from the inside, but you also need to spread it around. We have to get the class thinking of others beside themselves. We need to be generous with what we have.'

'You're absolutely right,' Lucy had smiled. 'It's what I was always taught as a kid. Spread happiness and it will come back to you tenfold, that's what my grandpa always said.'

'Sounds good to me,' said Kumari. 'Your grandpa must have been pretty wise.'

'He'd seen a lot and learned a lot. He was an explorer, Randolph Gillman.'

And now here Kumari was, fretting over what they had decided that day. Each member of the class would be buddied up with a kid from an activity centre for children with special needs. There was a risk the show could appear cheesey or patronising, but it was a risk they simply had to take. If everything worked as it should, both groups of kids would gain a lot from one another.

The Moreno class would have a chance to reach out with their new skills and, in doing so, fill in the final gaps of Happiness. In turn, the kids from the activity centre would have plenty to teach and learn. It could prove to be the tipping point they needed. At least then she would have achieved something. Why was it so much easier to witness Happiness in others than feel it yourself?

Perhaps, thought Kumari, *it's because I'm always worried about something. Maybe I need to just let go and trust things will turn out all right.* The trouble was, they hadn't, and not for a very long time. The shadow of the Ayah still hung over her. Vengeance seemed so very far away. All she wanted to do was free her Mamma and it appeared to be impossible.

Coney Island was not one giant theme park but rather a sprawling collection of smaller parks and rides. To make it easier to film, they had settled on Deno's Wonder Wheel. The park was home to a giant ferris wheel and the notorious Spook-A-Rama, a ride so terrifying kids had been known to run from it screaming. Raider's people had ensured the park was closed off the night before so that the crew could set up. When Kumari and the other kids arrived, everything was in place.

'Hey everyone,' said Kumari. 'It's the final one. Let's make it good. In fact, let's make it the best one ever. This is our last shot at achieving Happiness. And to help you do that, I've invited some people along. Here, they are, bang on time. Meet the kids from the Sunshine Center.'

As the cameras began to roll, the kids were helped from their minibus. Some walked unaided and some needed support. A couple of wheelchairs were lowered.

'You're kidding,' muttered someone in the Moreno crowd. Kumari glanced around sharply.

'This is so cheap,' said someone else. 'Like, typical TV schmaltz.'

Kumari remembered how they had called Raider a fake. Only this was no stunt; it was real. But how to get the kids to see it that way?

'OK, everyone, buddy up. We have a list here so let's get

moving.' Lucy glanced at Kumari as she stepped in. *Don't worry*, her look seemed to say.

While the Moreno kids hung back, the others had no such inhibitions. With no desire to appear cool, they reached out instantly to their new buddies.

'I'm Hannah,' said Hannah to her new friend and was immediately engulfed in a huge hug. Charley was already being tugged towards the rides by a kid whose T-shirt read *Keep Staring*. As he turned away, Kumari saw the back. Written across it: *I Might Do A Trick.*

This could work, thought Kumari, as her hopes began to rise. She saw Eddie being given a hard time by his buddy, a boy in a wheelchair.

'You're doing it all wrong, man!' the boy was saying. 'You gotta lift me from underneath.'

Eddie looked helplessly about.

'Are you going to get me on this ride or what?'

There was nothing for it but to lift him. The rules stated that the kids and their buddies had to look out for one another. Red-faced, Eddie huffed and puffed and finally hauled the boy on to the Wonder Wheel. As Kumari watched, the one-hundred-and-fifty foot high wheel began to turn. A huge grin spread across the boy's face. He was airborne, out of his chair, and all thanks to Eddie. As for Eddie, it looked like he had finally met his match.

With a smile, Kumari turned to the last kid off the bus. 'Hi,' she said. 'I'm Kumari.'

'I'm Dana,' said the girl. Her eyes did not meet Kumari's. She's in her own world, thought Kumari. A little like me, at times.

'Good to meet you, Dana,' said Kumari. 'Want to come and play on the rides?'

The girl stared at the ground. Taking her by the hand, Kumari led her towards the Wonder Wheel. Maybe a little fun would unlock her smile.

Then again, maybe not. Even as they soared high above the ground, Dana gazed into space. There was the ghost of something flickering about her mouth, but if it was a smile it was scarcely visible. *But maybe,* thought Kumari, *it's unfair to expect that. Just because she doesn't show it the way I do, doesn't mean she's not happy.*

From her vantage point high above the park, Kumari looked out at all the other kids. Expecting everyone to show Happiness in the same way was maybe too much to ask. Could it be that back home they were a little too conformist? The tenets of Happiness should be a blue-print, nothing more. And what she saw unfolding all around her was a bunch of kids doing it their way. It might not make the show a success in Raider's eyes but that was just too bad. Maybe, just maybe, they could succeed on their own terms.

CHAPTER 26

Razzle and the Ayah strolled towards the Spook-A-Rama, clipboards in hand. It had not been hard for Raider to smuggle them into the second unit. Today, there were many unfamiliar faces on set. The demands of the finale meant a whole new crew was needed to cover everything. So long as they looked busy and kept out of the way, no one questioned their presence.

They had so far managed to avoid the RHM. The man really did get everywhere. Razzle was glad he had knocked him out back in the Kingdom: one headache for another. Unnoticed, they slipped behind the scenes and along the twisted, snaking track of the Spook-A-Rama. Technicians were everywhere setting up for a shot. No one batted an eyelid as they passed.

They were heading for the darkest recesses of the ride,

where they had already set up a little trap. What made this particular spot so perfect was the presence of a devil figure holding aloft a curved sword. As the cars rounded a bend, the figure took a whack at the occupants – only in Kumari's case it would be no fibreglass dummy that assailed her, but the living, breathing Ayah holding the Sacred Sword.

The plan was so simple it was almost scary, but then all the best plans were simple.

'Help me with this!' hissed the Ayah as she struggled into the costume they had hidden the night before. Once her mask was in place, the Ayah was a reasonable replica for the original figure, horns protruding over an evil smile, red robes shrouding her portly shape. As she took up her position where the original had stood, Razzle handed her the Sacred Sword. One little nick, that was all it would take. And then Kumari was his.

Ten minutes after Razzle and the Ayah, the RHM slipped past the Grim Reaper at the Spook-A-Rama's entrance. He walked as fast as he dared, following the twisting track, trying to find a vantage point. The RHM was out of patience. It was time to force Kumari's hand. For so long now he had nursed his dream, his vision for the Kingdom. With Kumari at his side, he knew it could be a reality, but the girl was stubborn, devious and smart. She had thwarted him at every turn. Well, she was not the only one capable of deviousness. Kumari was about to learn the ultimate lesson, that destiny has a habit of catching up with us all. Sometimes it was better to turn and meet it rather than run and resist the inevitable.

* * *

'Kumari! Kumari, we want to film you on the Spook-A-Rama.'

She could hear Lucy yelling across the park. The crew were hustling her forward. Kumari looked about for Dana, but the girl had disappeared. Damn Raider and his demands. He had waylaid her as they left the Wonder Wheel, insisting he and Kumari have a word for a moment. And now she was needed on the Spook-A-Rama, her buddy was nowhere to be found.

'Where's Dana?' said Kumari.

'Someone took her to the bathroom.'

'We have to wait so she can come on the ride.'

'Don't worry about her. It'll be fine.' Raider was ushering her towards the Spook-A-Rama. Lucy was smiling at her, standing ready. She could see Chico and his buddy about to clamber into a car.

'Hey,' said Chico. 'We can ride together.'

'We need Kumari alone,' said Raider hastily. 'We want a final shot we can use for the credits. Kumari, you get in the last car. Isn't that right, Lucy?'

'If you say so,' said Lucy, distracted. There was a problem with her walkie-talkie. She had crew positioned inside the ride but, for some reason, they could not communicate.

'But what about Dana?' demanded Kumari.

'Who cares about Dana?' snapped Raider, suddenly testy. He was glancing at his watch, obviously in a hurry.

'I do.' In that second, the realisation hit Kumari. Raider had deliberately ensured Dana would not be in shot. Anger building, she glanced at Lucy, now speaking into her walkie-talkie.

Lucy looked up at her and smiled. 'OK, we're about ready, folks.'

Kumari clambered into her car, still seething over Raider's duplicity. The cars ahead were empty. All of a sudden, she heard a shriek.

'Hey, wait for us!'

Charley and Hannah were racing towards them, buddies in tow.

'There's no room,' called out Raider.

'What do you mean, there's no room?' demanded Charley. 'There's no one in those cars.'

'Like I said, there's no room,' snarled Raider. 'Now back off, kid.'

Lucy and the crew looked at one another.

'We need Kumari alone,' explained Lucy gently. 'But you guys can have a ride as soon as we're done.'

Kumari looked at her friends and knew this was the moment. As soon as the cameras started rolling, she would spring her surprise. She hated Raider now more than ever, hated him and his fake show. Still, she wasn't going to let it spoil her moment, although she really would rather not ride alone. The Spook-A-Rama was scary, but then again she had seen far worse. What could a bunch of fibreglass fakes do to her when she had faced down the Ayah?

At that moment Badmash leaped off his perch on the boom and flung himself into Kumari's lap.

'Hey, buddy,' she crooned. 'You want to come along?'

He looked up into her eyes and cooed.

'Give us a big, happy smile, Kumari,' Lucy called out.

Obediently, Kumari obliged. As she did so, she reached into her pocket and pulled out the cuttings Theo had given her. She was about to hold them up for the cameras when she noticed a man about fifty metres away walking purposefully towards Raider. He was nondescript, entirely ordinary, but there was something about the way he looked at Raider that was disturbing. Suddenly, he spotted her in the car. He stared for a second then speeded up. Lucy was moving in for a close up. The man broke into a run.

'Jack Raider!' she heard him shout. 'Or should that be Brother Joyful or John Monroe?'

Oh my god, the man knew as well.

'Jack Raider,' said Kumari to camera, 'is a fake of the worst kind. He's a conman, a rip-off artist. He may even be a murderer.'

She could feel the silence that fell; see Raider's face turn apoplectic.

'Here is the evidence,' continued Kumari, waving the cuttings. 'Your mayor was once known as Brother Joyful.'

'That's right,' said a voice off-camera. Kumari could see the man who had been running towards Raider. 'It was me who planted those cuttings. I have all the information you need. Recognise me now, John? Guess not. But then, you didn't on the Brooklyn Bridge either. It's me, your brother Mike. You know – your kid brother.'

With that, the cameras swung round to catch Raider lunging at the man. Never mind a reality show – this was history as it happened.

All of a sudden, the car in which Kumari sat jerked and shuddered. She was heading off into the darkness all alone. The last thing she heard was Chico calling out her name and then she was lurching downwards, Badmash trembling in her lap, past leering faces and dangling skeletons. A fiendish piano player bashed out his tunes. Shrouded figures leaned forward from coffins. Flashing lights lit up scenes straight out of nightmares.

Badmash squawked as they shot past a vulture, but there was no time for him to throw a scene. They were already heading towards a ghastly, stooped figure that clawed for them as they rounded a bend. Straight ahead, Kumari could see a devil, its curving sword raised as if to strike. At that very moment, the cacophony of shrieks and wails suddenly ceased. The car jerked to a halt and they were plunged into absolute darkness.

In the sudden silence, she heard an oath. Was there someone from the crew nearby? As her eyes adjusted to the dark, she saw a figure begin to move. How come the devil was still working when the power was clearly out? All her instincts were screaming at her to run. Something was obviously very amiss. But how to run when she could barely see what was around her? From out of nowhere, she felt her Power begin to rise.

Power 2, the Power of Extraordinary Sight. Once more, it was working all on its own. She stared at the devil figure and saw someone else move out from behind it, as if illuminated by a clear, cold light.

'You!' gasped Kumari in disbelief. She could see the Ayah's face now as she pulled off her mask.

'Well done, Kumari,' sneered the Ayah. 'Your Powers have obviously improved.' Beside her, Simon Razzle bared his teeth in a smile.

In that instant, Kumari leaped out of the car and began to run. She was racing along the track, trying to follow it back towards the entrance.

'Fly, Badmash!' she cried. 'Go get help!'

Behind her, the Ayah and Razzle stumbled along in the dark, handicapped by their lack of Extraordinary Sight. And then Kumari tripped and fell over one of the switch boxes positioned by the track. As she struggled to her feet, she heard a bloodcurdling cry and glanced back to see the Ayah advancing, the sword raised above her head.

All at once, someone hurtled through the half-darkness, pulling the Ayah to the ground. Horrified, Kumari watched the sword rise and fall as the Ayah hacked at her assailant. And then, as she staggered back, the other figure rolled on to one side and lay still. With a moan of anguish, Kumari saw who it was. Chico. His eyes were shut and his limbs lay heavy. Blood was starting to seep from his wounds.

Letting out a scream of pure hatred, Kumari turned on the Ayah.

'I'll kill you,' she shrieked. 'I'll destroy you!'

'I don't think so,' crowed the Ayah. 'This is the Sacred Sword, Kumari. And with it I am going to kill you.'

Behind her, Razzle smiled once more, his teeth shining white in the gloom.

'You coward,' cried Kumari. 'Hiding behind her. Well, come on then, do your worst.'

She could see Chico, but she could not reach him. The Ayah stood in her way, sword scything through the air as she aimed for Kumari's heart.

All of a sudden, the lights went up, dazzling them momentarily. Kumari could hear shouts and footsteps thundering towards them. Brave Badmash had managed to get help.

As the Ayah blinked, Kumari seized her moment, lashing out with all her might. Her foot contacted with the sword and sent it soaring out of the Ayah's grasp. As it hit the ground, Kumari leaped for it, but hesitated. If she picked up the sword, there was no going back. *What will it feel like?* she wondered. *Will it hurt?* She had no idea what happened when you became a full goddess. The RHM had always been vague about the facts.

'Leave it!' she heard a voice shout. The RHM's voice. He was emerging from behind a row of painted vampires, another sword in his hand.

'Take this one, Kumari,' he urged. '*This* is the Sacred Sword.' Raising his arm, he flung his sword at Kumari's feet. It landed with a clatter.

Kumari stared at the two swords both lying within her reach. Then another glint caught her eye. The Ayah had whipped a stiletto knife from her sleeve and was holding it at the RHM's throat. Simon Razzle pressed himself back against the wall, panic in his eyes. In that split second, Kumari made her choice. She bent and picked up the RHM's sword. She braced herself, wondering what would happen, but there was no rush of Power, no thunderclap from the heavens. The sword in her hand felt heavy but ordinary.

The Ayah laughed in her face. 'Wrong one, Kumari,' she sneered. 'But then, you always did make bad choices.'

Kumari glanced down at Chico and at that moment she heard him groan. Her eyes flicked to the Sacred Sword at her feet. If she grasped it, she would lose him forever. But it looked like she might lose him anyway. Chico was breathing fast, his eyelids flickering. Blood was spreading on the floor around him.

The Ayah was edging forward, holding the RHM at bay. Her eyes were fixed on the Sacred Sword. 'Kick it to me, Kumari,' she growled.

'Pick it up, Kumari!' commanded the RHM. 'Pick it up or die by it like your mother.'

Kumari's eyes whipped to the RHM's face. 'What do you mean?' she demanded.

Time seemed to stop for a moment. Even the Ayah was silent. They were all staring at the RHM.

'I had to do it,' said the RHM, his eyes shining with a strange intensity. He was plucking at his robes as he spoke, a smile playing about his lips. 'It was only a tiny scratch, but it was enough to kill her. She found out my plans, you see. My plans for you and the Kingdom. I knew that with her and your Papa out of the way we could make real progress. You see that the Kingdom has to progress, I know you do. You do understand, don't you, Kumari?'

'Understand?' croaked Kumari. 'All I understand is that you are insane.' She could not believe what she was hearing. It was too much to take in. The RHM had killed Mamma. He had done so with the Sacred Sword. But there had been no marks on Mamma's body. Was the RHM even telling the truth? Or had he simply lost his mind?

'Insane? I don't think so. I fooled you all, didn't I? Why do you think for so long you've been getting the wrong message? Your Mamma never saw who struck her. I made you all think it was the Ayah. I let you all go on believing that only someone from the Kingdom could wield the sword. You had no idea how she'd died when the instrument was right under your noses! The Sacred Sword does not leave a mark. It is the perfect weapon. If you'd studied properly, you'd know that, wouldn't you, Kumari?' He was panting now, his nostrils flared, his mouth drawn back in a snarl.

He is *mad*, thought Kumari. *Mad enough to kill my Mamma.*

'You louse,' snarled the Ayah. 'Although you saved me the trouble. I would have killed her in the end. All you did was get there first.'

The shouts of the crew were getting nearer, but they were still not close enough. It was as if the world were moving in slow motion and yet spinning very fast.

'I hate you,' said Kumari, barely able to speak above a whisper. The pain was crushing her chest now, squeezing out all the breath. This man, her teacher, had killed her Mamma – and for what? For some crazy plan, some wild idea. He must truly have lost his mind. 'And I feel sorry for you at the same time. I don't know what your plans were but they will never, ever work. And to think my Papa rescued you from the borderlands and brought you up as his own.' She shook her head, determined to stay dignified. She would not let him see her crumble.

'I wish he hadn't,' said the RHM. 'I wish he'd left me there, with my people. Then I would not have had to live as an outsider all my life, never knowing this mythical Happiness.'

'It's not mythical,' said Kumari. 'It's real and I've proved it. You can feel it here and you can feel it there. Happiness is a state of mind. But not for someone like you, someone so twisted and torn up. You killed my Mamma and all this time you let me think it was *her*.' She looked at the Ayah and saw nothing but hatred.

252

'It was for progress, Kumari,' cried the RHM. 'The Kingdom needs to change to have a future. You believe in science just like me. Your Papa, he clings too hard to outdated beliefs.'

'So you hurt him too, is that it? It was you who poisoned him that time?'

'Actually, that *was* down to me,' snapped the Ayah. 'It seems I did your dirty work for you.'

They had betrayed her, both of them. Without another thought, Kumari hurled aside her sword. As both the Ayah and the RHM dived for it, Kumari bent and snatched up the real one. Instantly, she felt a surge of Power. A light began to suffuse her from within. Her head felt light and yet oh so clear.

She glanced at Chico, lying on the ground, still and lifeless in a pool of blood. *He's gone,* thought Kumari. *He's gone and I never got a chance to say goodbye. Just like with Mamma, I'll never again know his touch, never hear the sound of his laughter.* The pain sliced through her heart like a blade. She was empty, bereft. Alone once more. In that moment, fury rose from somewhere deep inside, bringing with it her Power. Opening her mouth, Kumari let out a howl that resounded through the tunnels, directing its full ferocity at her foes, pinning them writhing to the ground.

As silence fell once more, Kumari could hear a wailing in the distance, the sound of police sirens. There would be justice of a kind, but not the sort she could mete out. Kumari felt something else rise alongside her Power, a certainty, a sureness. She would be judge and jury, exacting the punishment the gods expected. For the first time in her life, Kumari knew precisely what to do.

CHAPTER 27

Two slashes was all it took – two swift, precise thrusts and it was done. The Ayah and the RHM lay as still as Chico. Mamma was avenged at last. In the hollow, shocked silence that followed, Kumari stared at the figures slumped at her feet. There was no evidence of any wound. The Sacred Sword left no sign. So that really was how he had killed Mamma. Kumari was glad but also sorry. Sorry that she had had to take their lives; glad it was over at last.

Flinging herself down by Chico's side, Kumari reached for his cold, limp hand. There was one last thing she could do for him before she had to go, an act of restitution. As a full goddess, she could restore him to life. The tears poured down her face as she stroked him, willing him to breathe once more. But nothing happened; he lay chalk-white, unmoving. Was she to fail even now when it mattered the most?

And then it happened: he took a breath and then another. She watched his chest as it began to rise and fall. Slowly, like a butterfly emerging from a chrysalis, his eyelashes fluttered and then he was looking at her, meeting her gaze.

'Kumari?'

'Don't try to talk. You got hurt.'

He tried to lift his head, moaned and let it fall back in her lap.

'You saved me, Kumari,' he said. 'I died there. I know I did. I saw this light. It's the same light that's coming from you. Kumari, you're different. What's happened?' He looked at her in wonder. 'Oh my god. You did it. You became a goddess.'

'I had to,' sobbed Kumari. 'I had no choice.'

'Take me with you,' he murmured. 'You can do it, I know you can.'

She gazed at him for a long moment then sadly shook her head. 'You don't really want that,' she whispered. 'Your place is here, with your family.' She wanted to, so much, but she knew it would be selfish. Turning Chico into a god would mean being together, eternally. But, as Kumari knew, eternal life could be a blessing and a curse. Chico was mortal; he belonged here in the World Beyond. She could not, would not rob him of his rightful destiny even if it meant losing him for ever.

'I love you,' she said, slipping her amulet from her wrist. 'Take this to remember me by. If you ever need me, hold this and call out. Who knows, I might even hear you.'

His fingers closed tightly around the amulet. 'Don't go,' he whispered.

'I have to. I must. It is my destiny. A full goddess cannot

live outside of the Hidden Kingdom.'

A sudden roar drowned out Kumari's final words and she looked up to see a lion stalking towards her.

'Kumari.'

'Mamma!'

She was there, dismounting from her lion, holding her arms wide for Kumari.

'Kumari!'

There was someone else calling her name. She looked round and saw Lucy and a whole posse of people. At their head, the man, the one who had begun to run towards Raider. Others were crowding in behind them; Kumari caught sight of Hannah and Charley. And then she noticed the two police officers who held on to a handcuffed Raider.

'That's him,' said the man, pointing to Razzle, now crouched down against the wall, whimpering. 'That's the guy who hired me to hurt Kumari.' He looked at her then and blinked. *I'm sorry,* his eyes seemed to say. The police officers looked at the two on the ground.

It was time to leave, before the questions started.

Kumari looked at Chico. 'I have to go now,' she murmured.

'I love you,' he whispered.

'I love you too.' She bent then and brushed his lips, lingering to taste them one last time. Then, tearing herself away, she rose to her feet and walked into her mother's arms. They closed around her and held her tight and Kumari felt the warmth of her beloved Mamma at last.

'You're free,' she said, barely able to believe that it had happened at last. 'You're free. Oh how I've missed you, Mamma!'

'I am, thanks to you, my darling Kumari. I've missed you too, so much, so very much.'

They stood there for a moment, mother and daughter locked in their embrace. Kumari could hear her Mamma's heart beating. It was a sound she had longed for all this time. The blood flowing through Mamma's veins was her lifeblood too. The love between them was a bond that had never been broken, not for an instant. It was as if nothing and everything had happened, as if she had held Mamma only yesterday. And now they would be together for a little while before Mamma ascended the Holy Mountain – where, finally, they would share all their tomorrows. Kumari let out a sob of relief.

After a moment, Mamma gently released Kumari. 'It is time, my darling. We must go.'

She led Kumari to the lion and seated her upon it. Kumari gazed down at her friends, at Chico's beloved face. She could see Theo and Ms Martin. So dear to her, and she would never see them again. Her heart twisted as she thought of Ma, of CeeCee and LeeLee. They meant the world to her and she would have no chance to say goodbye. She had dealt with the RHM and the Ayah. The cops would take care of Raider and Simon Razzle. There was nothing more to do here; her mission was over. She had brought Happiness to the World Beyond, in her own way. She had avenged Mamma at last.

'I'll miss you,' she cried, tears streaming down her face. 'But I'll always be here, in my dreams.'

'We love you, Kumari,' called Hannah, her eyes shining, her cheeks wet.

'Don't forget us,' cried Charley.

'Never,' said Kumari, and her eyes met Chico's. In them she saw the love she had always wanted; the love that could never be.

And then she held her Mamma tight and they were heading out of the tunnel, rising up, soaring towards the Kingdom and Papa. Kumari looked for one last time at the World Beyond. She was going home, a goddess.

THE EIGHT GREAT POWERS OF A GODDESS

1. The Power to be Invincible in Battle with the Sacred Sword

2. The Power of Extraordinary Sight

3. The Power to Run with Incredible Swiftness

4. The Power to Become Invisible

5. The Power of Rejuvenation

6. The Power to Levitate or to Fly Through the Sky

7. The Power to Move Freely Through the Earth, Mountains, and Solid Walls

8. The Power to have Command over the Elements

THE FIVE GREAT
GIFTS OF A GODDESS

1. The Gift of Eternal Life – and the power to grant the same

2. The Gift of Beauty – inner and outer

3. The Gift of Tongues – the ability to speak or understand any language

4. The Gift of Courage – often exhibited *in extremis*

5. The Gift of Wisdom – usually displayed by the more mature goddess

GLOSSARY

The spelling of these words can vary.

Ayah
South Asian word for nanny or nurse-maid – comes from the Portuguese *aia*, meaning 'woman tutor,' which in turn is derived from the Latin *avia* meaning 'grandmother' (just in case you want to impress someone!)

Badmash
Hinglish (a mixture of Hindi and English) for 'naughty'.

Hoodoo
African-American folk magic

Karali
Ancient martial art still practised in some parts of India today.

Kumari
From the Sanskrit, meaning 'princess' or 'maiden.' Although there are living goddesses in Nepal known as Kumaris, there is no connection with our heroine.

KUMARI

GODDESS
OF GOTHAM

AMANDA LEES

'Manhattan Mystery Girl!' screamed the newspaper headlines.

New York is full of thirteen-year-old girls who think they're goddesses. But Kumari is the real deal. And she doesn't have a clue how she got there.

Kumari is a goddess-in-training who lives in a secret valley kingdom. She is destined to stay young forever, unlike people in the World Beyond. But Kumari longs to break out of her claustrophobic life at the Palace, where her only real friend is a baby vulture, and there's nothing to think about – except the mystery of her mother's death.

It's hard to kill a goddess, but someone did. And so Kumari steals away to the Holy Mountain, determined to summon Mamma back from the dead and to find out the truth.

But the next thing Kumari knows, she's in Manhattan. Surrounded by strange buildings and even stranger people, and running for her life . . .

The first book in the Kumari trilogy

'A magnificent debut full of wit and humour' Lovereading4kids

ISBN 978 1 85340 956 1

KUMARI

GODDESS
OF SECRETS

AMANDA LEES

Kumari is back home, but everything has changed.
Papa has been struck down by a mysterious illness and
the Palace is full of danger. The fires of Happiness
are dying and the Hidden Kingdom is in crisis.

What's a girl goddess to do? Kumari's still struggling to gain
her Powers, while her quest to avenge her beloved Mamma
seems tougher than ever. And she's missing her friends in
the World Beyond – here, she has none,
apart from Badmash, her pet baby vulture.

Then unexpected visitors bring terrifying news.
With disaster looming, Kumari has to work in secret.
Can she outwit the thieves of Happiness and
save herself, Papa and the Kingdom itself?

The second book in the Kumari trilogy

'*Powerful and touching*' Glasgow Herald

ISBN: 978 1 85340 989 9

Find out more about Kumari at:

www.amandalees.com

✰ Read the latest news about future *Kumari* books

✰ Enter competitions with fabulous prizes

✰ Download free *Kumari* wallpaper and banners

✰ Get to know author Amanda Lees

✰ Chat with other *Kumari* fans at the exclusive members' forum

www.piccadillypress.co.uk

☆ The latest news on forthcoming books

☆ Chapter previews

☆ Author biographies

☆ Fun quizzes

☆ Reader reviews

☆ Competitions and fab prizes

☆ Book features and cool downloads

☆ And much, much more . . .

Log on and check it out!

Piccadilly Press

☆